Rodney Ivan Crouse

Wind Song of the Little Smokies

---

first edition

By Rodney Ivan Crouse
Illustrations by Gary Bowden
Edited by Janeile Cannon

Published by Foxsong Publishing

Wind Song
of the
Little Smokies

All the characters in this book are fictitious. Any resemblance to actual persons, living or dead, is purely coincidental.

Published by Foxsong Publishing
Illustrations by Gary Bowden

Foxsong Publishing
1769 Pine Creek Circle
Haslett, Michigan 48840
877-339-6918

ISBN 0-9677000-0-0
Library of Congress
Catalog Card Number: 99 097709

From the Editor ~

Wind Song of the Little Smokies is the first book published by Foxsong Publishing. It is a perfect beginning place to feature writer Rodney Crouse and his first manuscript as a way to inspire new writers for whom Foxsong has been created.

When a writer pours time and talent into a story, he or she reveals what is valued. In these pages you will find lyrical word pictures of compassion, generosity and kindness. You will also find a network of different kinds of people cooperating with each other in their community living a modern day truth. Family is no longer defined by blood alone but also by spirit.

As I read through this manuscript for the first time, I could hear my father's harmonica coming to me from my childhood many summers past. I can still see the far away look he would get in his laser blue eyes when he was about to tell a story. Many times it would be about an experience in his youth which was spent in long hours on his family's farm in the rolling hills of southern Ohio. He would cross his legs and curl his body up to rest his elbow on his knee, Pall Mall red between his fingers and thumb planted in his right cheek. Old timey words like filling station and "chivolay" for Chevrolet flavored the warm tones of his Midwest speech.

Wind Song is written just the way my Dad would have told it in a richly detailed fashion of the time before TV.
As a little girl in the middle of six children, I would sit very still savoring every moment of the after dinner tale. Dad farmed and gardened in the day and worked second shift at the Gearworks at night. Mother did all she could and then some, to help us kids get up and go on into life's adventures. These quiet Sunday afternoons were very precious

I invite you to pull up a chair to the kitchen table and linger on the lines colored with nature's rhythms and the joys of the human experience. You'll leave the table well satisfied.

Janeile Cannon
Daughter, Publisher and Editor
November 7, 1999

Acknowledgments ~

To thank those who made it happen: my constant supporter for all the years, and hundreds of hours of editing, typing, and rewriting; my lovely wife Donna. For overcoming impossible difficulties, for caring, for her determination, for her fantastic ability to organize; I thank my daughter Jan. For all the members of my family who read, made suggestions and supported my ego, thanks so much for helping make this book a reality.

Signed,
Rod Crouse
November 8, 1999

Much thanks and appreciation to the following for their support and expertise in launching Foxsong Publishing:

Patrick Cannon,
Jamie Ottensman,
Crystalla,
Gary Bowden,
Candace Elliott Person, Attorney at Law,
Mary M. Moyne, Attorney at Law.

Signed,
Janeile Cannon

Preface ~

Raised on a general-purpose farm in southern Ohio, I was well aquainted with hard work and long hours which was the normal way of life for most farm boys.

Most of the animals in the Little Smokies were well known to the hill farmers and villagers near the Ohio River. The kind of farming practiced encouraged wildlife rather than cause harm. Many rural people were glad to have the quail, partridge, pheasants, turkeys, rabbits, squirrels and the occasional deer as supplements to their frugal diets. I was well acquainted with families whose main supply of meat came from the water, fields and woods.

Even as a very young child, I learned to set traps for fur-bearing animals and for edible game. Farm people used steel traps in a routine manner as common as picking berries or gathering wild mush-rooms for the table.

My childhood among the ordinary people of the Ohio hills gave me an opportunity to be part of nature in the raw. My older brothers were my best teachers when it came to hunting, trapping and fishing. Seining, setting trotlines or fishing with a pole, we managed to bring home enough fish for a good fish fry from time to time.

Learning to hunt at night with dogs and a lantern was a chilling experience I didn't like, but I did it because I didn't want to display my fears of the "bogey man" that children believed ran about at night.

We caught skunks, 'possums and 'coons in some quantities during the long winter season. A few mink contributed a relatively large amount of money when the furs were sold. I bought my first pair of hi-top boots with the money from my first mink. The sale of musk-rat furs bought a lot of shoes for my brothers and sisters.

I have lived in many places, doing many things to make my way in life, but always kept in touch with my roots and the wildlife around me. With at least a dozen dogs as pets over the years, I have learned to observe them for the pleasure of learning more about them.

Luckier than many young people of the time, I grew up in a very large family that had many kinds of domestic animals in large quantities. We had very little cash money but we were more than well fed by our farm and its animals.

Some abandoned dogs turned feral; roaming the hills, living on anything they could find or catch to eat. Lambs, pigs and small calves were killed and eaten by "wild dogs" on occasion. I have used similar incidents in my story.

I have reached the conclusion that canines of all kinds are much more clever than some believe. I believe canines and other animals communicate with each other in a manner impossible for humans to understand or replicate. I believe canines feel grief, pain, fear, joy, love and concern much as we humans. I think we humans lack the ability to comprehend the animal intellect. I have given many of these hidden qualities to some of the animals in the following story.

Rodney Crouse

Chapter one

Chapter one

Chapter One ~

A light rain was falling on the brush-covered hillside the first time he came out of the den under the old fallen beech tree. With eyes nearly closed against the glare of light, he cautiously made his way to the edge of the table-sized ledge above the swift flowing little creek. As his eyes became adapted to the light, he grew bolder and moved farther away from the mouth of the den to push his nose under shrubs and into clumps of dead grass and weeds.

Soon, four other little foxes came out to join his exploration of the area in front of their home. Within a few minutes they all began to play a game of rough and tumble wrestling, running, and jumping that quickly tired his two brothers and two sisters, but only made him eager for more action. After several attempts to get them to continue the game he realized they had lost interest, so he left them alone and began looking around for his mother.

The rain had stopped falling and a pale sun was shining through a thin layer of clouds. A breeze, moving through trees above and behind the den, carried his mother's scent to him and led him to a tunnel-like path through brush and small trees growing around the old beech log. He followed the path and the scent several yards away from the den. He was just at the end of the sheltered path when he was met by his mother.

Much to his surprise, she rushed to him and bowled him over with her nose, rolling him back along the path to the den. With nips of her teeth and sharp blows with her nose, she forced him back to the burrow. The sounds of his chastisement and yips of pain caused the other young foxes to tumble back into the den where his mother checked each of them with her eyes nose and tongue to assure herself of their well being. Satisfied, she stretched out on her side to allow the pups to suckle while she groomed them with her long, pink tongue.

As the days went by, the pups grew quickly in size and strength. As they grew, the mother watched over them and fed them with her rich milk and, gradually, with small animals which she brought home in her mouth. She was helped in her hunting and feeding by her mate, who came to the den to drop fresh-killed mice, birds and rabbits on the ground for the pups to worry, chew on, and finally to eat, as soon as they learned how good the meat tasted. By the time the pups were six weeks old, they were weaned from suckling, and began eating only game, vegetation and insects, which they had learned to catch for themselves in open woods close to their home.

By mid-summer the young fox had grown nearly as large as his mother. He was much larger than the other four pups and easily dominated them with his greater strength and speed. He frequently followed his father on his regular hunting trips into the hay and grain fields of nearby farms, while the smaller pups hunted with the mother closer to home.

As fall approached, the hunting skills of all the young foxes improved to the point where they were able to find much of their own food. Berries, peaches, apples, as well as vegetables from gardens and fields became as much of the foxes' diet as the mice, squirrels, rabbits and birds eaten in large quantities.

When the small game-hunting season opened in November, the loud sounds of gunshots could be heard in every direction, driving the young foxes frantic with fear. The adult foxes had heard gunfire many times before and knew how to deal with the problem. They led the young foxes deep into a tangled windfall of trees, blackberry briers and thorn brush at the foot of a rocky cliff. They spent each day there, for nearly two weeks, until the hunting activity died down to occasional shots. They sought food only at night.

Hunting for food during the night was no real hardship for the foxes but tried the patience of some of the pups, particularly the two young females, who were becoming more independent with maturity. They especially enjoyed an early morning meal of fat mice caught in a meadow or weed field. Then they curled up in the soft grass on a sunny hilltop for a snooze.

One afternoon, they went to their favorite hill for a nap, when two hunters spotted them. The callous hunters ended the young sisters' lives with twin blasts from their shotguns.

The following night, one of the young male foxes left the home territory to seek his own way in the animal world. He was followed by the other young male of the same size a few nights later. This left only the two adults and the big fox pup.

Winter came with cold nights, mild days and light snows. There was warm sunshine most days with just enough rain to keep the fields and woods from becoming dried out and noisy. Food was plentiful and the foxes were healthy with thick, glossy coats of new winter fur. The gun-hunting season for deer had come and gone without causing the three foxes any trouble. They stayed in the windfall by the cliff in the daytime, slaking their thirst at a tiny spring of cold water at the foot of a poplar tree. At night each fox went out to hunt and feed alone. Since gunshots were heard only in daylight, the foxes were careful to return to their lay-up before full light each morning.

~

Tim Buckman was a very calm, well-organized man. His wife, Lora, matched him almost perfectly. Both were medium height, brown haired, and had gray-blue eyes. They went about their lives in an unhurried way that aggravated some of

3

their friends and neighbors, who rushed about making and spending money as if their lives depended on how much they accomplished each minute.

Tim and Lora were married when they were twenty years of age. They moved into the old house on Tim's parents' farm, commuting to jobs in the city until Tim's dad was disabled in a fall from the house roof. Lora kept her job in the city while Tim operated the farm for three years.

Lora's parents had died in a plane crash while they were on the way to a vacation in Alaska. After the funeral, when the will was read, Lora learned she was the sole beneficiary of her parent's estate.

Later, in a family meeting with Tim's parents, a plan was worked out to buy an adjoining section of rolling, wooded hills and pasture just to the south of their farm. The idea was to go into a large-scale program of small grain, hay, pasture and cattle farming. Lora quit her job and worked side by side with Tim. Using money from Lora's inheritance, the land was purchased and fenced where needed.

Their house was modernized, insulated, and painted. Some of the old farm machinery was then exchanged for the kinds Tim needed for small grains and haymaking. The barns were modified for hay storage and cattle feeding. Within five years the two farms had been fully adapted into one large soil and water-conserving unit of eleven hundred acres.

All the lands previously used to grow corn and soybeans were now used for oats, wheat, barley and hay. Any land with slope enough to cause serious erosion had been planted with permanent grasses and long term alfalfa for hay and pasture.

With a cattle herd of three hundred to four hundred fifty animals, Tim and Lora also kept four horses to work cattle, check fences and for pleasure riding. The two mares belonged to Tim's mom and dad and the geldings had been a gift to the couple when Lora started helping on the farm.

4

At least once each week, Tim and Lora would get up before sunrise, eat a quick breakfast and go for a ride around their land. These morning rides could take several hours, but was always a pleasure for both of them. They loved being outdoors early in the morning when the abundant wildlife was most visible.

Raising cattle required repairing fences, helping cows deliver new calves, and rounding up animals in need of medical treatment. Sometimes this would take several hours, but they also found time to watch deer and other wildlife so common on their land.

Lora was able to enjoy the details of animal life with the field glasses she carried in her saddlebags. She had been able to catch frequent glimpses of a litter of fox pups at play on a hilltop meadow, near a stream on the edge of the woods. She had watched them throughout the summer and fall seasons while they changed from awkward, leggy babies to nearly adult specimens of great speed and agility.

Early one morning, while riding along a ridge above the meadow, Lora and Tim found a secluded spot where they could watch the playful family unobserved. A screen-like growth of young pine trees were dense enough to allow the Buckmans to come and go without being seen or disturbing the beautiful little animals.

As the fox pups grew it became obvious to Tim and Lora that one pup was superior to his mates. His size, speed and strength allowed him to win the rough games and mock fights the youngsters were constantly engaged in. When the cool weather of September brought out the foxes' winter pelts, the big pup was much darker in color than the other four.

The dark reddish-brown color of the big pup's fur gave reason for the Buckmans to start calling him by the name Chestnut. His nearly black face, legs and tail caused him to clearly stand out from his much lighter colored brothers and sisters.

Once, when the bright early morning sun was shining on Chestnut as he stood atop a tree stump, his coat seemed to glow like fire.

Using his telephoto lens equipped camera, Tim took several pictures which turned out to be nearly perfect. Lora had enlargements made of the photos and framed them for display on the wall of their family room.

Due to their love of wildlife, the Buckmans kept their land posted with signs to keep out careless hunters. Despite the "Hunting by Permission Only" signs, some hunters still trespassed in secluded areas of their farm.

It was trespassing hunters, carrying the two dead foxes back to their car, that Tim came across one November day. Angry, but still outwardly calm, he escorted the men off the property and advised them not to return, or be arrested. That incident coincided with the disappearance of the foxes on the hill.

~

John Buckman, Tim's dad, was feeling like a new man. An operation on his back had restored his ability to do some of the lighter work around the place. He had taken over the job of putting the big rolls of hay out for the cattle. The hay was stored in the barns and under shed-like roofs built at strategic locations on the farm. Using a specially equipped, four-wheel drive tractor, he transferred the hay from storage to feed bunks set on sled-like bases which made it easy to move them to cattle feeding areas. The feed bunks were moved every few days, to fresh, clean locations around pastures and feed lots.

The cattle had access to barns and rain shelters, but most of them preferred staying outside year-round. The Buckmans encouraged the cattle to stay outdoors because they seemed to stay in better health, and it reduced the amount of barn cleaning time and cost. Tim took care of the grain and supplement rations fed to those animals requiring the additional feed.

With a one thousand pound roll of alfalfa hay on the front of the tractor, and another on the rear forks, John was driving the hay burdened tractor out to the bull yard about one-half mile away from his home. It was a cold January day. The tractor engine purred quietly through the snow-laden trees along the winding farm road. His dog Pepper, a young, black coated female crossbreed, scampered ahead of the tractor, nosing into every brush pile and stand of cover.

Pepper was John's "cow" dog. Almost without training, she had learned to work the cattle in response to John's voice and hand signals. Most of the time Pepper seemed to know what to do even before John gave her a signal. Usually well mannered and gentle, Pepper could be fierce and determined if a truculent cow or bull resisted going the direction she was trying to make it go. Growling and snapping her sharp teeth, Pepper would charge right at the animal. If her bluff didn't get the job done, she actually bit them on the nose or heel to accomplish her purpose. Pepper could drive more cows by herself than three men could on foot, according to John.

On this day in January, Pepper was coming into her breeding cycle. Every few minutes she had to stop to urinate. Seeing what Pepper was doing reminded John of an offer made by his friend and neighbor, Paul Cross, to have Pepper bred to his registered Blue Heeler, in trade for one of the male offspring of the union. John decided to take Paul Cross up on his offer this year.

John placed the rolls of hay into the hay bunks and checked over the dozen bulls in the twenty-acre bull yard. Finding the animals to be sound and healthy, with plenty of salt and minerals in the covered feeder and the big concrete, spring-fed watering tank working properly, he was ready to return home. Rounding the corner of the hay bunk, he was stopped dead in his tracks when he saw Pepper and a large, dark colored fox making friendly advances toward each other.

Now John had lived in the country all his fifty-five years and had never seen anything like this. The dog was whining softly while bounding up and down on her front feet. Her tail was swinging back and forth in an excited manner, while the fox gazed at the dog in apparent delight. With his ears pricked up, his long pink tongue hanging slightly out of his open mouth, the fox almost seemed to be smiling at the dog. It was plain to see Pepper was familiar with the fox. She exhibited none of the normal animosity of dogs for foxes that John expected to see.

When John took a step toward the animals the fox merely trotted away a few yards and sat down on the snow again. Pepper started to follow the fox, but John called her name and snapped his fingers for her to return to him. She did not want to come at first, and John had to speak sharply to get her to obey. At this point, the fox got up from the snow and quickly ran away into the nearby woods.

Later, at home, John told Lora about Pepper and the fox meeting at the bull yard.

When John described the fox to her, Lora said, "That must be Chestnut."

She took John to her house to show him the pictures Tim had taken a few weeks earlier, but never got around to hanging. Looking closely at the pictures, John agreed that the fox was probably the one he had just seen in the bull yard. After some further discussion about Pepper's friendly attitude toward the fox, they decided Pepper thought the fox was just another friendly dog. Then John remembered Pepper was showing signs of coming into her heat cycle.

John left Lora's house, called Pepper, put her in his old pickup truck and drove to Paul Cross's home a few miles down the road. When he pulled into Paul's driveway, a frisky blue-gray dog came bounding out to meet them, barking to announce the arrival of visitors.

Paul came out of the house, pulling the earflaps of his winter cap down over his ears. His dog ran to him and sedately followed him to the truck. John and Paul shook hands and then discussed the reason for the visit.

Paul examined Pepper and told John he would have to keep her for a few days in order to mate her with his dog, the Australian Blue Heeler, who was showing much interest in Pepper.

With reluctance, Pepper entered one of several wire-enclosed dog pens, each with its own sturdy doghouse. The pens were located near Paul's house, in plain view from his kitchen windows, so Paul could keep a close watch over the dogs he kept there at all times. Pepper would be in good hands with Paul, for he loved dogs and enjoyed raising and training them to work livestock.

John couldn't keep from noticing how much some of Paul's dogs resembled foxes. "Maybe that was one reason Pepper had treated the fox, called Chestnut, as if he were another dog," John thought to himself.

John and Paul talked about dogs for a few minutes before he returned home. When he entered his house, he found Tim and Lora there to join him and his wife, Mary, for supper. This was a common but happy practice for the four of them to eat together in one of the two homes, which were separated only by a tree-filled yard at the top of a low hill just west of the barns.

Mary at fifty-four was a tall, slender woman with black hair and brown eyes. She had been a nurse in the local hospital when she and John renewed their friendship, after going their separate ways from high school graduation. A few weeks after the meeting, they were married and had lived on the farm ever since. Having Tim and Lora in the house next door suited her perfectly. Lora had become like a daughter to her, and treated Mary as if she were her mother.

While Lora and Mary prepared supper, John and Tim sat at the big kitchen table so all four of them could talk together. They discussed the incident between Pepper and the fox at length before the subject was changed to topics concerning the upcoming calving season. This conversation lasted through the meal and doing the dishes, in which all of them took part.

At ten o'clock, walking back to their house, Tim and Lora heard a fox barking on a nearby hill. Lora, jokingly, told Tim it was Chestnut inviting Pepper to come and play. The wind sang through the tall treetops as the young couple paused in their walk and looked up at some small clouds pushed along by the wind to briefly dim the silvery moonlight. The wind sounds rose and fell like the faint notes of a distant organ giving musical background for the fox's plaintive solo.

Chapter two

Chapter two

Chapter Two ~

Chestnut watched the man on the tractor and the small black dog leave the bull yard. Concealed from sight in a clump of brush on top of a hill, he waited until they had been gone several minutes before trotting down to sniff at the yellow spots of Pepper's urine in the snow. The scent caused a strange excitement in the young fox. At this time he was less than a year old, and was unaware of how these natural urges would influence him in the future.

Curious, he followed the dog's tracks to within a few hundred feet of the barns and houses that made up the farmstead. After watching the man and dog get into the truck and drive away, he trotted into a large open-sided building where he could hear mice among the rolls of hay stored there.

It didn't take Chestnut long to catch and eat enough mice to satisfy his hunger. The shape and size of the round hay bales made it easy for him to slide between them and snap up the mice. With his hunger satisfied, he slipped down to a little creek and had a drink of water. He returned to the hay barn, climbed to the top of the stack of bales and curled up to sleep.

Chestnut slept intermittently for a number of hours. Even while sleeping, he was aware of sounds and movement in and around the hay shed. Unusual sounds of any kind caused him to come fully awake and alert. A cat came into the building and spent a short time grooming it's fur before leaving to run to one of the barns, unaware he had been so close to the fox. Chestnut hadn't moved or made a sound.

Chestnut was sitting on the hill behind the barns when Tim and Lora were walking across the yard that night. Seeing and hearing them caused Chestnut to jump up, raise his head and give out with a few short barks.

13

Lora's laughing voice seemed almost like a reply to Chestnut. He sat back down on the hill and watched the couple enter their house. Soon lights came on in several windows. Chestnut had never been this close to a house before, but he was not afraid. He knew about dogs, was cautious about men, but had never been harmed by either.

The moon was shining bright and clear on the snowy land. The air was cold but pleasant to the fox. He watched the house and listened to the sounds coming from inside. Drawing closer, only thirty or forty feet from a French door, he could see a man sitting in a chair.

Chestnut soon tired of watching Tim, so he left the yard to circle around both houses, then the barns and other buildings on the farm. As he moved about the buildings, he was unknowingly filing away all kinds of information about the place. There were mice in the hay, muskrats in the creek by the barn, ducks and geese in a building by a tiny pond, rats under a pile of posts and logs near the granary. Here and there were smells of a dog but no sight or sound of one. He knew the black female was usually in the doghouse near the side door of the smaller house at night. He was disappointed not to find her.

Chestnut spent the night around the farm buildings and in the hay shed. Just before daylight he returned to the woods by the bull yard where he had established a new lay-up in a large pile of treetops left from a recent logging operation. He was now living alone since his father had become very aggressive toward him in recent weeks. Chestnut didn't know his father's seemingly harsh actions were only one of nature's ways of assuring the healthy breeding of unrelated animals. By driving him away from the home den area, he was sure to meet females from distant fox clans.

As the days went by, Chestnut often saw the man on the tractor taking hay and feed to the several herds of cattle. He kept looking for the dog, and finally was rewarded several days later by the sight of Pepper running through the snow beside the tractor.

Staying out of sight of the man, Chestnut barked softly at Pepper several times. At first she didn't hear him because of the noise the tractor was making. When she finally heard his call, Pepper was not sure what to do. She could smell him, hear him and for some reason she wanted to run to him. She hesitated due to some shyness developed through her domestic environment and to his wild male odor.

Finally, she started running toward the sound of Chestnut's urging voice. When she burst through a fringe of brush at the edge of a clump of trees, she almost bumped into the fox waiting there. Inches apart, motionless for long moments, the two shy animal's natural instinct caused them to step away from each other until Pepper's curiosity pulled her forward to sniff at Chestnut's flank. He remained perfectly still while she moved all the way around him, inhaling his scent and touching him lightly with her nose.

Satisfied with her investigation of the fox, Pepper sat down on the snow while Chestnut performed a similar inspection. With the amenities over, the two little animals trotted off toward the bullpen where John had just finished his work and mounted the tractor to return home.

John was not really surprised to see Chestnut follow Pepper into the feed lot. He was a little surprised when the fox followed her all the way to the hay sheds behind the barn.

When they reached the building where he had spent recent times sleeping on the hay, Chestnut turned toward the building and stopped to watch John and Pepper go on to the barns.

Pepper would have gone back to join Chestnut but John called to her and she obediently followed behind the tractor, which he put in the barn. He kept Pepper with him while he went into the repair shop where Tim was repairing a mowing machine in preparation for the next haymaking season.

After hearing John's story about Pepper and the fox, Tim wanted to look at the animal. John led Tim out to the, side of the barn where there was an unobstructed view of the hay sheds. Chestnut was still sitting on the ground in front of the shed, looking at the men and the dog without any sign of fear. After a minute or so, Chestnut calmly turned, jumped onto the first roll of hay and scrambled right up to the top roll under the roof. He simply lay down, put his head on his front paws and appeared to go to sleep.

When the men started walking toward the houses, Pepper trotted ahead and went into her own warm doghouse. From where she lay in her house, Pepper could not see Chestnut curled up on the hay sound asleep. Chestnut, with his superior eyesight, looked across the lot every time he awoke to make sure Pepper was still there in her little house. Pepper had just made a new and lifelong friend.

~

The two Buckman families spent considerable time in each other's homes. Both houses had been equipped with a phone system that permitted them to take all their calls in either house and to use the phones as a simple intercom. Pressing a button caused a bell to ring on the other phone.

One night, when John came back in the house from feeding Pepper, the intercom bell rang. John picked up the phone and was asked by Tim to look out the window by Pepper's house. When he looked out, he saw Chestnut coming across the yard. John called Mary to join him at the window as Chestnut ran right up to Pepper and her bowl of food.

As Chestnut came near, Pepper ran to him, touching him

on the nose and neck with her nose. After this show of welcome, Pepper ran back to the food bowl, then moved aside and lay down on the ground. Chestnut walked very slowly over to the bowl to sniff at the contents. He took a small piece of food in his mouth and cautiously chewed and swallowed the morsel. He then quickly ate several mouthfuls of the food before backing away. Pepper came back to the bowl and finished eating the remaining food.

Seeing the bowl was empty, John took a box of dog food from the cupboard, opened the door and stepped outside. The fox ran away a short distance, stopped, turned around and watched John pour food in the bowl.

John heard the buzz made by the automatic yard light coming on. He thought this noise and the sudden increase in light would scare the fox away, but Chestnut only gave the light fixture a quick glance, then ignored it completely. When John had gone back inside the house, Chestnut moved back to the food bowl to try some more of Pepper's evening meal. He seemed to know there was plenty for two, so he ate more the second time he fed.

In the following weeks, Chestnut became a familiar sight around the homes and farm buildings. He started coming to eat from Pepper's bowl every few evenings, so Mary and John took out another food bowl for the fox. He never ate much and preferred meat scraps over the dry dog food. He would not eat canned dog food at all.

~

One morning in late winter, Tim and Lora saddled their horses just before dawn to go for a long ride around the farm. With a weather forecast of warm, dry weather, they had decided to pack a lunch and check all the fences around the property. It had just become light enough for them to see well when they left the barnyard. Topping a small hill, they turned to look back toward the house just in time to see Chestnut enter the little grove of trees behind the houses. He was carrying a full-grown rabbit in his mouth and headed in the direction of Pepper's doghouse. Chestnut was taking food to Pepper.

"Well," Tim said. "The rabbit will help feed Pepper and her unborn pups."

"Yes," replied Lora. "But it doesn't explain why Pepper and the fox have become friends."

"It may be because both of them have been alone and need companionship," Tim said. "You know those hunters killed some of Chestnut's family," he added.

"You don't think they killed all of them, do you?" Lora asked.

"I doubt it," Tim answered. "Foxes learn fast," then added, "Chestnut's father would force him to find an area of his own, away from the old den. Chestnut seems to have found a place where he is welcome."

"But, aren't dogs and foxes natural enemies?" asked Lora.

"I'm not sure that's right," Tim said. "I've never seen or heard of foxes attacking dogs. Some people do use dogs to chase and kill foxes, but I don't know that dogs would chase foxes if they weren't encouraged by men," he said.

They found the fences were all in good shape, with only an occasional wire to be refastened or a tree limb to be removed. In places where the horses couldn't be ridden right by the fence, Lora would ride her horse and lead Tim's horse, going around the obstruction to rejoin Tim farther along the fence.

By noon, they had checked out more than half of the six mile-long boundary fence. The warm sun had caused them both to shed their coats and tie them to the backs of the saddles.

Stopping for lunch on the top of the highest hill on the property, Tim opened one of his saddlebags and gave each of the horses a small amount of grain. With their backs against the trunks of small trees, Tim and Lora sat down to eat their lunch.

To hear the weather report, a vital element of farm work planning, Lora took a small transistor radio from the lunch bag, turned it on and put it on a nearby tree stump. Lora tuned in to a radio station that featured farm news and the local events. She kept the volume turned down low until the announcer started giving weather information, then turned it up so both of them could hear the complete farm report.

"Today's weather continues fair and warm, with only a ten percent chance of showers. The high for today is expected to be in the upper sixties or low seventies. Tonight will be clear and cool with a low of forty-five degrees. Tomorrow will be slightly warmer, with a possible chance of showers late in the afternoon."

The announcer then gave the livestock prices for cattle, hogs, sheep and the current prices for grain. When the commercials started, Lora turned off the radio and put it back in the lunch bag. Tim passed the canteen to Lora, waited for her to drink, then took it back and drank of the cool water himself.

Finished with his meal, he turned to Lora and said, "That fox den, last year, was only a little way from here. Do you want to ride over there to see if there are any fox pups there this year?"

"Sure," Lora said. "I have a pair of binoculars in my saddle bag."

"I'll get them while you put the lunch bag away, said Tim."

Ten minutes later, they tied the horses to a fence post and, glasses in hand, crept quietly to a vantage point downwind from the fox den. Concealed from sight by a cluster of thickly growing, young pine shrubs, Lora and Tim waited and watched for any sign of the den being occupied.

The fox is normally a nocturnal animal, feeding at night when they feel safer. During the time of raising young, the adults will hunt during the day to satisfy the hunger of their growing pups.

Tim and Lora had to wait only a short time until they saw the old fox approach the den with a fresh killed grouse in it's mouth. He dropped the bird at the mouth of the den, whined and stepped away a short distance.

As Tim and Lora watched, the female fox came from behind a large log nearby, picked up the grouse and carried it out of sight behind the log.

"The babies may be too young to eat meat," Lora whispered.

"You may be right," Tim whispered back. "Let's slip away before they scent us," Tim added.

Careful to make little noise, Tim and Lora returned to the horses and rode back to continue checking and repairing the line fence. As they worked, Lora told Tim she thought Chestnut was treating Pepper like a mother fox. Tim agreed with her, adding,

"Animals may be a lot smarter than we think."

By three o'clock that afternoon, they had finished their work and were back home. While Tim cared for the horses and did his evening chores around the barns, Lora went to the house to prepare the evening meal.

~

The nice weather continued with only a normal amount of rain for the season. April came and the cows were already giving birth to their calves, night and day. John, Tim and Lora were busy most of the time, until the middle of the month, helping new heifers with difficult births and urging new calves to their feet to nurse the first time.

By the third week of April, all the cows had calved and the work eased up enough to allow the Buckmans to get more sleep. They now had over a hundred new calves, raising the total herd count to more than four hundred head.

The Buckmans had developed a reputation for having good breeding animals and sold many young bulls and heifers to other beef growers. The main selling period was in the spring of the year.

To keep the best class of livestock and their reputation, it was necessary to cull out and sell any animal that was less than perfect. This culling process took place each spring and fall. To further maintain and improve the quality of the herd, the Buckmans bought only the best "proven bulls" for herd sires.

Since the Buckman land was mostly rolling or slightly hilly, they did not raise corn. This meant they had to acquire corn by trading or buying from other sources. Most of the time they were able to trade with neighboring farmers to an advantage for both parties.

Nearly everything coming to, or going off the farm was by the truckload. For this purpose, large platform scales had been built under the roof of one of the storage sheds. Whether buying, selling or trading, everything was carefully weighed on these scales. The scales were frequently tested to assure accuracy. A weight ticket was made out for each load and an entry made in the scales record book. A complete, detailed description of everything weighed was maintained for the farm account books. These records were invaluable to Lora, who kept the farm books, did the taxes, and handled the banking for the family.

This year, to keep the herd size within the capacity of the farm, it would be necessary to sell or trade about two hundred head of cows, bulls, heifers and calves. By the first of

May, a load of cull animals of all ages was trucked off to a commercial livestock market. Next, some of their regular buyers came and purchased over a hundred young heifers and bulls for breeding stock.

This left the Buckmans with a herd of about three hundred head, some of which they had committed to neighbors, in exchange for shelled corn, to be delivered in the latter part of the year. The incoming corn would be mixed with the small grain raised on the farm, as needed, for fall and winter-feeding.

Each year, a ten-ton load of peanut meal was ordered from a supplier in Georgia. As the grain was ground, peanut meal was added to attain the needed protein level for calves, cows or other animals. Since the Buckmans didn't raise many animals for slaughter, they used the peanut meal more sparingly than would be for finishing beef animals. If, as occasionally happened, all the young stock weren't sold as breeders; the remaining animals were penned up and fed a richer ration to prepare them for the commercial market.

Late in June, the breeding cows and heifers were to be separated from the other animals and put in well fenced fields near the farmstead. The choice "proven" bulls would be put in with the breeders to start the calf production cycle all over again. The bulls were separated and taken back to the bull yard by the first of August. Cows that failed to breed were culled out and sold as soon as possible. This practice had been followed closely for years and it was now rare to have more than four or five barren cows each year. Since the Buckmans preferred the taste of mature beef to young beef, when a fat, barren cow was available, they would butcher her for home use.

~

Many things were happening on the Buckman farm this particular year. Mary brought home one hundred six-week old baby chickens and put them in the small, heated brooder house during the third week of March. Pepper delivered six little, furry, multicolored puppies the same day. She wouldn't let Chestnut come near the doghouse or eat from her food bowl. She spent all but a few minutes each day curled up around the tiny little pups.

To keep the doghouse warm, John covered it almost completely with bales of straw, leaving only an opening at the door. After a week had passed, Pepper had become less defensive and permitted the fox to come back to the food bowls, but always guarded the opening to the dog house until he had gone away.

Chestnut carried in mice, rats, birds and sometimes a rabbit or squirrel. Pepper preferred the food John and Mary had always given her, so she didn't eat the game Chestnut provided. John didn't know how to discourage Chestnut from bringing his catch to Pepper at first, but discovered that he quit supplying them when the animals weren't eaten.

When the puppies were three weeks old, John and Tim made a chicken-wire pen around the doghouse to keep the pups contained. Soon, the little dogs were eating from their own bowl and Chestnut gave up, completely, trying to feed them.

Two of the four horses the Buckmans owned were registered quarter horse mares. Both mares foaled that spring. One had a colt, the other a filly. To reduce the demands on the other members of the family, Mary took charge of the mares and colts.

Mary combed, brushed, petted, fed and watered the animals with such tenderness that she soon had both mares and colts eating out of her hands. She took some soft pieces of craft leather, using her sewing machine, and made little halters for the colts. By the time the colts were a month old, Mary could lead them all around the stables.

In March, the Buckmans contracted with a small construction company to build four large ponds on the farm. One of the ponds would capture the runoff water from the hilliest part of their land and create a twelve to fifteen acre reservoir. When all the ponds were full, approximately twenty-five acres would be covered with water. The contract called for all the work to be completed in six months.

One sunny day, Tim and Lora cashed in a five thousand-dollar Certificate of Deposit at the bank. They bought an International garden tractor, with a complete set of attachments, for John and Mary who would celebrate their thirty-fifth anniversary that summer.

Tim plowed and worked the garden with one of the older farm tractors. Using the new garden tractor and a precision planter, one of the new attachments, the Buckmans proceeded to plant enough gardens to feed themselves and many of their neighbors. Fortunately, the row spacings were wide enough to permit cultivating with some of the other attachments. They later hired a neighbor boy to come over and pull weeds out of the garden each week.

John traded his old pickup truck in on a small, new four-wheel drive pickup. Tim bought John's old truck back from the car dealer for seven hundred dollars. He knew the old truck to be in excellent shape, mechanically.

He then had a local farm repair shop install an auger-equipped feed hopper on the truck. The unit was ideal for filling the cattle feeders and made it easy for anyone to perform that demanding task.

Pepper's puppies grew very quickly and when Pepper weaned them, Paul Cross came over to select his pup. After looking the pups over for quite a long time, he offered to buy all five of the remaining young dogs. The four Buckmans talked it over and agreed to let Paul have a total of five pups, but would keep a cute little female for themselves.

For several days after Paul took the pups away, Pepper lay by the pen gate and hardly ate at all. She licked and groomed the last little puppy almost constantly in her loneliness.

When the hay season arrived, two part-time men became full-time employees to help with the farm work. Approximately ninety acres of hay was to be harvested this year. Most of the hay was alfalfa, which would have to be mowed and baled three or four times during the season. The mower-conditioner would make the hay ready for the round baler in one to two days after cutting, depending on how fast the hay cured.

When everything went right, one of the men kept mowing and the other ran the round baler. John and Tim, on the especially equipped tractors, hauled the huge round bales from the fields and put them in storage sheds or barns. Barring rain, the work would go on every day until each cutting was complete.

This year the Buckmans had thirty-five acres of wheat and fifty acres of winter barley to harvest. After the grain was combined, the fields were also mowed and all the straw baled in regular square bales. Some of the wheat straw was kept for barn bedding, but all the remaining straw was sold to various buyers as in prior years.

It was a constant battle to get all the hay and small grains harvested each year without losing too much due to heavy rains. They all listened to weather reports morning, noon, and night, but John had become almost an expert on predicting the weather. The Buckman farm seldom lost more than a few acres each year. Any hay damaged beyond use for feed was used for bedding in the cattle feeding barns and loafing areas.

~

Pepper's baby was a smart little devil. She figured out so many ways to get out of her pen, that John and Mary finally gave up and hooked the gate in an open position. With the gate left open, she appeared to be content to run and play until she tired, then return to the doghouse for long naps and her four daily meals. Her meals were small amounts of meats, cereals and milk. Anything not eaten at once was taken away immediately. When she was three months old, her meals were cut to three each day.

John and Mary could not agree on a name for the frisky pup for a long time. When either of them made a suggestion, the other one would come up with some reason the name didn't fit.

More and more, the little dog's speed, quick action, and even her appearance suggested the qualities of a female fox. They discussed calling her Vixen and then Vickie, and suddenly the pup had a name.

Vickie learned her name, and to come when called in just two days. With the use of treats, when she responded quickly, she learned other simple commands easily. The hardest thing to teach her was to stay in the yard, away from cars, trucks and tractors. The Buckmans all feared she would be run over and crippled or killed.

Pepper solved the problem. Watching Mary's and John's actions to keep Vickie in the yard, Pepper took over and administered some sharp toothed lessons to Vickie at the edge of the yard. From then on, Pepper was used as a teacher anytime Vickie needed special tutoring.

From the beginning of her freedom outside the pen, Vickie liked Chestnut as a great friend. Her persistent play, chewing and pulling on his ears and tail and other antics, caused

Chestnut to respond in kind. He would come to the yard every evening for an hour or so of games and mock-fights with the little dog.

At first, Pepper was worried about these roughhouse sessions, but soon joined in herself. The two dogs would join forces trying to catch the fleet footed fox but never succeeded. He sometimes put on daring displays of agility that amazed the watching humans. Running at full speed, Chestnut appeared to float over the ground. He could change direction in two strides with little loss of speed. Going all out, he would jump five or six feet up into the air, reverse his body and land running in the opposite direction. Chestnut seemed to be able to disappear in the blink of an eye. In the middle of a mock fight with the dogs, he would flash away to the tree-filled part of the yard, dart behind a tree trunk, and be lost to sight.

From their vantage point in the house, John and Mary could sometimes see Chestnut glide out of the trees, unseen by the dogs, circle and come back to hide in a place the dogs had already searched. Whether Vickie knew it or not, Chestnut had become her teacher also. Vickie loved the play periods and was learning many things that would affect her future life on and around the Buckman farm.

Vickie made attempts to follow the fox away when the evening play sessions ended. Each time, Chestnut would pick Vickie up, in his mouth, by the back of the neck and bring her back to the dog pen. Then, if she persisted, Chestnut would strike her with his nose, tumbling her back to the pen. The lesson was finally learned and Vickie only whined plaintively when Chestnut went away for the night.

~

Rats and mice are a fact of life on the farm. If many

precautions aren't taken, any place grain is stored soon becomes infested with the sharp-toothed, gray vermin. All grain and feed on the Buckman farm was stored in metal buildings with concrete floors and foundations. John always kept a few cats that were good for mouse control and would even kill some rats. Chestnut was a welcome addition to the cats in keeping the rat and mouse population down around the barns and storage buildings.

Like most farms, there were things like fence posts, logs and rough lumber stored outdoors in various places around the farm. Pepper examined these places for the scent of rodents, and would help John and Tim kill the pests anytime some of the wood was moved.

At night, the rats would travel from a stack of lumber to the pond or creek to get water. Chestnut would lay in wait by the water and make short work of any rodent caught in the open. He also caught many of the pests in the stored rolls of hay and bales of straw.

As Vickie developed in size and strength, she often followed Pepper into the field behind the houses. This field was pasture for the horses, and was only mowed to keep weeds down. A marshy, spring-fed stream flowed through the field, making a perfect environment for field mice, marsh rats, and some muskrats in the creek.

Vickie would follow Pepper and try to copy her pursuit of the little varmints. From the beginning, her sharp sense of smell made it easy for her to find mice in the grass, but her clumsy efforts to catch them seemed to be hopeless. Both Chestnut and Pepper were more interested in the animals in the marsh and creek, than in the mice in the field. They would dig into the spongy creek bank to expose whole nests of rats, which they quickly disposed of, seldom letting even one escape. At times, Chestnut would gather up several of the rats in his mouth and carry them off for some reason of his own. Pepper, usually, just dug a small hole and buried her catch.

Vickie sometimes tried to dig up what Pepper buried, but Pepper discouraged Vickie from this by snarling and snapping at her until she quit trying to dig.

With little help from Vickie that first summer, Chestnut, Pepper and the cats did an excellent job of reducing the rodent population around the farmstead. However, Vickie learned a lot by observing her mother and the yearling fox. By the end of her first summer, Vickie learned to trap mice in the grass with her front feet, and then finish them off with quick little bites or by grabbing and shaking them.

~

In August, when all the straw had been baled and removed from the fields, the stubble fields were well worked with disc and float drags, in preparation for planting the fields with alfalfa seed. A large combination seeder-fertilizer drill-was used to plant the new crop.

After the alfalfa was planted, other fields were worked down and the wheat and barley crops planted. The alfalfa, wheat, and barley would establish good root systems and enough growth in the warm, late summer and cool fall days, to make a good stand the following spring.

By mid-September, the hectic part of the year's work was behind them, and the Buckmans had time to take life easier and catch up on chores around the houses and barns. Everyone in the family pitched in to help harvest and store the late vegetables from the garden. The chickens were sorted, leaving forty pullets to put into the laying house, along with four choice young roosters.

The fryers that hadn't been eaten that summer were dressed and put in the freezer for later use. Two fat, barren heifers were sent to the local butcher, along with two pigs a neighbor had raised in exchange for a calf.

After the apples were picked, the best were stored in the basements, and several bushels taken to a nearby mill where the juice was bottled. Most of it would be used as cider and some to turn into vinegar, which Mary used to make pickles the next year.

Until late in the fall, the work on the farm kept everyone busy, but not overworked. The two full-time men had been kept busy mowing weeds, cutting brush and putting in field drain tile. The tiles would take excess water from some fields and run it into the just completed ponds.

One small pond was already filled with water from some ever-flowing springs in the hillsides. The other ponds were ready for the water from winter snow and rain.

Tim and Lora, now followed by Pepper and Vickie, often rode by the ponds, just to check them and to enjoy the sight of the slowly increasing amount of water held back by the earth, rock and concrete dams. Stocking the ponds with fish was planned for the future, after the ponds were stable and all the vegetation around them was restored. Already, the new grass was showing bright and green, through the straw mulch, on all the contoured earth around the ponds. The ponds were enclosed with woven wire fences, and cattle watering tanks had been installed below the dams. Water-level control pipes and irrigation hook-up pipes protruded through the concrete of each dam.

Lora was astride her horse on the bank above the large pond, early one morning, when she spotted Chestnut running toward his old home den. He had a mouth full of small animals, which he was apparently taking to his mother's half-grown babies.

Lora rode to the hilltop, where the young pines grew, and took out her binoculars to watch the den area. She was just settled when Chestnut appeared at the den. Through the glasses, Lora saw Chestnut drop the rodents from his mouth and heard him give a series of shrill barks. Out of the den came a thin female fox and two skinny, undersized fox pups.

Lora correctly surmised some disaster had occurred to the family. The old male had been caught in a long forgotten trap and the mother, forced to hunt alone, had been shot in the leg by an out of season hunter. All but two of the young foxes perished because they had been unable to feed themselves. The female and the two pups existed only because Chestnut had heard the pup's hungry cries and responded by bringing food to the den.

Several times after Lora first saw Chestnut take food to the fox den, she observed him taking muskrats, rabbits or other game, from near the farm buildings, and carry them away toward the fox burrow. She made a special effort to check on the foxes and was happy to find the mother fox had recovered, the young foxes were healthy and had grown to near normal size before the weather turned cold that fall.

Chapter Three

Chapter Three ~

By the first of December, the cattle had been separated and moved to their winter quarters. The last of the corn had been delivered and stored in the metal buildings. The meat for the winter was brought home and stored in the freezers. The new hens were laying more eggs than the Buckman family needed each day. The surplus eggs were given to the two hired men, who were cutting and stacking firewood for themselves, and the two Buckman homes. The daily chores only required a few hours each day.

For the first time in their lives, Mary and John were all set to take a real vacation. With the help of the two hired men, Tim and Lora would be able to handle all the farm work.

On December second, in a rented motor coach, John and Mary set out on a trip through the southern and western part of the country. The trip was intended to last for three to five weeks or, as John put it,

"Until we are good and ready to come home."

Mary promised to call home each time they selected a new destination, and at any other time necessary to keep Tim and Lora informed "as to their whereabouts". Mary called almost every night they were away.

For the first time since their wedding, the younger Buckman couple was alone on the farm. Now that the work was at a much reduced pace, Tim only needed help grinding feed or taking hay to the cattle. He took turns using the hired men to give each man some income. Mary saw to keeping them supplied with eggs, meat from the freezer, and vegetables from the big root cellar. Both men were very happy with the arrangements, especially after Tim let each one take a deer from the large number living on the farm. The men were cautioned not to reveal from where the deer came to avoid attracting other uninvited hunters.

Chestnut happened to be near when the first deer was taken early one morning. At the sound of the shot, he left the area at a dead run and stayed away for over a week. When he returned one evening, he was very shy and kept well away from the area of the gunshot.

Vickie had grown to a size somewhat larger than Chestnut, and had become quite a fast runner. As her winter coat came on, she acquired a smoky blue-gray color on her back and sides, while her underbelly, chest and throat became a lighter slate gray. Her black tail was white tipped and each foot had white toes below jet-black legs. She also had a dime-sized spot of white on her chin and another between her eyes. She had inherited features from both Pepper and her Blue Heeler father. The combination of her mixed ancestry had produced a well proportioned, strong bodied animal, with long tapered legs ending in wide feet with exceptionally strong toes. Her wide, deep chest indicated large lungs and endurance.

Vickie was no longer kept away from the barns. She had learned to keep away from moving vehicles and also to follow most of the commands of her human protectors. Vickie liked to receive the same praise Pepper got for performing well. As soon as she learned to follow any signal or command, the Buckmans made a point of petting and talking to her to reward her performance.

Vickie now followed Pepper almost constantly. When Tim left Pepper on guard at an open gate, while he drove the tractor or truck through with bales of hay or a load of ground feed, Pepper would keep the cattle from passing through the opening until Tim came back and closed the gate. At first, a large number of the big cows or bulls intimidated Vickie, but by copying Pepper's tactics, she soon learned the cattle could be controlled.

Any time Vickie did something to disrupt the cattle while being moved from place to place around the feeding areas, Pepper would snarl at Vickie, and even nip her, to teach her not to confuse the big animals. Vickie was still just a pup and made many mistakes, but she learned quickly and seldom forgot a lesson.

One important lesson Vickie learned the hard way was to stay clear of the heels of anything on the farm. One day she playfully ran up and barked at the back feet of one of the young colts. Instinctively, the colt lashed back with a foot and sent Vickie tumbling head over heels. Luckily, she had been very close to the colt's foot and was pushed rather than struck a hard blow. No bones were broken, but Vickie had a very sore shoulder for a few days.

A short time later, Vickie tried the same trick on a four hundred-pound calf and received a bloody nose and mouth for her efforts. Vickie was due to have some shots at the time, so Tim took her to the vet who checked her over and assured Tim the dog was alright. After those two lessons, she copied Pepper and did her barking far enough away to avoid the hard hooves of all the animals.

As Vickie grew larger, Pepper's house became too crowded for both dogs. Vickie had started sleeping on the rug of Lora's enclosed back porch. A pet door allowed her to come and go freely.

Lora found a large, wooden box in the workshop, which she put on the back porch for Vickie. The box was placed on its side with a small folded rug inside for padding. Vickie slept in the box or on the rug by the door until the nights became colder, then slept in the box all the time.

With John and Mary away, Lora assumed the feeding and grooming of Pepper and Vickie. She also took care of the young colts, now living in a separate lot and stable, keeping them from the older horses until they were weaned from nursing. The colts could still touch noses with their mothers across the board fence. Vickie, remembering to stay away from their back feet, liked to join the colts in their frolicking runs around the four-acre lot. They seemed to enjoy having the speedy dog join them and did their best to outrun her. At first, Vickie could only follow along behind as the colts raced around the lot. Then Vickie learned to run on the inside of the circuit, covering a much shorter distance and staying almost even with the young horses. By cutting across the narrow ends of the lot, Vickie seemed to be leading the race. Sometimes the older horses became inspired by the antics of the dog and the colts and raced around their own pasture field, bucking, kicking, snorting and farting as they ran.

To continue with the training of the colts, Tim and Lora bought a pair of regular adjustable halters for them. Every few days, they would put lead ropes on the colts and take them along as they rode out to check the cattle, or when going to inspect the ponds.

The colts were always glad to be out of the lot and willing to go, especially when Tim and Lora rode the colt's mothers on these trips. Tim made a practice of giving cookies or apples to the horses when he went to the stables. Vickie always begged a cookie if she happened to be near when Tim gave the horses their treats.

The riding trips made quite a colorful party for Tim and Lora. Riding two horses, leading the colts, Pepper and Vickie running ahead and Chestnut joining in sometimes amused them all.

~

The night of December twentieth, Mary called to say she and John were in Lexington, Kentucky, on their way home. Lora was not at all surprised, since she had detected a feeling

38

of homesickness in Mary's recent phone calls. Tim had often said to expect them home sooner than his parents' original intentions of several weeks.

Right after the welcome call, Tim went over to his parent's house and turned the thermostat up from fifty to seventy-two degrees. Lora came over to join him a few minutes later.

She had made a large cardboard poster, reading "Welcome Home-Merry Christmas" in red and green, surrounded by pine tree tips taped to the edges. They hung the poster from the living room mantle, then checked to be sure the house was in perfect condition before going back across the yard to their house.

At noon the next day, Mary and John drove the motor coach into the driveway, blowing the horn all the way. The dogs ran, barking loudly, to meet the vehicle. Lora and Tim, expecting them, were also waiting when Mary opened the coach door. Pepper rushed right through the open door to jump on John before he could even get out of the bucket seat. Vickie was leaping up and down trying to get Mary's attention. After a hug and kiss for Lora and Tim, Mary took Vickie in her arms and gave her the attention she was seeking. The two dogs kept jumping back and forth between Mary and John, while the happy group walked to the younger couple's house for lunch and much happy conversation.

The dogs begged to come in with them, so Lora spread a small rug by the back door and made them stay on it while the Buckmans had their meal. After a lengthy lunch,' Tim helped his parent's empty and clean out the motor coach, while Lora did the dishes. Then Lora and Nary followed the coach, in Mary's station wagon, as the men returned and paid the fees for its use. The dogs, still excited, rode in the back.

After returning the coach, the four of them did some quick shopping and then started home with John and Lora in the back seat.

John said, "I've had all the driving I'll need for a long while."

The dogs had their heads over the seat back, as if to take part in any conversation. John, halfheartedly, scolded Mary for opening a sack and giving each dog a piece of candy.

Two days before Christmas the weather became cold and windy. Heavy clouds moved in from the west and snow came swirling down to coat trees and fences. That night the wind ceased and the snow fell straight down to deposit an ankle deep layer of the white crystals on every surface.

At first, Vickie refused to leave the shelter of the porch the next morning. She had never seen anything like this before. After some hesitant steps in the snow, she finally decided it was safe to join Pepper in the yard. The snow had so changed everything that Vickie had to explore all around the houses and barns.

By the time John came out to start cleaning the steps, the dogs had made trails in the snow everywhere he looked. John expected to see fox tracks also, but didn't because Chestnut was still up on top of the hay in the storage shed. Sensing the change in weather, Chestnut had caught and consumed a foraging muskrat at dawn the day before. He could easily go another day without eating, if necessary. Anyway, there were mice still to be had in the hay stored in all the buildings. He could take life easy for many days, if he so desired.

There was a lot of coming and going by the friends and neighbors on Christmas Eve day. The Buckmans were popular with merchants in the area and received small gifts from many of them each year. The Buckmans also exchanged gifts with a few life-long friends on this day. In addition to all the established gift giving this year, large baskets of fruit, some of which John and Mary had brought back from Florida, were made. Apples, pears, oranges, and tangerines were delivered to the homes of the men who had worked for them the past several months. There were two decorated bushel baskets for each family and a Christmas check for each of the men.

Christmas Eve in Lora's kitchen eating area was a quiet, relaxed time for sandwiches of country ham and glasses of ice-cold cider. Later, with cups of coffee and pieces of apple pie, baked by friends, the four of them exchanged gifts and discussed pleasant happenings that had occurred since the previous Christmas. They all agreed they had much to be thankful for. It was a very nice evening on the farm.

It was snowing again on Christmas morning. Tim and his father spent all morning hauling extra hay and topping up the feed bins. All the cattle were given extra grain rations and the calf feeders were filled to overflowing. The men finished the work and came back to John and Mary's house in time to clean up for the big annual Christmas dinner. Mary, who hadn't done any cooking for three weeks, had insisted on cooking this meal all by herself.

Mary served baked chicken and dressing, rich homemade noodles, and mashed potatoes with giblet gravy. Homemade jelly, hot buns and country butter from another neighbor, deviled eggs, pickles and celery sticks, glasses of milk and cider, and pecan pie were served with coffee to wind up the meal.

After the meal, the men put the soiled dishes in the dishwasher while the women took care of the leftovers. When everything was all cleaned up, the four of them went into the family room and lit the fire in the fireplace. In just a few minutes, both Tim and his dad were asleep in their chairs.

It was still snowing when Tim and Lora went home at nine o'clock that evening. The old snow had settled to a firm layer, only a couple of inches deep, but the new snow had accumulated to a combined depth of about seven or eight inches.

Again, during the night it grew colder and a wind out 'of the northwest caused some drifting of the falling snow. By morning, most of the ditches and fence rows were accumulating deep drifts of hard snow. The temperature had dropped to fifteen degrees on the outside thermometer, but the wind made it feel like fifteen below zero.

In ski mask, insulated coveralls, parkas and double thick footwear, Tim and John fed the cattle and checked the water supply in every lot and field. Despite the extra warm clothing, both men were chilled to the bone by the time the work was done for the day.

Lora draped a thick, warm rug so it hung down over the open side of Vickie's box, as well as completely covering the rest of the surface, to help keep Vickie warm. She quickly figured out how to get in and out under the cover. Both dogs were given an additional amount of warm food that evening.

Sometime during the night, Pepper came and crawled in with Vickie. The air let in when Pepper entered the box was bitter cold. The warmth of two bodies in the box made for good sleeping. Sometimes a little crowding can be a good thing.

The bad weather continued right on to the end of the year.

Tim spent two whole days plowing out driveways and roads around the buildings and feed lots. Even using the largest, most powerful tractor on the place, at times it took many tries to break through some of the huge drifts and clear a passage so John could take hay through for the cattle.

New Year's Day was much warmer than prior days had been. The temperature rose to forty degrees. The snow started melting, settling down several inches in one day and night. On the third day of the month, the weather turned bad again with an intense cold rain that slowly turned to sleet.

It continued to get colder each hour with the sleet turning to hard fine snow, like grains of sand that stung the skin and brought tears to the eyes. The half-melted layer of old snow turned rock-hard and slick as real ice.

John and Tim put chains on the four-wheel drive tractor in order to get up and down the sloping roads to the feed lots. Where the roads had been plowed out before, the thawing and freezing had turned the slopes to icy chutes, too slick to even walk on.

As the old snow became hard frozen, the cattle could walk on it, but often fell down and had trouble getting back to their feet. To reduce the number of possible injuries to the pregnant cows, all of them were shut into the lots Where the wasted hay from the feed bunks was spread out to make paths to the water tanks, feeders and cattle shelters. Sand was hauled in and spread so the feed truck could function.

The water tanks were spring fed and did not 'freeze, so the animals were content to stay confined to the areas where food and water was always available without the hazards of walking on the treacherous, icy fields.

The dogs were always out with the men in good or bad weather. Their coats were thick and warm enough for the coldest conditions. Their sharp toenails penetrated the ice enough to provide good footing. This ability made it easy for them to keep the cattle away from open gates while the men moved in and out of the pens with loads of hay and ground feed.

Vickie loved to ride in the old truck, with the auger-equipped feed bin mounted in the back. As soon as John or Tim opened the truck door, Vickie would jump right in and get up on the seat, put her front feet on the dash, and stay there until the truck was stopped at the first gate. When the truck door was opened, she would dash right up to the gate as if she was anxious to take up guard duty.

By the middle of January, Vickie had learned the job well enough to leave her at one gate while Pepper guarded another one. Once, Vickie became distracted from her duty by a red squirrel on a nearby tree. Pepper saw Vickie leaping at the squirrel and calves going toward the open gate. Pepper drove the calves away and then jumped on Vickie, thoroughly trouncing the younger dog. Vickie was forced back to the open gate where she crouched down in the middle of the opening until Tim drove back with the truck.

Vickie didn't get back in the truck after Tim closed the gate this time, and she took care to stay well behind the older dog as they trotted back to the garage where the truck was parked. An extremely docile Vickie followed Tim to the back porch, entered her box and stayed there, licking the places Pepper's teeth had painfully pinched her that day. From that day on, Vickie never abandoned any place she was left to guard. At this time, Vickie was only about ten months old, but she was well educated for one so young.

Since late fall, the Buckmans had been putting out food for the birds and squirrels around the farmstead. When the severe weather struck, Tim called a farrier to put special shoes on the two gelding horses. Tim and Lora then could safely ride them to take food to the woods for the wildlife that spent the winter in the shelters of pine, spruce, cedar and vine covered, brushy hillsides. Every few days Tim and Lora, each carrying a sack of grain, rode the geldings over safe trails through the woods to feed the wild birds and animals.

The deer came right into the feed lots to help themselves to hay and grain, some becoming almost tame as the bad weather continued all through January. Wild rabbits also came into the open buildings and feed bunks for the food they needed for survival. Their regular supply of grass, hay' and saplings were encased in ice or buried in snow. Foxes came to the feed lots to catch rabbits, but also helped themselves to the rich ground feed in the calf feeders. 'Coons and 'Possums learned to eat the calf feed as the cold winter progressed and more snow fell on frozen creeks and ponds.

The long awaited January thaw finally came the last week of the month. The air temperature rose to just above freezing and a bright sun melted the snow and ice from trees, power lines and fences. The snow on the ground softened on top and settled down into the bottom layer of solid ice. At night it became cold again to solidify the softened snow.

The mild weather only lasted three days before the clouds and cold north wind brought more real winter days and frigid nights, but only a small amount of snow.

~

The Buckmans had surplus hay to sell most years. They stored all the hay in barns and sheds to keep the quality of hay at the maximum for their own animals, so the hay would bring top prices when sold. The hay could be safely stored for one or two years, if necessary, and retain a good level of nutrition. When selling, the older hay was disposed of before the new crop was offered.

The long, severe winter had caused a demand for cattle and horse feed, with a higher than normal price, especially for alfalfa. John and Tim planned to sell a hundred tons of alfalfa hay at this time, while retaining an ample supply for their own animals.

John made a few phone calls to previous buyers and arranged to sell all the hay at one hundred twenty dollars per ton, with the buyers furnishing their own trucks or wagons. John and Tim weighed the hay as it came from storage, before loading it on the buyer's equipment.

The hay selling activity kept Tim busy for several mornings, so Lora took food out to the woods for the wild animals by herself. Naturally, the dogs went with her each time and were joined by Chestnut when they neared his lay-up in the pile of treetops behind the bull yard.

Vickie always stayed very close to Lora, but Pepper and Chestnut would go off by themselves out of Lora's sight. Unknown by the Buckmans but soon discovered, Pepper was in heat. Not quite ready to accept a mate, Pepper still attracted Chestnut, was now almost two years old. He was mature enough to be interested but not old enough to actively seek a permanent mate among the wild foxes.

Out of sight, Pepper and Chestnut were going through all the preliminary actions of courtship. Pepper was careful to stay within hearing distance of Lora on the gelding, and to catch glimpses of her from time to time. Several times Chestnut made timid attempts to mount Pepper, but she always whirled away and snapped at the fox in pretended anger.

~

Lora turned her horse to ride back along the fenced lot where the calf herd was being kept after she finished putting out the wildlife food. When she reached the back corner of the lot she found a dead bull calf, it's head caught in the fence, two feet above the ground.

Lora tied the horse some distance down the fence and walked back to inspect the calf. The calf's forequarters were held off the ground by the head thrust through the fence. The stomach had been torn open and partially eaten away. The back end of the calf had been badly chewed, with the hipbones exposed by whatever had been feeding on the carcass and blood had seeped from punctures in the neck.

Lora mounted her horse and started home, calling the dogs as she went. Pepper came running at once and Chestnut trotted back to his nest in the old treetops.

Arriving at the scale shed, just as the men finished loading a big truck with hay, Lora informed them of what she had just found. After Lora gave them all the facts about the dead calf, Tim got on the horse Lora had been riding and set off to see the dead animal and check the rest of the calf herd.

Tim rode through the herd, inspecting all the half-grown animals, but didn't see anything wrong with them. Then he tied the horse to a hay bunk and started walking toward the most distant corner of the twenty-acre lot. As he walked, he kept a close eye to the ground. At first, near the feeding area, he found only hard packed snow, beaten down by dozens of calf feet. As he neared the back corner, he found many other kinds of tracks made by wildlife, but very few calf tracks.

When he was only a hundred yards from the farthest corner of the lot, Tim found many dog tracks and some fresh blood by a place where a calf had fallen and then got back to its feet.

There appeared to be three or four sets of dog tracks following the path of the apparently fleeing calf. He found another patch of bloody snow in a cluster of pines where the dog prints obliterated the calf tracks.

When he came to the partially eaten calf with the head caught in the fence, Tim had the details of the calf's death pretty well worked out in his mind. When he turned the body so he could see the back legs, Tim was sure he was right. The tendon on one back leg had been bitten almost all the way through. In trying to evade the dogs, the calf had run its head through the fence, trapping itself for the killers. He left the dead calf where it was and rode back home.

Back at the house, Tim related what he had seen and his conclusions to the rest of the family. John agreed that Tim was probably right and that there might be a really severe problem facing them.

"Normally, the dog pack would kill enough deer for food,

but the hard frozen snow that's on the ground lets the deer escape," John said. "Now, the dogs have learned how easy it is to kill a calf and if we don't get them, we'll lose more calves," he concluded.

"Can't we trap the dogs?" Mary asked.

"I don't know how," John replied. "I'll call the sheriff, the game warden, and the dog warden to see if they have any ideas," John stated, as he picked up the phone.

"Well, I know where I'm going to spend the night," Tim said. "I sure wish it wasn't so cold," he added. Those dogs will probably come back to the calf to eat again tonight. I plan to be there with a shotgun when they start feeding," he emphatically stated.

When John had finished his calls, he wasn't too happy. All three parties contacted had advised him to "go ahead and shoot the dogs". The game warden said he would come and help if necessary.

"But, what if the dogs are some of our neighbor's pets?" Lora asked.

Tim answered her by saying, "Those dogs ate at least thirty to forty pounds of calf meat in one night. I don't believe our neighbor's pets would be that hungry. I feel sure we have a pack of feral dogs on our hands.

"So do I," John supported Tim. "I wonder what kind of dogs we're facing?" John asked Tim.

"I don't know, but only one set of tracks appeared to be made by a very large dog. The other tracks were only medium sized like a large Beagle or a Pointer," Tim replied. "Anyway, I plan to find out tonight, and I'd better get ready," he added.

"Now just a minute," said Mary. "We're all in this together, so let's work out the solution together," she chided Tim.

"Right," said Lora, "and since we're all here, I'll fix supper while we make some good, safe plans.

"That's a fine idea, Lora," said John.

"What do you have in mind, Tim?" Mary asked.

"I gave it some thought while I was out at the calf lot and while riding back," Tim replied. "I think I'll take Dad's four wheeler, park it down wind five or six hundred feet, and then walk up close enough to shoot if I see or hear the dogs at the calf," Tim explained.

"I have a suggestion," said John. "Why don't we go out right now, taking enough bales of straw to make a warm blind down wind for a place to keep you from freezing in this wind."

"Okay. If we hurry, we can be back by the time Lora has supper ready," Tim said as he rose from the table.

John and Tim loaded the truck with bales of straw and were ready to leave, when suddenly John said, "Wait Tim, let me get that little tarp. We can put it over the top to keep the wind out and cut down on any sound we make in the blind, tonight."

"What do you mean by 'we'?" Tim asked.

John just chuckled as he went to get the tarp. When he returned, he had the tarp under one arm, some one- by- four strips under the other, and some short two-by-four blocks and a roll of baling twine in his hands.

Arriving at the bull yard, they found a good level spot forty yards from the calf's body, just in front of some young cedar trees. Using the bales of straw, they quickly constructed a little straw house, about four by six feet inside. The side facing the calf was three bales high and the rest of the walls were five bales high. An opening, about one and one-half feet wide, was left for a door in the side away from the dead calf. The door opening was braced with the two-by-four blocks and one-by-four strips were tied in place with twine to the outside corners of the bales to keep them in place. Two strips were laid across the top to act as rafters.

The tarp was slipped over the top of the whole thing, pulled down to the ground and stretched tight with more twine tied into the bottom bales. One flap of the tarp was left untied at the opening for access.

One bale of straw was opened and spread on the ground inside the blind, and two bales of straw placed as a seat for the person sitting inside. The remaining bales were opened and scattered on top of the snow to form a path for several yards behind the blind. The straw would prevent the snow from crunching underfoot while approaching the blind.

Last of all, John used his pocketknife to open a vertical seam in the tarp on the side where the bales were only three high, facing the anticipated targets.

Tim went inside and sat down on the straw bale seat and propped the tarp slit open with a two-by-four block. He could see the target area perfectly. Before leaving the blind he removed the block from the slit and left it lay on the top bale, with the few remaining blocks.

Before leaving to go home, the two men walked part way down the hill toward the calf, turned and looked back at the blind. The dark green tarp blended right in with the cedars, completely hiding the bales of straw. As usual, John's thinking had produced good results.

Tim punched his dad lightly on the shoulder and said, "Great job Dad."

"When it gets dark, that little structure will just about disappear," John replied.

They were all four seated at the table in Lora's kitchen eating their evening meal just as it became dark outside.

"We should keep the dogs here at home tonight," Mary said.

"Yes, we will," Lora replied. "I'll shut Vickie in on the back porch. Pepper will stay here, near her house, if you' are firm about it."

"Right Lora, I'll put her 'on guard'. Pepper won't leave the yard until I release her." John said.

Finished eating, Tim went to the gun cabinet in the hall. He took out his twelve gauge automatic shotgun with a thirty-inch long barrel, a box of buckshot shells, his shell bag and a pair of shooting mittens. He then dressed in heavy insulated clothes and arctic boots. Lora and Mary had his flashlight, a sandwich and a thermos of coffee in a small box sitting on the kitchen table, ready for Tim to take with him.

John came in from the back porch to say, "The dogs are taken care of for the night. We won't have to worry about them following us. Tim, you take the first part of the night. I'll come out to relieve you about midnight, then you can come back out there about four o'clock in the morning, if that suits you," John said.

Tim hesitated, but agreed to John's timetable after Mary and Lora supported John's suggestion. Tim pulled on a pair of lined gloves, wrapped a scarf around his neck, put the shell bag into the cardboard box and said, "Well, I'm ready to go."

Giving Tim a hug, Lora said, "Now you be careful. Don't stay out there too long and get too cold."

"I won't," Tim answered, then picked up his shotgun and headed for the door. John carried the heavy little box of supplies out to the' truck, wished Tim "Good luck" and re-turned to Lora's warm kitchen.

Vickie whined and barked for a few minutes, then settled down quietly to sleep in her box on the porch.

"I'll put Pepper in with Vickie when it's time for me to go out to relieve Tim," John said. "In the mean time, I'd better go home and try to get some sleep. This could turn into a long night," he added.

Pepper peeked out at John and Mary as they crossed the yard to their house. Mary commented on how much less wind was blowing as they entered the door. The thermometer on a post in the yard was setting on ten above zero. A full moon was trying to shine through thinning clouds as Tim drove with lights out past the feed bunks in the calf lot. Turning the ignition off, he let the truck coast in neutral down the slope to the first clump of trees. He left the truck parked about three hundred yards from the blind. With the shotgun in his right hand and the box under his left arm, he moved slowly toward the northwest corner of the lot where the dead calf lay.

The snow crunched and squealed under his boots, no matter how careful he was, until he reached the straw path. When he drew near the blind, Tim estimated the wind speed had dropped to only five or ten miles an hour. Inside, he put the cardboard box on the floor to the right of the opening, placed the flashlight and the box of shells on top of a bale, before pulling the heavy tarp back in place to close the opening.

Leaving the flashlight on the bale, he turned it on so he could see to load the gun. Then, pushing the safety button on safe, Tim put ten more shells in the shell bag and put the remaining shells back into the cardboard box on the floor. He then placed the shell bag, flashlight, mittens and thermos bottle out of the way, but close to hand on top of the straw bales on each side of the slit in the tarp.

With one of the short two-by-four blocks, Tim wedged open the slit in the tarp so he could see out. He then stacked up the other blocks under the slit to act as a support for the gun. With the shotgun resting on the blocks, the barrel pointing at the target area, Tim could be more relaxed than if he held the cold gun in his hands.

Pouring himself a cup of coffee, Tim sat down on the bales to wait, watch and listen. The moonlight was stronger now. He could just make out the dark shape of the calf on the snow.

He sipped the coffee, holding the hot cup between his hands to absorb the heat. The last swallow of coffee was only lukewarm, so he put the cup back on the thermos and put the mittens on over his gloves.

An hour passed, and then another. Tim was getting cold and sleepy. High in the sky, the wind tore the clouds apart to let the wintry moon shine through, making everything around Tim stand out in sharp relief above the hard white snow.

As Tim watched, three light colored foxes came up silently, outside the fence to stare for long minutes at the dead calf and the area around them. The larger of the foxes slipped under the fence, sniffed at the cold meat and then began feeding on the exposed rear quarter. The other two foxes joined the first one and tore at the opened stomach area.

Tim concentrated hard on the feeding foxes so long that he became mesmerized by the spectacle so near to him. The slight wind brought only the sound of teeth on flesh and bones for the next hour. Tim nodded off to sleep for just seconds, then jerked wide-awake to find the foxes gone.

Despite dropping off to sleep for a moment, Tim was sure he hadn't made a noise to scare the foxes, but why had they left so suddenly, he wondered. Tim stood up carefully, removed his cap to uncover his ears and then leaned close to the slit in the tarp for a wider view and better hearing. Only some faint, muffled sounds from the calf feeders reached his ears. He could see nothing moving in front of the blind except a large opossum moving silently toward the abandoned carcass. The gray-white scavenger crawled right inside the open body cavity of the frozen calf.

Tim's ears hurt with the cold and his eyes watered from the wind coming in through the slit. He sat down and put his cap on, but left the earflaps loose so he could still hear well. He waited. He ate his sandwich and drank more coffee. The opossum, satisfied, left the carcass and waddled past the blind out of sight. Time passed slowly. Tim's head dropped to his chest. It was eleven P.M.

Chapter four

Chapter Four

Chapter Four ~

Just over a mile west of the calf pen, in a jumble of hills, rocks and cliffs on the edge of a state forest preserve, a large, red Doberman dog came out of a cave at the rear of a rock ledge. Her right ear ragged and bloody, hung down behind her bulging head painful and useless. Blood was crusted above the eye on that side. She had an annoying sound in her other ear and the sight in the left eye was slightly blurred as she looked out over the ravine below and to the east of where she stood.

Two more dogs, her nearly grown, mixed-blood offspring, soon joined her.

The previous winter, her careless owner had ignored the Dobermans heat cycle, leaving her in his backyard while he went to work. Normally the, sometimes vicious, dog would have killed an intruder, but due to being in heat, she had welcomed a neighbor's male dog, a pure bred racing Greyhound.

Three days in a row, the greyhound sailed back and forth over the six foot high yard fence to mate with the amorous, now gentle, red dog.

One day, the Doberman's owner came home and found the dogs locked together in his back yard. Enraged, he beat the dogs until they separated, then threw the greyhound over the fence and grabbed the red dog by the collar to put her in the garage.

The mistreated dog turned on her owner, biting him severely as she forced him to flee the garage. He locked her in the building for several days without food or water, until she became weak and nearly helpless. Using the clothesline prop, the man slipped a choke chain on the dog, choked her and threw her into his car trunk.

It took the still angry man two hours to reach the state park, east of Cincinnati. He drove around the park for another half-hour until dark, then opened the trunk, removed her collar and choke chain and prodded the Doberman out on the snow by the park road. He closed the trunk lid and drove away without looking back.

Her owner wasn't the first person Dutch the Doberman had bitten. At age two, her first owner sent her away to a school for guard dogs for training. Dutch paid no attention to the padded sleeves the trainers wore. When taunted, she always went for the legs or neck of the men. After three weeks without success, the school manager called the owner to come get the dog. Learning of the animal's bad habits, he authorized the manager to dispose of the large, untrainable dog.

When Jarvis, her tough acting, prospective buyer came to the school for a "big, mean dog," he left with Dutch and a "no warranty, no return" receipt for his two hundred dollars. Jarvis didn't even ask for the papers on the dog. The papers gave her name as Duchess Elga Von Scheer. "Dutch" sounded just like the dog Jarvis wanted.

In the following two years, Dutch attacked the mailman, the meter man and a friendly, dog loving, policeman who came to see Jarvis after complaints by neighbors who had been chased into their houses by the Doberman.

Since the policeman's visit, Jarvis kept Dutch in the house basement or on a long chain in the back yard. Dutch's constant moving and jerking against her chain and collar tore them up in short order. Jarvis made a trip back to the dog school where he paid another fifty dollars for a very strong, hardened chain and a special leather covered, steel lined collar to keep the powerful dog confined.

Dutch had never had but one friend, the lady next door. Her name was Wilma. Wilma gave Dutch the only meat she had ever eaten. She also gave Dutch water when Jarvis forgot to fill the pan under the faucet at the rear of the house. Sometimes Wilma would roll her wheelchair under the cherry tree by the fence and talk to Dutch while she knitted or crocheted things for a craft store.

Dutch would lay on the ground by the fence and watch for the lady to come down the ramp in her wheelchair. She liked the way Wilma smelled, like flowers and fresh grass except when she brought meat. The scent of the meat caused Dutch to drool and lick her lips. At times the meat was raw, fresh from the butchers. Even the cooked meat was good, but Dutch liked the raw meat best.

When the water pan was empty, or even low and stale, Wilma would take her aluminum clothesline pole, poke it through the fence and hold the lever down on the faucet until the water overflowed the pan. Dutch would always lap at the water pouring down from the faucet.

Wilma watched every day as the two dogs mated in the yard next door. Now that there was snow on the ground, she preferred not to go out in her wheelchair, but she could open a window to talk to the Doberman and toss her pieces of meat. Most of the time, in cold weather, Dutch stayed in her doghouse, but always came out when she heard Wilma open her window. Luckily for Dutch, Wilma could still reach the faucet with the pole, which she kept propped up in the corner of her kitchen. Wilma was happy to think Dutch would have babies. Maybe Jarvis would treat her better now.

Wilma had gone to the craft store to deliver a carton of things when Jarvis beat and put Dutch in the garage. She noticed Jarvis had a bandage on one hand, but never knew why. She didn't see Jarvis put the dog in the trunk of his car because the garage concealed the car from her sight.

Wilma missed Dutch, but never found out what happened to her. Jarvis didn't speak to any of his neighbors.

~

Luck played a major role in Dutch's survival the winter she was discarded. The park had numerous fresh water springs and clear running streams, flowing too fast to freeze solid, therefore, she never lacked for water. Even in winter, many local townspeople and tourists from more distant cities visited the scenic preserve to walk along paved paths and well-marked trails. Some of these visitors threw food out along the roads and paths, or put uneaten food in the many containers provided for waste items.

Dutch found water and then food within minutes of her abandonment. She drank cold spring water from a stone trough only fifty feet from the road, and then literally stumbled over a nearly full box of fried chicken in the snow by a path leading away from the trough. Dutch was so weak from privation, she was barely able to chew up the chicken bones.

After eating, Dutch found a stack of picnic tables chained to the side of a low, brown painted storage building. Leaves had almost filled the space under the bottom row of tables. She forced her way through the leaves until she reached the side of the building. There she turned around and around, pushing at the leaves with her nose, until she had a nest large enough to curl up in for the night.

Before dawn, the first morning, the big, gaunt Doberman left her nest in the leaves to slake her thirst and find more food. After filling up on water at the stone trough again, she found a trash barrel overflowing with the previous day's refuse, and turned it over. Among the plastic containers and paper bags, she found and devoured hot dogs, hamburgers, empty buns and many other bits and pieces of meat, a large package of sweet rolls and a container of potato salad.

Her hunger for food seemed to increase each day. Not because she didn't find food, but because running free her body was burning up more calories as she became more active. Also, her metabolism was changing as the ten peanut-sized fetuses developed in her womb.

The second night Dutch spent in the park, she came upon a large raccoon in a trash barrel. She now took this stranger as an invader in her private domain. When the 'coon dropped from the top of the container to the ground, snarling aggressively at the big dog, Dutch dived at the 'coon and instinctively sank her teeth into the furry demon's neck and crushed it to death.

When the blood from the expiring animal reached her taste buds, Dutch liked the taste. It was even better than the meat the lady, named Wilma, had given her over the years.

Dutch carried the raccoon's body into the woods and began chewing on it. The tough skin resisted her teeth until she began ripping at the belly, then she found by holding down with her feet and pulling with her teeth, she had no trouble getting at the warm meat inside. Within the next two days and nights, Dutch consumed every morsel of the twenty-five pound beast except the hide, tail and large bones.

Dutch changed considerably in the first month she spent in the forest. All the exercise she was getting converted the fat and flabby muscle tissue in which she came to the park, into sound flesh and long, stringy muscles. She learned to use stealth to catch unwary squirrels, and her growing speed to bring down fat, lazy rabbits. One morning she tried to sneak up on a fox that was busy digging into the top of a muskrat house. The muskrat's house protruded about two feet above the ice, a few feet from the shore of a small lake.

The fox knew from experience to first, dig directly into the underwater tunnel used by the muskrat to enter the space above water, inside the house of reeds. By digging in and blocking the tunnel to prevent escape, the digger could then open up the way into the den area and take the occupants as they scrambled out on the ice.

Bellied down behind a bed of' dead reeds, Dutch eased forward on the snow toward the fox. The fox saw the dog coming through the woods when the dog was more than a quarter of a mile away. The fox kept on digging. As the dog came closer, it suddenly crouched down in the brush. The fox knew he had been seen by the dog, but kept right on chewing and digging at the reeds.

At a hundred yards, the fox could smell and hear the dog coming through the brush. The fox ignored it. When the dog was only fifty or sixty feet away, the fox tore open the den, plunged his head into the opening and snatched out a young muskrat. One by one, while Dutch came within twenty-five feet, the fox caught and killed two young and two old muskrats.

When Dutch smelled the blood from the kills, she couldn't maintain her patience any longer. She charged through the reeds to find the fox trotting away over the ice with the old male 'rat in his mouth. Thinking the fox was the source of the food smell, Dutch changed directions to intercept the now running, fox.

With its head start and familiarity with running on ice, the fox easily beat the dog across the lake into the woods. Inside the woods the fox scooted in one end of a hollow tree, dropped his prey and ran out the other end. By accident, Dutch spotted the fox headed back to the lake and chased after it.

The dog and fox made two more fast trips between the muskrat house and the hollow tree before Dutch gave up on the fox and carried off the last rat as her only reward for a hard morning's work.

Dutch's good luck continued to serve her. The park employees had seen her at the trash barrels and knew she was responsible for the mess made around the containers. The truck driver and his helper kept a shotgun in the truck, hoping to kill the big red dog when they came around to collect the trash.

The truck driver had his chance one day but made a simple mistake. He loaded the shotgun with light birdshot. Dutch was almost completely inside the overturned container when the driver spotted her. She heard the squeal of brakes as the truck came to a stop fifty feet away. By the time the driver grabbed the gun and jumped out to shoot at her, Dutch was more than a hundred feet away and running fast for the woods. A few of the tiny pellets struck her with the first loud boom of the gun. The sting of the pellets encouraged Dutch to run even faster, and by the time the truck driver got off the second shot, she was well out of range.

The skin on her hip stayed irritated until the wounds festered and the pellets worked out. Dutch helped the process by biting and licking at the sore spots.

She didn't come back to the scene of her wounding again that winter. She gave up her nest under the picnic tables and found a new sleeping place farther from the road where Jarvis had dumped her. The new site was southeast of her first nest by about one mile, still two miles from the Buckman farm. She still raided the trash containers along some forest roads for part of her food.

Dutch occasionally gave chase to deer living in the protected forest, but had no success until one evening she came upon a young doe that carried an arrow in her left back leg lodged there for days and causing infection. The arrow had been shot into the deer by one of many illegal crossbow hunters who frequented the hills of Ohio.

Dutch came across the place where the sick, wounded deer had lain down to rest. The ground and leaves were rank with the smell of blood and drainage from the deer's leg. Dutch followed the trail south along a stream for more than an hour before catching sight of the young doe. The deer had been aware of the dog for some time and was trying to escape down the stream.

The doe was exhausted when Dutch came upon a large pool of blood where she had paused to regain her wind. Caught between a sheer rock face, on her right side and a high bank above the frozen creek on her left, the terrified doe plunged down onto the shallow ice only to break through into the frigid water below.

The doe lunged and struggled across the creek to the far side, but all her strength was gone when Dutch, running on the unbroken ice, bit through the tendon of the deer's uninjured back leg. The death battle extended several yards from the creek, back into a tangle of brush and vines.

With one back leg useless from the arrow and the other crippled where Dutch had torn away the tendon, the doe, her rear quarters on the ground, still tried to strike at the dog with her sharp front hoofs. For the first time, Dutch met with real resistance, but she pressed her attack until she was able to sink her teeth into the valiant doe's throat. After that, the deer quit resisting and gave up her life to the still silent, red killer. Dutch hadn't barked once during the chase or the time of her first major kill.

Dutch found the deer hide to be much more difficult to cut through than the small animals she had killed before, but after some effort she had the belly open and fed on the hot entrails. She ate many pounds of the meat and then walked over to the creek to drink at the channel the deer had made in the ice. She spent the next few days guarding her kill, eating huge amounts of flesh and sleeping at night in the base of a hollow sycamore tree, only feet from the dwindling carcass.

~

The big Doberman's first deer kill took place in the most remote area of the forest preserve. The area was almost primitive because the broken terrain had not been farmed in the past, and real roads had been too costly to construct. Even logging had not been profitable to the landowners. Only small amounts of timber had been harvested in the last hundred years, and no timber had been cut since the state had acquired the land.

Rattlesnakes and Copperheads infested the area from the warm weather of late spring until the cool nights of late September, when the temperature drove the snakes to hunt shelter underground. Therefore, hikers and campers were rare in this wilderness of dense woodlands, thickets, vines and rock jumbled ravines during the summer.

The relatively light human traffic in this wild haven was made up primarily of park personnel, game control officers and a larger number of hunters and fishermen in season. Trapping was not permitted, but still occasionally practiced by some area residents.

Poachers hunted deer, night and day, all year round in this part of Ohio. Local law enforcement departments made halfhearted attempts to control illegal killing of deer, but realized many area poor people hunted from necessity. It would have kept an army of officers busy patrolling the thousands of acres of hilly country. Governing officials frequently pondered how to pay for such a large number of officers to patrol the dense, remote area.

Following the land acquisition by the state, there had been a general increase in the wildlife population of the entire Appalachian foothill country. The deer herds increased many times over the decades, while also spreading out over lands surrounding the forest preserve. An annual deer-hunting season was established after World War II. Legal hunting and illegal poaching kept the deer herds from increasing beyond the capacity of the land to support them.

Bobcat and coyote sightings and even reports of black bear were heard around places where hunters congregated. In fact, the wildlife in general had increased tremendously, drawing thousands of people to the many parks and forests.

Good paying jobs in the city drew away many of the young people growing up in these foothills. Many others found employment with contractors building power plants and highways close by. The number of people supported by farming was reduced each year until only a fraction of the number tilling the soil in bygone years remained. For far too many, tobacco was the only cash crop. A few determined souls sought out a living cutting timber and selling it to local sawmill operators who made only marginal profits.

By the time Dutch came to the area referred to as "The Little Smokies," hundreds of farms had been allowed to grow back into woodlands. She could travel for miles in some directions outside the park itself without encountering more than an occasional, occupied farmhouse. She would instead, find dozens of weekend cabins and hunters shacks used by the non-resident owners for all kinds of purposes.

~

Dutch finished with the deer carcass, then traveled on down the creek in search of more food. She soon came across a female raccoon caught in a steel trap at the bottom of a muskrat slide on the creek bank. The trap chain was fastened to a wooden stake, driven into the gravel beneath the swiftly flowing water of the rapids, about two feet from the creek bank. In her efforts to escape, the raccoon had entangled the trap chain around the stake and would have drowned in time. The animal was clinging to the top of the stake to keep her head above water.

Dutch waded into the chest deep, chilling water and quickly killed the unresisting, mask faced animal. She easily pulled the stake out of the gravel, then carried trap and all to the top of a nearby bluff to eat her latest prey.

The big red dog lived well, for a few days, off the fur-bearing animals she found in traps along the mile long trap line. Alive or dead, the animals were kept fresh by the cold air or by the nearly ice cold water. She had been an the wilds for over a month now, getting stronger and more wise in the ways of her ancestors who roamed the forest of Europe and Asia for thousands of years before a breed called "Doberman" existed. Dutch still carried the genes of her hunting forebearers. The skills of the hunter were being reshaped in her brain and the capability in her body.

When the' out of season' trapper found his traps missing or empty, he was furious. He lay in wait all one night with a high powered rifle to kill the trap raider. As bait, he tethered a pet 'coon by the creek in an opening where he could get shots at the fur thief from his vantage point in a tree. On a portable deer stand, thirty feet up the tree, he sat for hours in the cold, moonlit night. When Dutch finally came in sight, the trapper opened fire as soon as she grabbed for the raccoon.

Just as Dutch picked up the docile little animal to crush it's head in her jaws, a bullet struck the raccoon in the shoulder. The heavy, fast traveling slug delivered a terrific wallop to the raccoon, transmitting the force to the dog's jaws. Knocked over by the impact of the bullet, Dutch instinctively retained her grip on the animal and rolled back to her feet. She barely felt the slight pull as the tether on the raccoon parted.

Bullet's flying past, Dutch left the scene in great lurching bounds, her prize flopping from her mouth.

Unscathed until she reached the first of the trees along the creek bank, almost safe, the last bullet from the rifle ricocheted from a tree, burned across the top of her neck and almost severed her right ear. The soft nosed bullet had mushroomed, in the sapwood of the tree trunk, to almost an inch in diameter before striking the dog. The slug-like projectile passed through the root 'of the ear, coming apart in the process. A dime-sized piece of lead was left under the skin between the right eye and ear.

Badly hurt, Dutch ran until she had put a lot of distance between herself and the shooter, who didn't know he had almost accomplished his objective. Dutch still had the 'coon in her mouth when she stopped to rest.

Dutch had been running toward the rising sun, which was causing the sky to lighten when she finally dropped the 'coon and lay down on the cold ground. Blood stained her head, neck and shoulders as it seeped from the mutilated ear. She tried to lick at the ear with her tongue, but couldn't reach it. Twigs and leaves became matted in the bloody hair of her neck and head. Blood licked from her shoulder made her thirsty so she picked up the dead 'coon and moved toward the sound of water falling over rocks, somewhere ahead.

Dutch came out of the timber on top of a bluff running north and south at her feet. Below, she could see water falling over slate ledges in a small brook. The water came from a hole in the ground beneath a rock to her left. She started down over the bluff to reach the water, but was stopped from completing her descent when the path turned to the right along a sheer cliff parallel to the creek. Dutch had almost walked off the cliff.

She followed the path south along the top of the cliff for thirty or forty yards. Here the path she was on dipped back and opened into a large cavern created by an overhanging ledge of limestone, fifteen feet deep and twenty-five or thirty feet wide, along the cliff side. The solid slab of rock forming the roof of this half-round room was about four or five feet above the crumbling stone and powdery clay floor.

At the rear of the cavern, almost hidden behind a deep drift of poplar leaves, was the top of an almost square opening. The sun, just peeking over the eastern hills, sent rays of bright golden light into the gloom of the opening. Dutch, in pain, tired, and now feeling an urgent need for water, dropped her burden on the leaves and came out to the path that continued south along the cliff. She followed the, now downsloping path to a point where she found a place she could descend to the brook.

Dutch lapped at the cool, sweet water for a long time. Then she waded right into a shallow pool of water and coarse gravel and rolled around to cleanse her matted coat. Careful to protect her injury, she switched back and forth on her back until she had scrubbed away most of the irritating incrustation on her neck and shoulders.

The water came from a deep spring, in the ravine and was nearly sixty degrees, but the air temperature was only about twenty-five degrees this February morning. Dutch came out of the pool and repeatedly shook herself to throw off the water then rolled in a bed of pine needles to finish drying her coat. After drinking again, she made her way back up to the path and returned to the room-like place above the cliff.

Hungry and weakened by loss of blood, Dutch fed on the 'coon and then curled up in the pile of poplar leaves to sleep away most of the day.

Her womb now contained only nine mouse-sized babies. The other one had failed to develop and had been absorbed by her system. In just a little over a month there would be puppies born. At the Buckman farm, Pepper was also waiting to have her first litter of pups. The two mothers were destined to meet in the future.

~

While the big red Doberman slept, a routine, but almost miraculous event occurred. As the sun rose higher in the eastern sky, a warm mass of air moved into Ohio from the southwest. By noon, the temperature had climbed to sixty degrees. The snow melted away from protected sunny areas to expose layers of sodden leaves and bare ground. By four o'clock the temperature reached seventy degrees and the warm wind kept blowing across the land.

In her rock house, the dog stretched and yawned, then dozed again for a short time. Somewhat dizzy from the ugly, swollen mass of her wounded ear, she made her way back to the water below to sip and lap at the refreshing liquid. The water felt good on her wound as she turned her injured ear down and held it in a tiny pool. The cool water helped ease the throbbing pain.

At dusk, Dutch ate most of the solid meat on the 'coon carcass before going back to her bed. She was already feeling better. Her body was strong and her will to live, stronger. Again she slept.

The next several days of late February were warm and bright. Birds appeared as if by magic, to scratch in the thawing earth for seeds, bugs and worms. Chipmunks and squirrels competed for hidden acorns, beechnuts and hickory nuts. Many rabbits had survived the winter and now came out at dusk to feast on saplings, shoots and still green plants uncovered by the melting snow of which very little could be found.

Dutch came across a bonanza in the form of a farm recently converted to soil conservation, just a short run from her cavern. Most of the fields had been planted in grasses to control erosion. The elderly couple living in the farmhouse only did enough mowing, with a rotary cutter pulled by a tractor, to keep down weeds and prevent the intrusion of the adjacent forest. The only crop raised was two or three acres of tobacco. It grew on a flat section of land near a group of weathered barns and small buildings behind the small white house.

In search of food, three days after her injury occurred, Dutch came to the edge of the woods and looked out over the nearest open field. Coming toward her, along an intersecting farm fence, was an old buck groundhog. She didn't know it, but she was between the groundhog and his burrow by a tree just behind her.

The "woodchuck," as most people called them, was not in the least bit intimidated by the dog. He had fought several scraps with farm dogs and easily won them all. Stopping under the barbed wire fence, ten feet from Dutch, the surly acting, odd smelling, brownish animal raised up on his back legs and chirped a warning to the dog blocking the den.

Dutch responded to the chuck by charging, striking him in the stomach with her nose and gaping mouth. The twenty pound rodent, struck by over eighty pounds of speeding, hardnosed dog, was knocked breathless back into the field. Her momentum carried Dutch right through the bottom strands of rusty wire. Before the groundhog could gather its senses, she had him firmly gripped by the neck. Dutch found the skin on the 'chuck to be the toughest of any small animal she had eaten so far.

The unusually warm days gave way to more normal weather as March came in. Some snow, rain and wind mixed with gradually milder weather and more sunshine, thawed out the earth and green came back to woods, fields and yards. Grouse, squirrel, rabbits and groundhogs were plentiful on and

71

around the farm, which became like a pantry to Dutch.

The Doberman's ear healed and the plugged up ear canal opened to drain when she gently rubbed her paw against the tender crusted area of her head. The hearing improved as the inflammation disappeared. The pulpy knot above her right eye, caused by the chunk of lead, stayed sore and tender. The ragged right ear hung down over the back of her head, but the pain had gone away.

The weight in her belly was starting to slow Dutch down and also affected her ability. As a result of the decrease in physical ability, she began to be more patient and stealthy in her approach to prey. By trial and error she perfected her ability to stalk game. The more patient she became, the more successful she was, especially with 'chucks and squirrels. Her sense of smell was now brought into full use finding bird nests and young rabbits in their tiny sunken pockets in the sod of open fields.

~

Dutch had often stuck her head into the dark, square hole at the back of her cavern on the cliff. She disliked the odor emanating from the hole and did not venture inside. In addition to the smell, there was a low, disquieting sound apparent deep in the gloomy hole.

One day, Dutch came back from her trip to the farm to find a huge, dark, furry creature and two very small, fuzzy miniatures of the large one, coming out of the hole. The huge animal charged at Dutch, giving out a loud roar as she bore down on the dog. Dutch fled back down the path as fast as she could run.

She stayed away for two nights and then cautiously returned to peer toward the hole. Slowly, she crept to the open-

72

ing to sniff and listen. The smell was faint and the cave was perfectly silent. Fearfully, Dutch entered to explore the cave. Cool air came in behind her to waft away through some unseen outlet above her head. Away from the opening, her eyes adjusted to the dim interior, Dutch followed the curve of the cave wall until she was back at the opening. The cave was a long, narrow oval much larger than Dutch's outside cavern, but the roof was only about three feet above the floor. In one place, a hollowed out bowl filled with the scent of the strange animal, Dutch took time to empty her bladder.

One evening, Dutch found a freshly killed buck below the hill behind the cave. She had heard a gunshot just before dark. The sound seemed to come from the place where she once slept under the picnic tables. Curious, she ventured in that direction. Halfway from the cave to the old stone trough where she once drank water, more shots rang out in the dark woods.

Dutch was scared now, not curious. She turned and ran away from the sounds. Nearing the hill behind the cliff, she found a large clot of fresh blood and more blood was spattered on leaves to the right of the trail she was running in. Dutch followed the scent of deer and blood as it circled away from her original path and then almost back to the same trail several hundred feet from the point where it first caught her attention.

The blood spots ended but the hot scent of the deer was still plain to her sharp nose. She followed the deer smell to a narrow, deep ditch leading to the brook in front of the cave. The buck lay in the bottom of the ditch his stubby antlers encased in soft, spongy velvet. Not really hungry, she ate only part of the vital organs, then followed the ditch to the brook for a drink of water.

Birth contractions began before Dutch got back to the cavern. She nosed out a new hollow in the poplar leaves and lay down, only to get up and pace the cavern floor. Sharp pains

73

forced the air from her lungs. Dripping pink fluid, she waddled back to the new hollow in the leaves. Moaning softly, she curled into a ball and licked at the pink fluid oozing from her rear. Another spasm of pain struck accompanied by a gush of warm, thick fluid. This brought temporary relief to the panting dog but the pains soon returned.

By first light, eight sausage-shaped little pups were pulling at her nipples. One stillborn pup had been consumed with the placenta. The other eight had all been washed clean by her tongue and nudged into the warmth of her curved legs and belly.

At mid-day, Dutch slipped away from the squirming, whimpering pile of whelps to drink water and eat from the nearby deer carcass. She had only been gone ten minutes but the pups were complaining shrilly when she returned.

Fortunately, the nights were frosty and the deep ditch kept the sun from heating up the deer carcass. Fox, 'possum, mice, and one bobcat ate some of the meat, but the food lasted all the meat eaters until the buzzards cleaned the bones in less than a day. The handy food supply was gone.

Eight hungry pups, though only five days old, require a lot of milk. To make the milk, Dutch had to consume a lot of food. This meant that to get the food, Dutch had to leave the pups alone. Dutch stayed close to the cavern one more day, chewing on the smelly bones from time to time. On the seventh day, she returned to the old couple's farm to hunt.

Her strength and agility were both subnormal, due to her recent ordeal, but Dutch had far more drive and determination, now that she had the large litter of babies to feed. She stalked her game with a new cunning and silent wariness. The casual, almost playful times were put aside. She had to have meat.

There were no human hands to pet and fondle, feed, water and groom as in the days of Duchess Elga Von Scheer's

74

puppyhood. Nature however, had imbued Dutch with the instincts to survive and to care for her own.

Like a wraith, the gaunt but dug-heavy red dog ghosted through the woods on the way to the farm. Watching, listening, silent and sure-footed, Dutch mentally catalogued every bird and beast she saw, heard or smelled along the way.

For more than an hour, hunting the brushy fence line between the woods and fields, she found only one chipmunk. Shortly after eating the chipmunk, she arrived at a field of young clover and orchard grass bordered by a creek and an old farm road.

She left the fence row to move along the old sunken road beside the short, lush, new growth of clover and grass. A plump yearling groundhog was feeding on the tender vegetation some distance from the weed bordered road. Dutch stayed in the road until she was even with the 'chuck and then slid through the weeds to begin her stalk of the careless rodent.

By the time the young 'chuck saw her, it was too late. Dutch rushed the last few yards to catch and shake the fat, young beast. Not stopping to eat, she ran silently back to the brook, paused to drink, then climbed quickly up the path to the waiting mouths of her hungry litter. With pushing feet and vacuum tongues, the pile of demanding whelps welcomed Dutch home. When the pups were satisfied and back to sleep, Dutch fed on the 'chuck.

~

With the coming of April, spring was well established. There were still light frosts, but the days were growing warmer. Some days were filled with showers, but the sun beamed golden light over the forest and fields much of the time.

The damp floor of the woodlands aided Dutch in her

game stalking. The rotted leaves and softened twigs made little sound under her creeping feet. Between feedings, the pups were content in the bed of leaves on the ledge. Dutch had dug a much deeper bed down into the knee high mass. The sides of the nest were steep, and deep enough to keep the now open-eyed, curious whelps safe and hidden from the sharp-eyed hawks that flew by the open-faced cavern.

At the peak of her physical and mental condition, Dutch hunted several times each day to satisfy her demanding system. Leaner than ever, her speed and stamina was phenomenal for an animal that had spent such a short time in the wild.

As the pups grew larger they began to clamber out of the deep bed to waddle about the dirt floor of the cavern. They soon learned to chew at the rabbits, 'chucks and squirrels. Dutch brought to the ledge. She would rip open the small animals and place them where the pups could find them, which they learned to do in short order.

As the young dogs' eyesight and strength improved, so did their appetites. Soon, Dutch was hunting more of the time than she spent in the cavern. She was now gone for longer periods of time because she had to range farther from home to find food, having thinned out the game in the immediate area.

Dutch was returning to the cavern one morning, a pair of young rabbits an her mouth, when she met a coyote coming down the path with one of her dead pups clutched in his mouth. Dutch was instantly enraged. She dropped the rabbits and charged the coyote. In trying to turn to escape back up the slippery path, the dog-like creature stumbled over a loose rock and momentarily lost his footing.

The savage Doberman was on him in a flash. She sank her teeth into the coyote's left hip and bit down with all the strength in her massive jaws. Muscle and bones in the hip were crushed in an instant, but the coyote whipped around and slashed through the skin on the dog's neck, then fastened his teeth into Dutch's shoulder. She released the crushed hip, grabbed the coyotes left front leg and all but bit it off. Whipped and mortally crippled, the coyote struggled to escape. Dutch had a death grip on the back of the coyote's head, when the coyote slid off the narrow path.

Intent on killing the rank smelling beast, Dutch increased her grip on his neck and was pulled over the edge also. Locked together, the pair of predators rolled, bounded and slid to the bottom of the cliff. Stunned by the impact of striking a large rock in the ravine, Dutch held her grip on the coyote until his struggles ceased. Then, holding his head down with one front foot and his body with the other, Dutch bit, ripped, and tore the coyote's head from his body.

On three legs, Dutch hobbled over to the nearest pool to drink and to cleanse the wound in her shoulder. She couldn't reach the cuts on her neck with her tongue, but the bleeding stopped with little loss of blood. Before leaving the ravine, Dutch managed to scratch and kick some old leaves, pine needles and loose twigs over the coyote carcass.

The little pup's body had been knocked off the path during the battle. It was lodged on a protruding rock, halfway down the cliff face. The pup forgotten, she picked up the two young rabbit bodies and hobbled up to the cavern.

There were no pups in sight. Dutch searched the pile of leaves in vain for a frantic minute. The coyote's pungent odor was everywhere. Faint sounds from the cave opening came to her ears. Warily, she entered the hole to peer into the gloomy half-light ahead.

~

The curious, prowling young dogs had finally summoned up the courage to explore the dim, silent cave behind the cavern. First one, then another, sniffing and nosing pup made its way through the opening and down the short ramp of dirt and stones to the floor of the cave Within minutes, the eight little animals had taken possession of the dim space.

They found the bear's hollowed out birthing place at the farthest part of the long, narrow sanctuary and a deep, thin but wide opening extended back under the cave wall. The opening was too shallow for the little dogs to stand erect, but they all filed into the opening in crouched and crawling eagerness. Darker than the cave itself, still smelling faintly of bear cub urine and feces, the pups sniffed about in search of anything edible, or just to chew on.

The old male coyote had been aware of the dog and her litter of pups for some time. He had seen her hunting and bringing her kills back to the cavern in recent days. He also knew the big red dog would be a formidable adversary and therefore avoided a confrontation with her. The coyote wasn't afraid of being caught by the dog, but he would be careful to avoid injury if she cornered him.

When the coyote did come to the cavern, he came when the wind would carry the scent of the dog up the slope to him in time to be forewarned of her return. He checked the empty leaf nest, then tracked the pups into the cave. Following the scent and sound, he came to the pups' hideaway behind the bear hollow. Jamming his head under the rock, he was able to reach the tail of one pup. Dragging the yelping whelp out by his tail, the coyote bit him through the head and tossed him aside. The other pups had forced their way as far back in space as was possible to do. He could not reach them with his teeth, but was able to rake the back of one pup with his sharp toenails.

Fear of being caught in the cave caused the coyote to give up digging at the hard roof and floor of the slot. He picked up the four-pound body and fled to the cliff edge where he looked both ways before running down the south path. The scent of the pup in his mouth camouflaged Dutch's smell as he neared the bottom. Picking his way over the rock-strewn ledge, he rounded the sharp turn of the path, to come face to face with the big red dog.

~

Dutch stopped just inside the cave then heard the whimper of the injured pup in the slot. She moved toward the sound and the strong odor left by the digging pup killer. It took a long time to coax the seven remaining pups from their hiding place. When she had licked the blood from the split skin of the wounded pup, she then groomed the other six before stretching out in the bear's wallow for the litter to nurse.

From that time on, all the young dogs were content to stay in the cave when Dutch was absent, except for the injured pup. When Dutch left, the little sore-backed creature would go back out to the cavern until her mother returned. The only runt in the group, she was only about half the size of her mates. The week after her injury, she was plucked from the ledge by a cruising hawk.

Favoring her sore shoulder, Dutch fed on the coyote carcass for two days. That night a torrential rain fell on the forest. A small flash flood swept the coyote remains away downstream. The pup's body was dislodged from the rock on the cliff and also disappeared in the swift water below.

There were only six to feed now, but they were growing fast. Their need for meat increased. Dutch forced her sore shoulder to function and continued to hunt frequently.

The female coyote, now the sole provider at her den, was driven to find food at the nearby car parking area with all the trash barrels. The mess she made there by scattering litter, caused the truck driver to load his shotgun with high powered shells filled with buckshot.

The morning after the flash flood, the driver of the truck threw her riddled body into the compactor at the rear of the truck. Shortly after that, her two hungry, half grown offspring made their way to the same site, only to be killed by a single blast from the same shotgun.

The truck driver didn't brag about his three kills. It was illegal to carry a gun or kill wildlife by any means in the picnic areas of the forest, but he kept the loaded gun in the truck in case he spotted another barrel robber. After all, the park ranger was his cousin and they often shared venison with each other.

~

By the end of May, her six pups had a combined weight equaling that of a much thinner Dutch. Their gap-toothed mouths were hard pressed to deal with the tough hides of ground hogs or large deer, but had little choice if hunger was to be assuaged.

Twice the big red dog had found young fawns hidden in the tall grass along the tumbling brook. These she was able to carry to the den, but they lasted only one day each. By traveling to the far sides of the farm, she could still stalk and catch groundhogs but the fields nearest the cave, were nearly cleaned out. The few remaining 'chucks had learned to use sentinels to warn of Dutch's presence. Her efforts to run down large deer only speeded up the elimination of her milk and she now had no milk at all.

Experience taught Dutch to cut across the arc of circling deer to reduce the distance she had to cover when in pursuit of the big, fleet animals. She was lighter and stronger since her milk had dried up. Everything she ate now was utilized for her own benefit, rather than that of the offspring.

It still took Dutch most of one night to run down her first grown doe, one that ran on only three legs. This deer had been shot in the left front ankle when only a few months old, but had survived to bear a fawn.

Dutch passed very close to the hidden fawn while stalking the doe. When the chase started, the doe led the dog away from the hidden young deer and never came near it again, but the fleeing doe's loops and circles came within a hundred yards of the fawn several times before the chase ended. Sometimes reaching a distance of a half mile from her baby, the crippled doe led Dutch a five mile chase before giving up to her tenacious pursuer.

Dutch fed, drank water and fed some more. She rested and slept for a short time before trying to drag the carcass toward her den. By the time the sun came up, she had been able to move the one hundred fifty-pound body only a few hundred feet. Dutch was now completely exhausted from the chase and her attempts to take her kill home.

Tired and concerned for her pups, Dutch made her slow way back to them and finally led them to the doe's body. They stayed near the kill until it was nearly consumed, spending their first nights away from the cave.

Sometime in the third night, a mother opossum, babies clinging to her back, came to the now odiferous remains to feed. Dutch was away hunting again, but the six young dogs were sleeping beside a downed tree only ten feet away.

The pups woke up and attacked the small gray invaders. They were much smaller than the mother 'possum to drive them away as they had other varmints over the past three days. To the pups surprise, the 'possums seemed to die without a fight. "Playing possum" didn't do the little rat-like creatures any good. The pups ate them anyway. In the excitement of their first kill, the pups let the old 'possum sneak away and climb to the top of a redbud tree.

Unlike foxes and coyotes, dogs do not normally mature to the point of learning, or being able to hunt in a few months. But among her litter, Dutch had one precocious female that displayed some talent when she was only four months old. She had more of the features and shape of her Greyhound father than any of the pups. Long legs, long lean body, slender tapered tail, pert ears, small feet and a creamy tan coat distinguished her from her heavier bodied, dark colored mates with their thicker tails.

From birth, the tan pup had been the most active. Venturesome and aggressive, she became the dominant one. They started playing puppy games and having puppy fights.

Soon after the one-sided skirmish with the opossum, a thunderstorm struck the forest. Thunder and lightning intimidated the young dogs who were unsure of what to do in Dutch's absence. Unperturbed, the tan female led her littermates back to the warmth and safety of the cavern.

When Dutch came to the cavern at dawn, carrying a dead raccoon, five pups were asleep in the cave but the tan one was waiting in front for the thoroughly soaked Doberman. The tan pup set to work grooming the big red dog, removing most of the water from her coat, before feeding on the 'coon.

That summer in August, Dutch had her first and most frightening experience with a rattlesnake. One day she was leading her troop of six offspring up a rocky canyon-like stream bed, during the hottest time of the year. The stream was very low, but most of the pools held a few to several inches of fresh water. While wading in a pool, the tan pup was the first to catch one of the fish they came across. Some water still trickled down the very bottom, but not enough to allow the fish to escape, so her capture came easy. The pools contained pike, perch, bass and catfish. The entire group of dogs ate their fill of fish and then followed Dutch under some wide-spreading spruce limbs to rest in the shade.

The rattler was also under the tree to escape the hot sun. Gorged on fish, the snake was headed for an opening under a rock slab when the big red dog stepped under the tree. The snake, thinking he was being attacked, buzzed his inch long rattles and struck at the same moment. Hampered by the large amount of fish he had just consumed, the strike was off target as Dutch jerked her head back, but one venomous fang penetrated her upper lip on the right side of her mouth. The snake's single fang completely penetrated the lip as it clamped down with its mouth to pump the venom into its victim.

Most of the venom squirted over her teeth as Dutch snapped her head around to dislodge the reptile. The snake's fang was ripped right out of its head and stayed in her lip as she jumped backward into the creekbed.

Dutch whined, gasping in pain, while she rubbed her mouth against the sandy ground, then dug at the painful lip with her right front paw. One of her toenails hooked the glob of flesh on the snake's fang and pulled it free, but the pain grew more intense until she pushed her nose into the nearest pool of water.

She slashed her open mouth right and left through the water, washing the venom out of her mouth and the open wound where the fang had ripped her lip. The water in the shallow, rock pool was hot to the touch from the direct rays of the sun. The hot water helped increase the flow of blood from Dutch's lip. The flowing blood carried most of the poison out with it, reducing the burning pain.

The pain became bearable in a short time, but Dutch's anger was still evident when she abruptly left the water and headed for the rock the snake had gone under. The rock was only an inch or two thick and about two feet square. Dutch pawed the rock aside with one powerful tug of her feet. The snake was there.

Now Dutch had killed snakes before, but never a rattler and knew she had to catch the snake in her teeth, very close to the head so it couldn't turn its head to bite her. She had learned this lesson when killing a big rat snake earlier in the summer.

With the snake exposed, Dutch teased it into striking repeatedly at her snarling mouth, each time darting in and out to easily avoid being bitten again. After awhile the snake's striking speed was reduced to slow motion and only inches in distance. Too fast for the eye to follow, Dutch smashed her feet down on the snake's head and bit into it's body close to her feet. She stepped back and grabbed the rattler behind the head with her teeth, crushing and chewing until the thrashing snake dropped free, minus it's head.

Spitting out the poisonous head, the big red avenger turned her back on the three foot long, writhing serpent's body and trotted away to find some cool water to drink. The unusual five-minute ordeal was an invaluable lesson to the six half-grown feral dogs.

~

The tan female and the largest male pup were flanking their mother, with the other four following close behind, when Dutch detected the large fawn, motionless and almost scentless, in the fence corner. She froze in her tracks causing the flanking dogs to stop also. The other four copied the front three. Dutch looked left at the tan dog, then right at the black dog, then over her shoulder at the four behind her. The ones at the rear come silently up to spread out beside the front group.

The fawn was trapped between the dogs and the four-foot high, woven wire fence. The big red dog looked at the tan dog again. The tan dog moved slowly forward, placing her delicate feet very quietly on the ground. The tan female locked eyes with the fawn in the tall grass. She made two more careful steps, and her first deer kill. The litter of pups had become part of a dog pack on this warm September day.

At sixty pounds, Tan outweighed the fawn by several pounds and was much stronger. With only a show of teeth and a single warning snarl, Dutch kept the other dogs away while Tan ate her fill. When Dutch snarled, the gap in her lip opened up to expose fully the teeth in her upper jaw. The poison from the rattler bite had festered, the lip swelling and turning black. Digging at the lip with her toenails had opened a groove that never grew back together. Now this gap made Dutch look particularly vicious when she flared her lip in a snarl.

The big red dog and her pack made a meal from Tan's kill and slept the afternoon away in the sunny fence corner, while, less than three miles away, the Buckmans were digging potatoes and storing vegetables for the coming winter.

Tan and her long legged brother could actually outrun Dutch for a short distance, but hadn't developed the stamina to keep up with her on a long chase. Dutch had also learned that a steady loping pace produced more kills than a fast, short run which tired her and made the deer leave the familiar territory.

First Tan, then her largest brother, began to follow Dutch in the chase. In the beginning, Tan would charge full speed ahead when a deer was jumped, only to lose the deer and be lost from her mother in some distant place. Dutch would find the lost dog and bring her back to the deer track before taking up the chase again. Tan soon learned to use her nose as well as her sight to keep on the track, giving up some of the excitement of the high-speed chase.

As soon as Brother joined in the pursuits, and learned to stay on the deer's trail, Dutch would break off for a time while the two young dogs kept the deer moving. Tan picked up this tactic also, and in a short time the three tenacious predators could bring even the strongest deer to bay in a few hours.

By the time the leaves on the trees had turned from green to a rainbow of brilliant colors and frost had killed the weeds along the home area brook, all seven of the dogs were involved in the running hunts for deer. They perfected a system of alternating with each other in the runs and added another tactic whereby some of them would head off or deflect their prey to hasten the kill.

Bow hunters, with their almost silent but deadly arrows, came into the forest as autumn progressed. Dutch's wariness of the hunters was transmitted to her big pups, now almost as tall as their mother, but part of the pack would now hunt without her at times.

One cool evening at dusk, Tan's only sister and one of her brothers were trotting along the top of a hickory and beech covered ridge when they came across the smell of a hunter's feet in the leaves and on the ground. Their curiosity pulled them along the man scent trail to a point ten yards away from the tree where the hunter had his platform-like tree stand.

Dressed completely in camouflaged clothing and equipped with a powerful camouflaged crossbow, the eighteen-year-old, first-time hunter saw, what he thought was two fawns come in to the range of his seventy-five pound pull weapon.

The female dog heard a slight sound, raised her head and looked up in time for the arrow to miss her chin and let the broad-head tipped, razor sharp projectile slice through her throat and bury itself in her chest. The other "fawn" ran all the way back to the cavern on the cliff.

The hunter climbed down on the sixty-penny spike nail steps he had driven into the tree trunk, walked over to the body and blinked his eyes in surprised disbelief. He kicked the dead dog several times then walked away in the near-dark woods.

Dutch came to her dead pup that night, whined and licked at the still warm face, and for the first time in her life, howled at the sky.

Some distance away, Chestnut heard the mournful cry of Dutch's grief and yapped back his sympathy for the grieving mother. Dutch's plaintive wail added a heart-rending sound to the song of the night winds of the Little Smokies.

~

The Grants were in their seventh decade of life when they decided to accept the County Soil Conservation Department manager's recommendation to put their farm into the erosion control program. Several other agencies were involved with the plan, but in the end, they would receive enough annual subsidies, along with their social security, to provide for most of their needs.

One small field, near the barns, was exempted from the plans to leave space for the yearly tobacco crop, pasture for one calf and a few pigs. The tobacco would be raised "on the shares" by a young neighbor, thus leaving the elderly couple with only some chores and keeping the fields mowed to occupy their time.

The Grants, Henry and Melba, had seen first Dutch, and then Dutch and her pups, hunting 'chucks and rabbits on their farm. They assumed the dogs belonged to one of the nonresident cabin owners in the area and did not object to the dog's help in keeping the "pesky critters" under control around the farm. But something took place that changed the Grant's tolerant attitude that fall.

Three of the young pack dogs were trailing along behind a small spike buck when it broke from the woods to jump the fence into the calf lot behind the barn. As the pursuing dogs came under the fence, a thoroughly frightened beef animal let out a bellow and ran across the lot in front of the dogs. Distracted from the young buck's trail by the big calf's action, they all took out after the calf.

Henry heard the calf's bellow, looked out the kitchen door and saw what was taking place. He loaded his shotgun with deer-slug shells, ran out behind the barn and blazed away at the dogs.

With the first boom of the gun, the dogs headed full speed back to the woods. Aiming well above the dogs to allow for drop, he fired away. One of the slugs hit the last dog going under the fence. The heavy, slow moving, down-slanting slug still had enough force to smash the heart of one black coated, would be calf killer.

Henry buried the dog, shut the calf in the barn and kept his gun handy for several days but the dogs never came back again.

~

Now there were only five of the original nine members left in the family of man-made predators. All were capable of killing anything crossing their paths except the old black bear.

The bear had moved to a new territory during her summer wanderings. Her one trip back near the old den resulted in near disaster when she came upon two nighttime poachers. One carrying a powerful light saw her glowing eyes in the brush and fired a number of shots at her. She was several hundred yards up the ravine that went past the old den when the shooting occurred. One cub was killed by a random bullet, but the old female and the other cub got away in the dark. The poachers didn't even look for the dead cub. They thought they had shot at and missed a deer. They weren't about to go in the heavy brush to hunt a wounded deer. After all, they might run into a bear, if one could believe some of the stories told down at the store. Besides that, there were hundreds of deer around. "Why worry about one that was only crippled?"

The wild pack of dogs didn't need to kill as often now that there were only five members. The cold night air helped keep the carcass fresh enough to eat for at least two or three days, so two large deer would last about a week.

One huge buck had escaped from the dogs many times that fall. He had eluded the big red dog the first time he was chased simply by running in an almost straight line, at times deviating for obstacles. He ran for a half-hour in his ground-beating stride directly away from the place where he had been bedded down.

Dutch followed the deer expecting it to circle back toward the starting point of the chase. Deviating only to avoid anything that would slow him down, the wise old "Mossy Horn" kept going. In time, Dutch gave up and went home.

On one occasion, far from home, the old buck was caught napping. The buck's bed was high up on the pointed, end of a jutting escarpment of brush and rock with sides too steep and high for the deer to jump down. Two of the young male dogs, traveling upwind toward the buck's bed, partially blocked the escape route of the huge antlered animal.

When Old Mossy Horns had bedded down for the day, the wind had been coming from the east, but shifted to come from the west as he dozed in the normally safe retreat.

When the buck heard and then saw the dogs coming, he rose to his feet, facing them with his polished antlers lowered in the fighting position, before the dogs even knew he was there.

Old Mossy Horns charged out of the brush, knocking one dog head over heels before he could get out of the snorting deer's way. The other dog leaped aside, opening the escape path the deer needed.

One dog followed the buck for a short distance then came back in search of its mate. His mate was recovered enough to walk, but a gouge in his ribs bled and he limped, almost dragging one back leg, as they returned to more familiar scenes.

The injured dog moved slower and slower as time passed. All at once the dog was unable to breathe and slumped to the earth. An eruption of blood burst from the dog's nose and mouth. He twitched and convulsed, dying in spasms as he drowned in his own blood. The splintered ends of his broken ribs had pierced his lungs.

Once again, the size of the pack had shrunk and Dutch came to howl her grief.

Other attempts were made by the dogs to kill the old buck with the "ivory tree on his head," as some unsuccessful human predators referred to the beautiful antlers, but the dog pack was not successful either.

~

When the regular season for deer hunting opened, the booming of shotguns was continuous for hours. Just before daylight the first early-bird gunners opened up with a wide variety of weapons. Except for some primitive rifles only shotguns with solid slugs were legal. Despite the gun regulations, rifles and high-powered handguns were carried by a few men, willing to take the risk of being caught and having to pay a small fine.

Leading her three remaining offspring down the cliff path to the slate-bottomed brook for an early drink, Dutch heard the distant gunshots and knew the deadly sounds meant trouble for the pack.

Most of the non-resident hunters stayed close to the roads

in the forest preserve and on public highways around the forest, but a few bolder or more familiar nimrods penetrated a mile or more into the primitive hills and valleys of the woodlands.

The dogs had not eaten since the morning before the season opened and were eager to find game. They drank their fill of water, but did not leave the ravine. Made cautious by one gunshot much closer than the first faraway ones, and her own painful experiences, Dutch kept her family close to the cavern den. Brother and the other male dog soon became impatient with the delay, their growing hunger causing them to run back and forth along the brook, trying to tempt Dutch and Tan to follow them.

Dutch refused to be tempted and finally started back up the cliff path to the den. Tan and brother soon joined their mother, but the other dog, his dark gray-brown coat shining in the first light of day, ran up the ravine out of sight.

The big red dog stood on the ledge in front of the cavern and barked out the "come back" signal to her errant young, in vain. By this time the seal colored dog had struck the trail of a night-hunting raccoon and her five progeny. He tracked the 'coons through spring fed pools and potholes of water as they fed their way up the ravine to a side-branching gully leading off to the west.

Where the gully entered the ravine, a stand of persimmon trees with fruit ripe and sweet to their taste, had occupied the little troop of bandits for some time. Their scent was all over the grove in confusing patterns that delayed the gray-brown dog for a time.

He accidentally found a much hotter trail as he nosed among the fallen fruit in the upper side of the grove. He knew the scent was fresh and followed it at an easy run until the trail ended at the base of an ancient white oak tree.

On the side of the tree nearest the gully, a huge maverick limb grew out and down, almost touching the ground on the far side of the gully. At the base of the tree, a hole larger than the dog's head revealed the hollow in the interior of the white oak. Just above the out-jutting limb, another hole could be seen. The dog circled the tree, sniffing and whuffing at the hot, fresh smell of the raccoon family inside the tree out of reach.

Biting and clawing at the bottom hole, he tore out an opening large enough to force his body through the shell of the old oak, to the hollow center. The cone shaped cavity reaching up over the dog's head was about ten or twelve feet high and tapered to less than a foot in diameter, just above the top hole. Inside the cavity many old knots had rotted away providing ample nooks and niches for the 'coons to lie in, safe from the lunging, gray-brown 'coon tracker inside the tree below them.

With his persistent efforts to reach the creatures above him, the dog clawed and tore down large chunks of the dry, decayed heartwood of the ancient tree. This only drove his victims farther up the cavity, but one six inch thick, four foot long piece fell in such a way that the dog was able to use it like a ladder. This enabled him to reach a height of seven feet into the tree cavity.

The raccoons moved higher and prepared to leave by the top hole if the dangerous jaws came any closer. Suddenly, the dog's tenuous support collapsed. Scrambling at the punky wood, the surprised dog fell, yelping, back to the bottom of the cavity.

As the sudden loud noise burst from the falling dog, the 'coons started leaving through the hole above the large tree limb near the top of their den. Quickly digging the debris away, the frenzied dog came out the bottom hole, thinking to catch them on the outside of the tree.

The old mother 'coon and four of her young were

perched on the limb near the tree trunk, but one was running out the horizontal limb across the gully. The little 'coon jumped from the limb, almost directly into the mouth of the pursuing dog. While the dog ate the baby raccoon, the mother and her four babies reentered the top hole of the oak tree.

The angry mother chirred and chattered at the feeding dog. Only half appeased when he finished, he jumped onto the top of the foot in diameter limb and carefully walked its length to the main trunk of the tree. Near the trunk the limb was more than two feet in diameter. As he approached, the angry, scolding mother withdrew her head and backed out of sight.

Confident he could get another of the tasty creatures, the dog pushed his front feet and head right into the nine-inch wide hole, but didn't find anything near enough to catch. His body almost blocked the opening as he slid further in and down toward the 'coons below. One more shove from his back feet sent him in another six inches to where the right angle bend between the hole and cavity stopped the dog with his back feet barely touching the top of the huge limb.

Try as he might, he couldn't reach his prey. Every move just jammed him tighter. Pulling and scratching with his front feet, he drew his back feet completely off the tree limb. Further struggles wedged him to the point he could barely breathe. Efforts to back out of the hole were futile. The sixty-pound dog was hopelessly trapped in the tree.

Late in the afternoon of opening day of hunting season, two footsore, weary hunters walked slowly back to their camper parked by the stone trough where the cool water flowed from an artesian spring. Despite not getting to shoot at the huge, old, mossy horned deer they had seen at daylight that morning, they had thoroughly enjoyed the beautiful, early December day.

Most of the trees were bare, but the few remaining leaves on oak and sweet gum trees were still brilliant in the pale sun.

Tired from the exertion of walking to their remote, "private" hunting site and then back out, they sat down to rest on a tree limb that reached from the old tree all the way across the little gully at their feet. One man simply leaned back and half-sat on the limb; the other straddled the limb facing the tree.

Thirty feet away and three feet above his head was one of the most unusual things he had ever seen. The man astride the tree limb stared so long he finally caught the other's attention. Blinking his eyes at the legs and tail hanging motionless from the side of the tree, the second man said, "I think that's a 'coon dog."

The first man, who owned a service station next door to his wife's dog kennel said, "I believe it's a big Greyhound, and he looks dead to me."

The service station owner crawled slowly across the tree limb, placing his hand on the dog's hip. He felt warmth. "He may be alive. I'll pull him out and hand him down to you," he told the man on the ground.

The man on the ground, who was afraid of dogs, said, "That may be a vicious dog. You better put a rope around his backend and tie it to the limb."

"You may be right," the man on the limb replied, as he took a small coil of strong nylon rope from the game bag of his hunting coat. "I may want to take him home with us if he is okay, so we'll tie him up good when we get him down," he added.

With much tugging and some apprehension, the inert body was pulled from the tree and lowered to the ground. In just seconds, the dog's chest started moving and his long legs began to twitch as if he were running. Luckily, the service station owner frequently assisted his wife with her kennel operation. He knew just what to do to control the big dog and keep him from hurting himself or anyone else.

Pulling out his hunting knife, he cut off a piece of the

soft nylon rope and tied all four of the dog's legs together. The dog was breathing much better but was still unconscious. Satisfied with the dog's breathing, he then cut a one-inch diameter, twelve-inch length of green maple from a nearby sapling. He tied the length of wood crossways in the dog's mouth, just behind the long canine teeth in the dog's upper and lower jaws. Very careful to avoid injuring the dog's mouth or slow it's breathing, he wrapped more of the soft rope around the dog's nose and jaws, behind the stick, all the way up to the dog's ears, completely covering the eyes.

Over an hour later, the very tired hunters reached their camper with the struggling dog, which they alternated carrying all the way. By checking among the many other hunters parked in the picnic area, they found and paid a total of twenty dollars for a heavy choke chain, a collar and a light tow chain much used but still strong.

With a lot of advice and some help from other campers, they managed to secure the dog and remove the stick and ropes without anyone or the dog getting hurt.

Vic, the man who had climbed up to free the dog, could never explain what made him decide he would keep the animal but never had reason to regret the decision. From the first bowl of water he placed near the chained dog to the last bowl of water he would ever give him, he would remember this day. Within an hour after Vic gave him the water, "Seal" had a name and a drink from the stainless steel stew pot.

Seal's back feet were in bad shape. Before losing consciousness, he had continued to flail away with his back feet to get free from the clutch of the hole. The only results were broken toenails and bloody feet. He woke up bound tight and helpless, but felt no pain from the ropes. His tongue became sore and swollen by the time the stick was removed, but he hadn't associated the stick with the feel of hands on him or the sounds and smells of the men.

When the man placed the bowl of water near his head, the dog bristled and flexed his lip at the man, but did not snarl. He urgently wanted the water. When the man moved away, Seal raised his head from the ground and sniffed at the strange scent that somehow seemed familiar. He sensed no danger, only a growing thirst. He slid forward on the ground, touched the water in the bowl and began to lap up the delicious liquid. The water came from the same trough Dutch had drunk from during her first hour in the forest.

Later that evening, a hunter brought Vic a deer liver. Vic gave it to Seal and the dog ate every morsel. The next day Vic got a fat, four point buck. He dressed the deer and saved all the vital organs for Seal. He gave him some of the organs that day and saved the rest for the next day. On the third day, Vic stayed at the camper while his friend, Art, went back to the woods to try again.

During the morning, the park manager came driving by in a pickup truck. Seeing the dog, he stopped and walked over to Vic. During the ensuing conversation, Vic learned that Seal was probably the offspring of a big red dog that was running free in the area. The man also indicated his satisfaction that Vic planned to keep the dog, taking him home after the hunting was over.

Art killed his deer and was back with it in mid-afternoon. It was a nice spike buck weighing only about one hundred pounds. Art dragged the deer out by himself making him very tired. The two hunters in their one ton small bed truck pulling a camper, carried the deer and dog in the flat bed with side racks out of the park at four-thirty that day to drive to the deer tagging station before heading back to Columbus.

Seal had been tied up between two trees, the choke chain to one and the makeshift rig to the other for nearly forty-eight hours, when the time came to put him in the truck. He resisted being led to the truck, but never offered to bite Vic or Art.

With one man on each side of him, holding the chains firmly gripped in their hands, the men stepped up on the truck bed. To their surprise, Seal simply squatted down on his bank legs and, despite his sore feet, hopped right up between them.

The men fastened the chains to the side racks close to the cab where they could see him through the window. Seal lay down on the bed, staying there until they were close to home.

Seal finally got up, looked around and put his front feet up on top of the cab. He rode in the back of that and other trucks for dozens of trips over the following years, usually with his front feet and head on the cab.

~

Dutch, Tan and Brother stayed at the cavern all day. There hadn't been any shots really close by, but there were shots all around the area until after sundown on opening day.

When it became dark and quiet in the woods, she signaled Tan and Brother to come away, then trailed her missing pup to the old oak tree. The scent of dog and man was all over the ground and tree trunk.

Dutch followed the strong man scent, and the faint scent of her pup, back to a point near where she first set foot in the forest. There were many men, trucks, cars and campers there. The burning campfires, loud laughter and the constant movement of the people prevented her from approaching Seal.

Dutch moved off into the woods a short distance and lay down on the ground. She was hungry and the scent of raw and cooked meat was carried to her on the breeze.

Two hours later, a man came near Dutch and threw a heavy object into a ditch between her and the campfires. When the man left, smelling meat on the air, Dutch went to the ditch to investigate. She found a large pile of deer parts, discarded from a deer butchered for camp meat.

Dutch fed from the discarded meat before moving closer to the, now quieting, campers. Dropping to her belly, she crawled up behind the old stone water trough. Alert and wary, she whined softly to her son, only fifty feet away. Seal answered her and strained against the chains, trying to reach her. Dutch knew what the sounds of the chains meant and soon crept away, just before Vic came out to check on Seal.

Dutch spent the days in the cavern, but came back each night to be near her nearly grown pup. Tan and Brother came with her the second night. There was an even larger amount of deer meat in the ditch, so they all fed from this supply.

After the first night, Seal didn't try to get away, only coming as close as the end of the chains to whine softly to the three dogs in the dark behind the stone trough. The third night Seal was gone. Dutch, Tan and Brother came back each night for a week before giving up their vigil.

~

Although only a few hunters came deep into the woods to hunt, the majority staying close to roads, farms and camping areas, the hunters who went farther afield were more experienced. As a rule, they wounded far less game than the less skilled novices near the roads did.

The experienced hunters knew to gut and bleed their kills before dragging the much lighter carcasses out of the deep woods. The colder December weather kept these piles of deer entrails edible for many days after the kills. The dog pack, now just three, fed at night from these discarded organs closest to the cavern, but went farther afield as time passed.

Dogs, coyotes, foxes, opossum, bobcats, raccoon, mink,

mice, weasels and many kinds of birds fed on the hunter's leavings. They also found dead deer among fallen leaves.

The large predators continued to hunt only at night for many days. Finding food was easy for any of the meat eaters. Within two miles of the cavern, more carcasses and wounded deer were available to the three dogs than they had all killed since Dutch came to the forest. More deer continued to perish from gunshot wounds, but many of the crippled deer were easy to catch, making the chases short and the killings acts of mercy for the suffering animals.

~

On the day the Buckmans gathered in Mary's kitchen for their Christmas dinner, Dutch and her two big followers were in excellent shape with their coats sleek and glossy from the plentiful and nutritious venison.

Tan and Brother took the snow and cold weather in stride. Conditioned by the rugged life and continual exercise, and the speed inherited from their Greyhound father, both young dogs easily kept pace with their mother as the pursuit of deer resumed. The longer legged, smaller footed young dogs could now course through the roughest parts of the forest for any length of time necessary to bring their prey to earth.

Tan, by far the fastest runner, most often ran on the outside of the circling deer with the black dog, Brother, directly behind the deer. Dutch would also follow the scent trail until a pattern developed, then cut across to intercept the swift animals. No matter what the deer did, if it circled, it was caught by the tireless dogs.

Unlike their ancestors, the dogs seldom howled but when the voices of the wild coyotes sounded on clear moonlit nights, the dogs would reply in angry warning in defiance of their smaller cousins in the hills. The coyotes were not too successful in their attempts to kill healthy grown deer, but had pulled down many of the wounded ones they came across following the hunting season. Now they occasionally contested the deer killed by the three dogs. The coyotes, smaller and quicker moving than the dogs, usually escaped the savage rushes of Dutch and Brother, defending the meat. Tan, not nearly as aggressive, stayed by the carcass to guard against other coyotes that tried to slip in to eat when Dutch and Brother were distracted.

When the severe, bitter cold weather came that winter, the dogs would return to the cavern or cave to find warm shelter. The coyotes then gorged on the deer carcass left unattended.

Dutch hated the coyotes, and their scent, which was left on anything not consumed at a kill. The coyotes sometimes urinated and marked the meat left after their bellies were filled. When this happened, the dogs would not eat the rank, smelly meat.

During a break in the severe weather, the dogs took shelter under the root clump of a large windblown pine tree leaning against some other trees. The earth filled, root mass, with it's resulting saucer shaped depression, provided a temporary den for the dogs within sight of their last deer kill.

Dutch had tried to drag the large buck's body close to the leaning pine, but the widespread antlers caught in a tangle of vines so she couldn't drag it all the way. When she quit pulling on the deer's haunch, the recoiling vines slid the deer a few feet down hill on the icy hard snow covering the ground.

After eating, Dutch and Tan curled up in the leaves under the tree roots to rest or sleep. Brother lay down on the still warm carcass, guarding it from all corners.

When the two adult and four younger coyotes appeared, he snarled and barked at the raiders in hysterical fury. Tan ran directly to her brother's side, adding her strident voice to

Brother's, now bolder, defiance.

The two older coyotes were well in front of their off-spring, who hung back in uncertain caution. One young coyote, the only two year old, left his yearling mates and circled around to one side of the two dogs while one of the adults went the other way. The three yearlings came closer, seeing only two dogs surrounded by the older coyotes.

Dutch, silent as usual, had angled away from the altercation at the carcass, to come in on the flank of the incoming raiders. Dutch came very close to the yearling animals before making her rushing attack. She killed one yearling by slashing through his throat, grabbed a second one by the neck and cracked its spine with one quick shake of her head. Almost in the same motion, Dutch's charge carried her toward the old male coyote, behind which the last yearling had fled.

Dutch's onslaught had completely upset the coyote's tactics. The inexperienced yearlings had cowered down in fear on the icy snow when Dutch burst out of the brush upon them. The two-year-old coyote turned to look at the one-sided fray, exposing its neck to Brother. Before the second yearling hit the ground, Brother had his adversary by the neck in a death grip.

Both of the old coyotes plunged in to protect the little yearling, unaware of the dying two-year-old, hidden from sight by Tan and the buck's carcass. Dutch leaped away to avoid the slashing teeth of the old coyotes, following closely, trying to get her between them.

Tan, never the one to jump into unknown danger, finally entered the battle by jumping on the last young coyote. Tan's body slammed the lighter animal to the rock-like, icy snow, rolling and sliding it down the short bank of a frozen stream. Tan didn't follow up the attack, merely snarled at the young coyote, then returned to the carcass. The little female coyote fled into the night.

When the two-year-old's struggles ceased, Brother sped off in the direction of Dutch's battle in the concealing brush. Too busy to bark, Dutch, leaping in and out, back and forth, bided her time waiting for the right moment to kill the hated, aggressive little wolves. Dutch paid no attention to the newly ripped, tattered ear, or the patch of hair torn from her neck.

She had only one opportunity. The fight took them into the frozen streambed with an undercut on one side. Backing into this undercut to protect her rear and one side, she could keep both attackers in sight. Trying to draw Dutch out of the protective cut-bank, first one then the other coyote would dart in and jump back. Dutch waited for an opportunity to kill within the protective curl of frozen earth.

Thinking the big red dog was afraid, the old male lunged even closer to Dutch before flashing away; his feet slipping on the polished ice under the dusting of snow. In the blink of an eye, Dutch had him by the neck.

Seeing the fate of her mate, the courageous female leaped in to sink her teeth into Dutch's skull, just above her eyes. The female's canine teeth grated on Dutch's skull. One of the coyote's upper canines pierced into the soft tissue below her left ear and the other hung in the skin and bone above the left eye.

The coyote's lower canines ripped through the lump of skin and tissue containing the dime-sized piece of lead Dutch had been carrying in her forehead for almost a year.

Brother came flying from the creek bank at that same instant. He knocked all three of the fighting animals apart. In landing, the seventy pound, forty mile per hour projectile nearly broke the neck of the female coyote. Even one second more and the female's teeth would have punctured the fierce, big red dog's brain shell.

Their spirits broken by Brother's reckless attack, the coyotes fled, glad to be away from the two incredible animals that had just reduced their numbers by half. Brother gave half-hearted pursuit but quickly returned to his mother.

When he came back to the streambed, Dutch was stretched out on the ice, with Tan licking the blood from her mother's head and eyes. Less than three minutes in duration, the fight had been fierce and decisive, but painful for Dutch. The coyote's teeth had hurt Dutch very seriously. One fang-like canine had penetrated the eye socket of her left eye and another one had dented the fragile skull just between the left eye and ear. Her lower jaw teeth had ripped a flap of skin loose between the dog's right eye and ear.

The piece of lead, enclosed in a sack-like growth, the color and shape of a button mushroom, came loose under Tan's ministrations and fell to the snow. The last few swipes of Tan's tongue pushed the flap of skin down, shutting out the cold air and reduced the flow of blood.

Dizzy and almost blind, Dutch staggered up the little creek to a place where the water, still open in a tiny rapids, soothed Dutch's dry tongue and throat. Dutch made it back to the temporary den under the tree roots, which was less than a hundred yards from the creek, but by the time she got there, her eyes were swollen shut. Her forehead burned and ached from the coyote's teeth, and the pressure from its jaws. Less than a one-inch long section of normal tissue now held her right ear to her paining head.

For two days and nights she made her way in and out of the den to urinate and empty her bowels and to lick at the icy snow for moisture. The second day, just at dawn, Brother carried a fat squirrel's body up to her and dropped it at her feet. Dutch ate the fresh meat and went right to sleep. When she awoke, her left eye had opened slightly, just enough to permit her to avoid hitting her head against trees and brush on the way to the creek and back.

The wound on the right side of her head began to heal

and the sight in her left eye returned enough for Dutch to see fairly well, but not nearly as well as before she had been hurt. She began to eat the half-frozen venison, but Brother continued to bring her fresh rabbits or squirrels from time to time. Tan stayed with Dutch, her soothing tongue often stroking the sore places on the red dog's head.

By the time the worst weather of the year came, the three dogs were hunting together again, but Brother now did the actual killing. Dutch's sight was not good enough to avoid hoof or antlers of the deer. With Tan at the heels and Dutch acting as a decoy, they kept the deer confused until Brother slipped in to pull the prey to earth.

~

Bad weather conditions increased as January grew older. One long storm piled snow up so deep it made it very hard for the dogs to hunt. Many deer left the woods to feed on rolls of hay, left in the fields of isolated farms. Some deer moved right into cattle lots at night, feeding there until dawn, before leaving to bed down in cover close to the food supply.

Squirrels came down to the ground only to seek water. Since the ground was buried under layers of ice and snow, there was no chance of them digging under leaves for nuts and seeds. But the chattering little animals didn't starve as they had hoards of nuts inside hollow trees, as well as tree tips and buds to eat until the ground was bare again.

Rabbits kept their groundhog-hole dens open by going out each night to gnaw on the bark of trees, shrubs and berry vines, getting enough moisture from the inner layers of bark to maintain their systems. At times the rabbits ate snow to supplement their need for moisture.

The 'chucks slept the long weeks away, deep down in

their warm burrows. Raccoons sought out corn cribs, mangers and feed bins, as well as hay stacks and open field tiles in their search for food. The few open streams provided little food in the long cold winter. The 'coons living on or near farms were better off than those that lived in the forest where livestock feed was not available.

Nature loving people saved thousands of woodland creatures through their thoughtful practice of feeding wildlife in the wintertime. Hunting clubs hauled hay and corn to spots where deer and turkeys and other game would find it.

Late in January, the severe weather eased up to thaw and melt some of the heavy layers of ice and snow. All the predators in the forest and fields were out seeking food in the much-diminished larder, but in the peculiar way of the world, many balances occur that benefit nature. The numbers of predators had also been greatly reduced.

Four nearly grown raccoons left the old oak, with the long maverick limb, the third night of the January thaw. They had been back to the grove of persimmon trees recently, stripping the last of the frozen, sweet, plum-sized balls of fruit from the tree limbs.

The past several weeks, the young animals had spent most of the time sleeping in a nest of decayed wood in the base of the oak. Two feet of solid ice blocked the bottom hole in the tree, making it a safe place to "almost hibernate."

When the hungry 'coons reached the persimmon grove, they set to work digging for the buried fruit, oblivious of everything but their hunger and the delicious smell coming up through the foot thick carpet of lightly crusted slush.

The big dogs caught wind of the busy raccoons in time to start their stalk before the 'coons became aware of their approach. Only one heard their final rush and he made it up a tree to safety.

The starving dogs ate the other three, the only meat they

had found in several days. Even the muskrats in their dome-shaped houses on the lake escaped as Dutch dug through the snow, ice and reeds, trying to copy the fox of the winter before.

Dutch had led her ten-month-old pups far from home that morning. The little raccoons eaten the day before, thin from lack of food, had been mostly skin and bones. The weather had been so severe in the past few weeks that the dogs had not been able to find anything for days at a time. The forest animals seldom ventured out of their den trees or burrows. Only a few deer remained, mostly big, fleet animals, whose size made it possible for them to stand on their back legs to reach edible tree branches.

Due to her wounds and the lack of food, Dutch had become the least effective of the three dogs. Her vision had improved and the buzzing sound in her head was only intermittent now, coming back with irritating regularity from exertion. Even this disappeared after a long rest or sleep.

Since the forest roads had gone Unplowed, even the trash barrels filled with ice and frozen snow. There was no tourist or casual traffic to discard human food of any kind near the dogs.

When Brother found the scent of Old Mossy in the thick stand of young maple and poplar saplings, he gave the "come to me" bark to Dutch and Tan, behind him.

That day, in desperation, they chased Old Mossy Horns farther than ever before. Except for brief rest periods, Tan was able to keep pressing the huge deer until he escaped by jumping the fence into the calf lot. Tan wasn't able to get through the six-inch mesh wire. The frozen crust on top of the snow concealed the foot high space between wire and ground. As she waited for Dutch and Brother, she could hear a chorus of coyote howls on the hill not far away.

~

Old Mossy was thinner than in the fall before, but had fared much better than most animals in the woodlands. He had ranged far and wide, finding enough tall marsh grass to maintain his strength. Standing on his long back legs, he could reach eight feet up to feed on the sweet tips of tree limbs. In recent days he had been feeding on grain from a group of feed bins on the big farm just outside the forest area.

When the wise old buck heard the dog's brief bark, he began trotting directly away from the sound. He moved with extreme care to prevent his huge antlers from striking the saplings and brush, His head was tender from the beginning of shedding, which took place each winter.

The three dogs spent several minutes figuring out the maze of deer scent in the crusty snow of the deer's feeding area. Tan found the fresh, hot trail and gave the "chase" call. The dogs had recognized the old buck's scent and knew they had a long run ahead.

The buck's flight led him away from the Buckman farm. He ran swiftly, but unafraid of being caught, far into the tall hills of the blue tinted Little Smokies. He paused frequently to look and listen for the dogs, expecting them to give up at any time, but Tan had taken the lead of her small pack and clung to the even hotter scent of deer.

Now Old Mossy was tired, and lay down to rest at the top of a long, thinly treed ridge. The dogs kept coming, not barking, but still making enough noise to alert the keen-eared deer. For the first time since the chase started, he changed directions running at a right angle to the morning's trail.

Tan was close enough to the deer's bed to see him jump up and run down the side of the ridge. She sniffed at the bed, pausing long enough for Dutch and Brother to join her. All three of them lay down to pant and eat some of the sun-softened snow before taking up the trail again.

Leaving the ridge, the old buck came out in a log strewn clearing with a snow-covered dirt road crossing it. He followed the unused road, winding between the hills for over two miles, before it reached a gravel road that had been cleared by a snowplow.

At the sound of children playing in the bright afternoon sun, Old Mossy stopped to investigate the sounds. He saw wood smoke rising above the trees across the plowed road, then noticed other sounds and smells of an occupied dwelling. He turned right and ran parallel with the open road. He was now headed back to the starting point of mid-morning.

Despite his habit of running in a single direction to escape pursuit, there were many objects to avoid and impassable places to detour around as he fled southwest on the first leg of the huge triangular journey he made that day. When he ran down from the ridgetop, he was moving alongside a country road that led southeast until it turned left, away from the old deer's homebound course.

Considering all the zigzags around objects, he had traveled well over ten miles when he had heard the children's voices. The dogs stayed together until they came to a clearing where logs were piled. On one side was a small, open-sided, slab shack with a plain board roof. The smell of food came from the open shack.

Hungry and tired, the smell drew the dogs to a large plywood box just inside the rough little building. The four by eight by two feet deep box was nearly filled with oily cans, plastic bottles, old brown paper lunch bags and dozens of styrofoam containers from fast food places. It was all the rubbish from the loggers' activity around the log yard.

The deer was forgotten during the hour the three big dogs spent cleaning out the edible contents left by the mice living under the box, lapping water from the puddle of melted snow water below the sloping roof and resting on the littered saw-dust floor of the shack.

With the immediate pangs of hunger tempered and thirst slaked, the tenacious trio again picked up Old Mossy's trail. When the scent trail left the log yard, Dutch knew the deer would turn again to go back toward it's starting point.

Signaling her offspring to "hunt on," Dutch turned off the track to cut across country, saving her tired legs and sore feet from some extra miles. Dutch came across the deer's scent trail at the place where the gravel road veered left away from the old buck's straight-line run home. She had missed intercepting him by only minutes, but had to stop for rest. She was three miles from the Buckmans' calf lot.

The sun had gone down behind the blue cast hills and the air grew colder with approaching night. When the two tired young dogs reached Dutch, the little pack followed together on the buck's scent trail. Sensing the old deer's increasing exhaustion, Tan increased her speed trying to catch the prey that was in sight, at times only a hundred feet ahead, in the pale light of the full moon.

The "ivory tree" on the buck's head felt so heavy it made him hit the top strand of barbed wire when he jumped into the calf lot. He landed awkwardly, almost flipping over. This caused his unusually long, forward thrusting brow points to be buried in the mixture of half-frozen hay and snow. Already loose, the antlers separated from the head of the now helpless Old Mossy of the Little Smokies.

When Dutch and Brother loped tiredly up to the anxious, prowling Tan, blood was again pouring down the right side of Dutch's head. Spurred on by Tan's yipping "come, come," barks, Dutch had plowed right through the low broken limbs of a dead cedar. One of the sharp ended, broken branches had cut right across the mass of infected tissue, which closed her right eye. The resulting sharp pain had been only momentary and' the spurting blood was purging the matter from the old wound when she stopped at the fence.

Tan licked away the blood and whined softly, ministering to the spent Dutch while Brother moved along the fence, searching for a way to enter the enclosure. The forty-eight inch high woven wire fence was topped with three strands of barbed wire, spaced four inches apart, far too high for the exhausted dogs to jump or climb.

When the deer and dogs came on the scene, the calves had run some distance away, turned and stared back at the dogs. The big "hornless" deer had staggered along with the retreating calves until he was behind one of the hay bunks, out of the dog's sight. There he collapsed on scattered hay, gasping for breath.

One curious bull calf left the large herd of his peers, cut across the lot and followed along the inside of the fence, keeping pace with Brother, ten feet away, on the outside of the fence.

~

The old female coyote had "come in season" with the first mild day of the thaw. During her heat cycle, she had driven her yearling female pup away from the den. The mating accomplished, she called out in the early moonlit night, urging her daughter to return to her. Not far away, the yearling howled back her willing acceptance.

~

Chestnut had been in the old treetop lay-up by the bull yard. He heard the deer and then the dogs run up the gully below his part-time home. He recognized the deer's scent on the air, but the acrid odor of the feral dogs was alien and alarming to the, soon to be, two year old fox. He knew better than to accost the dogs by the pen, but he did bark out warnings, which the dogs ignored.

Brother came to a place where the snow was much thinner on the ground due to wind action, which swept most of the snow away as it fell to the ground. At the corner of the lot there was only a little ice on the ground, leaving nearly a foot of space between ground and wire.

The calf had stopped following him at the top of the slope, ten yards south of the corner. When the red dog and the tan dog came by, the little bull followed them a few yards closer to the corner. All three dogs sat down on the ground, tongues lolling from their mouths.

The dogs were bone weary and in need of food. Their systems not conditioned to properly utilize the scraps from the litter box found at the little shack, the food had done them little good. The increasing cold wind chilled them quickly. Their bodies were hot from the punishing run of many miles and hours.

The calf, much larger than a deer, moved back up the hill a few yards to get behind the small grove of pines, out of the cold wind, and lay down on a scattering of pine needles.

The coyotes continued their eerie conversation from a closer point than earlier that evening, causing Dutch to growl and wrinkle her lips at the sounds. The tired, old deer seemed to have disappeared, leaving no available food except the strange smelling creatures on the other side of the fence. Their scent was overpowering to the dogs despite their upwind location.

First Brother, then Tan, crawled under the wire, the more cautious Dutch holding back to search the air for danger. At last Dutch bellied under the fence and went toward the bull

111

calf, which now rose to his feet in delayed concern for his safety.

Tan and Brother quickly circled around the calf and closed in on him, with trepidation for his size and unfamiliarity to them. Dutch made a mock charge to get the calf's attention, expecting the docile animal to run for the herd behind Tan and Brother. A half-grown bull calf is not afraid of anything so small it can crawl under a fence, so the bull calf lowered it's head and charged right at Dutch.

Tan and Brother leaped in, grasping flank skin and leg tendons, to upset the calf and bring him down on the slippery surface underfoot. The terrified animal regained his footing and fled toward the corner of the lot, but the hungry predators prevailed. The prey sealed its fate when it tried to charge right through the fence in the corner of the calf lot.

The hungry dogs fed well before making their way through the cold wind, back to the snug cavern on the cliff.

~

Lora found the stricken calf at mid-afternoon on the first day of February. Tim and his father had been up very early that day to feed and check the water supply for all the cattle before the first hay customers of the day came to the farm. It was still dark when they came back for breakfast, and they had not seen anything wrong at the calf lot.

~

Deer and calves paid slight attention to each other as Old Mossy drank from the water tank and ate grain and hay from the ample supply close at hand. Hunger satisfied, the old buck remained in the calf lot, resting for a long time in the protection of the hay bunk, away from the frigid wind.

Hearing the approaching tractor, he got to his feet to stand on trembling legs and shake his unusually light-feeling head. The big deer trotted past his fallen antlers to leap easily over the fence. The decreased weight of the missing antlers made the jump easier than his entry jump of the night before.

The sound of the tractor had driven Old Mossy back into the forest on this cold, first day of February.

Chapter five

Chapter Five

Chapter Five ~

Tim was almost asleep, his chin resting on the thick wool scarf around his neck. The wind fell to a whisper, improving his comfort and making it easier to hear.

When the three coyotes appeared among the few bare-limbed trees beyond the fence, Tim assumed they were dogs. The two females, the yearling almost as large as her mother, came first to stand by the calf's head and peer around, sniffing at the slight breeze. The male coyote, a third larger than the females, glided up, paused, then slipped under the wire to begin pulling at the calf's open flank. The old female then slid under the fence and started eating on exposed meat at the dead calf's rear. The shy young female, newly returned to the family, sat down outside the fence to wait her turn at the carcass.

Trying not to make a sound, Tim put his gloved fingers through the openings in the mittens and picked up the gun. He only had to move the gun a few inches to bring the sights to bear on the animal at the calf's head outside the fence. Easing the safety to the off position with his right thumb, he took up the slack in the trigger.

As Tim's finger tightened on the trigger, the young female dropped to her belly behind the carcass. That move saved her life.

Tim fired at the moving "dog" once, then, as fast as he could pull the trigger, he shot at the two animals inside the fence by the dead calf. His second shot sent five of the pea-sized pellets into the head, neck and shoulder of the old female coyote. The third shot knocked the back legs out from under the old male as he turned toward the fence to flee. The fourth shot struck the big "dog" just as his head went through the six-inch mesh of the woven wire fence.

The first animal was out of sight behind the carcass, when the old female fell. Tim thought it was dead as he fired at the biggest one by the dead calf's flank, but the young coyote had not been severely hurt.

Only one of the nine pellets hit her. The other eight struck the calf or flew harmlessly over her back as she prepared to go under the fence to join her mother, feeding at the calf's rear. When the ear piercing sound of the second shot boomed out, the yearling coyote put the twelve-inch diameter corner post between her and the fire spitting gun barrel, to streak for the protective trees and brush nearby.

Concentrating on the "big dog," Tim caught a glimpse of the gray shape bounding away and fired two final rounds at it. None of the thirty caliber pellets touched the young female, but her tail flopped to the snow each time her feet came down. One pellet from Tim's first shot had ricocheted from the pipe used to brace the corner post, glancing down to break a vertebra in her tail.

The young female coyote survived to become a legend of her own in later years, as "Old Crooked Tail," the most widely known predator in the Little Smokies.

~

A few minutes before eleven, that evening of February first, Mary awakened John, dozing on the couch, to get ready to relieve Tim.

Lora came in the back door just before John was ready to leave the house. With a thermos bottle of coffee, a package of sandwiches, and a flashlight in the big pockets of his coat, John picked up his ready shotgun and opened the outside door.

Lora was standing in the open door while Mary stepped out on the little porch to give John a final caution "to keep

118

warm," when all three of them heard the shotguns prolonged thunder coming over the hill from the calf lot.

"That's the end of the dogs," John said, handing the gun to Mary. "I won't need this shotgun," he added. "Wait for me to grab a coat. I'm going with you," said Lora.

"Me too," stated Mary.

John gave in to them with a shrug of his shoulders and ran to get the old truck with the feed hopper on the back.

Pepper and Vickie were fastened in on Lora's back porch, barking to be let out, when they drove out of the barnyard headed for the calf lot. They could see the lights of the small pickup when they drove past the calf barn, so they kept right on in the old truck until they were near the straw and tarp blind at the northwest corner of the lot.

Opening the truck door, John advised the women to "Stay in the truck where it's warm," then went to where Tim had dragged the long, furry-haired bodies of the dead predators.

Tim had driven the small truck up beside the blind and was ready to put the "strange looking dogs" in the truck bed when he saw the lights of the other truck coming toward him. He waited for John to walk up, then pointed his flashlight on the dead animals at his feet.

"Well, I've heard them howl many times, but this is the first time I've seen or touched one of them," John said in awe.

"Do you mean what I think you mean?" asked Tim.

"Yes, no doubt about it, these are real coyotes," John emphatically stated. "But it sure seems strange that they would take on a five hundred pound bull calf," he added.

Mary and Lora, feeling left out, had gotten out of the truck and walked up just in time to hear John's last questioning statement. Shining the other flashlight down, Lora said, "They're beautiful. How could anything that pretty kill a calf?"

"They look like wolves to me," remarked Mary. "See

119

those long, sharp teeth?"

"I guess you're almost right," said Tim. "Dad says they're coyotes, and I agree," he finished.

"Let's take them back to the garage before they start to freeze," John suggested.

"Okay, let me get some sacks out of the feed truck to put them in," Tim replied.

They put the animals in burlap bags, loaded them into the back of the small truck, picked up the items in the blind, then drove both trucks back home and parked them in the garage. John set the thermostat for the garage heater on low before they all went into John and Mary's house to discuss Tim's night out in the cold.

It was only a few minutes after midnight when they sat down at Mary's kitchen table to review the recent event. The first thing Tim did was to tell about the "one that got away," then related in detail his story about the foxes, the 'possum and the brief, but violent moment of the coyote's arrival and demise.

Like all things, the topics of that night's events were soon exhausted, as were all the Buckmans. Tim and Lora returned to their house and John and Mary, soon after, went to bed for the night.

~

The wind ceased at ground level, but a bank of clouds moved in to block out the moon as the Buckmans lay sleeping in their beds. A milder breeze from the south brought a warmer quality to the air passing in front of the rock cavern where the big red, the long legged tan, and the strong bodied black dog stood looking out at woodlands across the ravine below them.

The dogs had not heard the gunshots earlier that night.

120

The distance and wind and intervening woods and hills masked the sound.

Dutch's right eye was almost completely open now, only thirty odd hours after puncturing the inflamed swelling while chasing Old Mossy. Tan had continued her therapeutic nursing sessions with her healing tongue, removing the suppuration when it appeared. The pain and buzzing sound in her head receded with the long rest and sleep of the past twenty-four hours. The big dogs were hungry again. Brother led them back to the woods behind the calf lot at about three A.M. that second February morning. Dutch arrived last, having paused several times to empty her bladder on the way. Her heat cycle was late this year, due to her poor health, but the cycle was starting.

The young dogs stopped well back in the trees, both disturbed by the strong smell of blood and coyote stench in the air. Brother was wrinkling his nose at some drops of blood and coyote tracks when Dutch reached his side.

Alert to every sound, Dutch approached the kill in the fence, the young dogs well behind her ready to go back into the woods at the first indication of danger. With the big red dogs signal to "come," the others crept to the carcass to feed. One dog always stayed on guard against anything that might come near.

The meat was harder to tear away, being partially frozen, but their powerful jaws soon tore away enough hide to have access to the rich, fat beef beneath.

Their apprehension became less and less as they took turns eating and guarding the kill, but when a fox barked from a place near the calf herd, all three dogs became slightly alarmed thinking the fox was signaling a warning.

Chestnut's keener hearing had discerned the call of a distant fox trying to locate it's absent mate. He barked an answer, understood only by others of his own kind. Pepper, on

121

the enclosed porch, heard Chestnut and renewed her efforts to open the pet door. All at once the little door popped open. Pepper slipped out, to have the door swing back and latch shut in Vickie's face. Vickie whined a few times, then returned to her warm box to sleep again.

Pepper ran to find Chestnut. The little black dog and the dark coated fox had become almost full mates recently and now Pepper was in full estrus. The urge to mate exerting an overpowering influence that Pepper could not resist.

Chestnut had been near the enclosed porch earlier that night, but left to run back to his lay-up where he had left a partially eaten rabbit the night before.

Chestnut heard Pepper, coming and ran to meet her near the calf barn. Mating between the two little animals took place at once. Later, the pair of them, running together along the west side of the calf lot, suddenly came upon the big red dog as she slid under the fence. She was the last to leave the carcass.

Chestnut turned and retreated south several yards, but Pepper only stopped to stare at Dutch. Dutch, still crouched on the ground, stared balefully at the little dog but made no threatening sounds or moves. The little dog was no danger to her, and Dutch was on "foreign ground" causing her to be much less defensive than if Pepper had been on Dutch's home ground.

Pepper whined and wagged her tail in a show of friendliness. Dutch came to her feet and slowly approached Pepper, who exuded the same estrus scent Dutch carried with her.

In nature's peculiar ways, the two female dogs sensed a kinship. They circled each other, cataloguing the various points of identity, filing the information away for life.

Satisfied that they were compatible, the two females squatted to leave yellow splashes of mutual acceptance on the hard packed snow.

Dutch loped off to the northwest while Pepper trotted

south to reassure Chestnut and to be immediately mounted again by the happy, bright eyed, lusty fox.

~

It was broad daylight when Tim and Lora woke up the morning after the coyotes were shot. Lora buzzed Mary on the intercom, asking the older Buckmans to join them for a quick breakfast before the men went out to begin the days work.

John followed Mary in to say the temperature had improved during the night and that he had turned off the heater in the garage, a building used in common by both families.

While waiting for his coffee to cool, John brought up a subject for discussion that was already on Tim's mind.

John began by saying, "If word gets out that there are coyotes in the hills, will the news attract a swarm of trigger happy hunters, shooting at anything that moves in the area?"

For a time there was no answer to his question, then Lora asked another question. "What are we going to do with the two in the garage? We can't leave them there very long," Lora finished.

At that time Mary made a suggestion that temporarily satisfied them all. "Why don't we call the game warden to come out and help us with both problems?" Mary asked.

"That sounds like a great idea, Mom. He is one of the people who advised us to shoot "those dogs," Tim ended on an uncertain note.

Lora, sensitive to Tim's tone of voice, asked, "Do you think there may be a legal problem, Tim?"

"We'll call him and find out," Tim answered.

Tim called the warden, catching him at breakfast also, asking him to stop by as soon as possible. When asked why, Tim, wise in the ways of country phones, avoided a direct answer. Tim just said, "In regard to the matter Dad called about last night".

The game warden, also knowledgeable about party line phones, paused, then said, "Okay, I'll be there in an hour." Tim thanked him and hung up the phone.

John and Tim left the house after finishing breakfast to feed the animals, each taking a tractor loaded with round bales of hay. Their first trip was to the calf lot where they carefully inspected every calf for any signs of injury or health condition requiring attention. They found all the young stock to be in fine shape, so they drove one of the tractors to the place where the calf carcass was. They also planned to roll the remains into the loader bucket on the tractor for removal and disposal.

Much to the surprise of both men, when they reached the northwest corner of the lot, they found a much-reduced carcass from what they had seen just a few hours before. Most of one back quarter was eaten and one side reduced to mostly rib bones. Some intestines were pushed or raked away from the body cavity.

The semi-frozen snow was starting to soften, but the packed and trampled area around the carcass was a confusion of faint imprints from all the activity around the fence corner, making it impossible for John or Tim to identify any particular predator or scavenger tracks.

The sound of an approaching vehicle was heard as the Buckmans stood there. John walked back to the top of the rise in the lot and saw a small four wheel drive truck coming in his direction, which he recognized as the game warden's.

John motioned for the warden, a man named Ken Kella, to drive around the outside of the lot to the fence corner where Tim waited by the carcass.

Ken parked his truck, got out, exchanged greetings with John and Tim, then walked up to look over the fence at the mangled remains of the slaughtered calf.

~

Ken Kella was a rarity among men. He had spent his childhood near Cleveland, in a house by the lakeshore. From his earliest memories, the gulls, ducks, geese and small animals that were so common on the lake and along the shore, had fascinated him.

All the sick or wounded birds and animals Ken found while playing about the area were brought home to his father, a doctor, to repair or to otherwise treat. By the time he was nine or ten years old, Ken was almost an expert in the art of splinting legs and wings, stitching minor cuts and nursing a wide variety of birds and small animals. His mother, as a result of Ken's constantly changing menagerie, became a good wildlife dietitian providing food to appease the hunger of the little creatures Ken brought home.

At age thirteen, Ken's father was killed while serving as a field doctor with the Army in Italy. The following year Ken and his mother returned to her home, a farm where her parents lived. The farm fronted on a small river that flowed, after joining a larger one, into Lake Erie.

The farm and river gave Ken exposure to a much wider variety and larger quantities of wildlife than his first home.

By the time Ken entered high school, he knew he would study for and become a wildlife specialist or a naturalist. He read everything available at school, the local library and books from a nearby college on botany, biology, zoology and ornithology that time and availability permitted.

He entered college at age sixteen and by the time he completed six years of formal education and two years of field work in related areas, Ken was mature and well prepared to take up his chosen work.

Ken's growing expertise, his sound logical methods and

his quiet, but outgoing, personality opened doors to opportunities for many interesting positions across the country. His longest and most satisfying assignment was with a large forest products company. This company owned and operated immense tracts of land in a dozen states from Maine to Oregon and from Florida to Michigan.

Fortunately, the company was very concerned to preserve, renew and maintain the environment in every sense of the word. Ken's work assuring the company objectives brought the company and him worldwide recognition and acclaim.

Ken's published nature articles provided him with the funds and the opportunity to travel all over the world, observing and studying nature.

In his late thirties, Ken met and fell in love and married a young widow with two children, a girl and a boy.

His wife's hometown spread along the north bank of the Ohio River. On trips to visit her family, Ken became more and more interested in the huge areas of forest and parklands, the big blue-tinted hills and the number and variety of wildlife in the area.

The work Ken had spent years doing made it impossible to have a normal family life. He took a closer look at the requirements for his family future and decided to apply for a position that allowed him to be home most nights and weekends with his wife and adopted son and daughter.

Ken accepted the comparatively modest position in the State Department of Natural resources. He bought a small property in the midst of the Little Smokies, and became a regular family man while still young enough to enjoy and join in with the development of the two teen-aged children.

~

Ken Kella didn't say much as he leaned on the top of a post studying the maze of prints on the snow around the fence corner. Stepping up on the corner brace pipe with one foot he swung lightly across the three strands of top wire and down to the ground. After thoroughly inspecting the soft, top layer of snow, the animal carcass and the hair stuck to the wire where animals had crawled under the fence, Ken climbed over the fence again. He studied the less cluttered snow between the fence and the nearby woods.

After his lengthy perusal of the entire immediate area, Ken came back to the Buckmans to relate his observation.

"I believe this carcass, pointing to the calf, has been utilized by a very large number of animals for food over the last two nights. I can identify several sets of dog, fox, coyote and opossum tracks. There are two sets of bobcat tracks between here and the woods, and many sets of skunk tracks going to that open tile over by the trees," Ken said.

Pausing to fill and light a long stemmed corncob pipe, he continued while squatting down by the calf's head, "These punctures and tears in the calf's throat were made by a set of teeth and jaws that seem to be much larger than any coyote I have ever seen. I think the marks were made by a large dog," Ken said in a matter-of-fact voice.

"How do you distinguish a dog bite from a coyote?" Tim asked.

"Based on my experience only, I think you will find these canine tooth punctures are much wider than the ordinary coyotes," Ken responded. "Look at this." He then placed his hand on the calf's neck. The first three fingers of Ken's right hand barely covered the tooth marks. His thumb lacked by two inches reaching the marks on the opposite side of the calf's

127

neck. "I've never seen a coyote with a mouth this big," Ken said, holding up his rather large hand to illustrate the size.

"Then we may still have a real problem to deal with," John stated. "We'll have to move the calves up to the empty hay-barn. They can use the colts pasture in the daytime and be safe in the barn at night," he added.

"That'll work out fine. The colts are weaned and can go back with the older horses now," Tim remarked.

"If I were you, I would occupy that blind at night until the killers come back to eat again," Ken advised. "I'll come over and take a night on watch for you, if you'd like," he added.

The three men worked out a schedule for manning the blind, then returned to the garage to decide what to do with the two dead coyotes. Arriving there, Ken assured the Buckmans that the shooting of the coyotes had been done under proper authority. He would see to the handling of them by sending the bodies to the "lab" for study.

Before leaving, Ken discussed the possibility of dogs and coyotes hunting as a combined pack. It was unlikely the pack was a crossbreed of dogs and coyotes producing offspring with the predatory genes of both species, however, they discussed ways to protect against wild animals or just plain feral dogs.

Ken said, "I have to do some research on all these things. Give me a few hours and I'll see what I can learn."

After Ken left, the men went in to have lunch and to call Bob and Clyde, the farm hands, to come help move the calves and feedbins after lunch.

~

It took most of the afternoon to relocate the hay bunks and feed bins, put the colts in with their mothers and to move

128

the calves to the horse lot.

Moving the calves was not an easy thing to do. Pepper and Vickie who were directed by John aided Tim and Lora, riding the geldings. The calves would start out all right, but turn back when they came to the open gate, then break back for the calf barn or the familiar feedlot.

After three attempts to drive them, the calves "discovered" the opening and walked through it like a herd of old cows.

Out in the big open pasture the calves wanted to run in every direction but the right one. Thanks to the dogs and much hard work with the ice-caulked shod horses, the slipping, sliding herd of skittish animals was driven into the colt pasture.

With the chill of early evening upon them, they closed the gate on the calves, brushed down the horses and watered and fed them before going in for supper. Bob and Clyde joined them.

Mary had another of her good hot meals on the table by the time everyone had shucked boots and coveralls in the garage, washed up and entered Mary's kitchen. An hour and a half later, four well-stuffed men went back to the barns to put the few straggler calves inside and secure the doors. They opened all the vents and windows high up on the building before sending the hired men home for the day.

Tim went to his house and John to his. Tim took a hot shower, went to bed and slept like a log. John took his shotgun and drove to the blind.

~

Earlier this same day at the picnic area in the park, the roads open now, two lady bird watchers took turns getting out of the big station wagon to blow a whistle and call their dog.

The dog, a beautiful black and white Alaskan Malamute, was their personal guard dog that they had owned for three years.

The dog liked to go with the women anytime they visited wooded areas. Given the opportunity he would chase the squirrels up trees, barking in plain delight, or pound after rabbits until the whistle was blown or either of his mistresses called him to come back. Usually he was kept on a leash, securely fastened to a tree.

This time, attracted by a number of Piliated Woodpeckers, the dog had been fastened to a small tree while the bird watchers eased closer to the seldom seen birds. The dog waited patiently for a lengthy period, then backed away from the tree. His loose collar slipped over his head to swing back and forth on the leash from the tree limb above his head.

Free, the large five-year-old Malamute, with one blue eye and one brown eye, went bounding into the woods away from the bird watchers.

At first the playful dog was uncertain about leaving his busy owners and even stopped twice to listen for the whistle's "come back" tweet.

Just running over the snow was ecstasy to the part wolf, Arctic bred and reared dog. His loping strides covered a mile of hills and valleys in only minutes. Suddenly, his city-dulled nose picked up a scent to which even he quickly identified and responded. It was the urine splatters left by Dutch just moments before the excited male reached the big red female's trail.

Dutch had not gone into the leaf pile to sleep at dawn, following their second feeding at the kill. The call of nature was telling her to seek a mate.

Signaling the young dogs to "stay", Dutch trotted on up the cliff path then turned toward the west to prowl the forest.

The day was mild with practically no wind as she made

a big circle through the forest. Leaving her sign frequently, she continued to search. Her trip for the day almost completed, Dutch stopped to urinate before starting for the cliff path a few hundred feet away.

Pulling his nose out of the yellow snow, the Alaskan gave out with an excited, keening, muted wail.

Dutch heard his keening call and turned to watch the black and white dog scuttling toward her. The dog's performed the introduction shuffle before running away shoulder to shoulder seeking a courting and mating place, north along the ravine.

~

After hours of waiting and calling, the two tired bird watchers drove to town to report their lost dog. The well-mannered deputy sheriff assured them he would notify all local agencies to be on the lookout for the missing pet. After filling out the information form, they drove sadly home.

~

At midnight Tan went to the top of the hill behind the den to howl for Dutch who had been absent from the den area for many hours. Dutch heard and responded at once. With the reply understood, Tan knew to "stay away." In a little while, Tan and Brother started southeast toward the "kill". They passed under the fence to feed on the calf for a third time in as many nights.

In the brilliant moonlight, Ken Kella winced in remorse as he quickly pulled the trigger four times on Tim's shotgun.

John had just stopped to say goodnight to Lora and remind her to wake Tim at four o'clock, when the staccato sounds of the shots rolled over the hills.

Ken knew the big dog wasn't one of the two at his feet, the minute he looked at the bodies. These two had feet too small to have made the largest tracks he had seen on his first trip here.

Having spent part of the day reading up on hybrids, he had halfway expected to see a "coyote" or "coydog" as some references called them. He had examined one of the reported cross breeds in the Upper Peninsula of Michigan some years before, but wasn't sure the animal had been a hybrid. Ken had been disturbed, thinking nature was being changed by the influence of mankind. Now he was glad the dogs at his feet were just that - - dogs.

The calf lot was as bright as a perfect moon could light it as he put the long, lean animals in the back and drove toward the Buckman homes. He was not sorry now for killing the dogs. He didn't want word of cattle killing coyotes to spread over the region. He would be sure the stories spread would be about feral dogs, not about the few "little wolves" in these hills. The least he could do was to delay their slaughter.

~

Having spent the night with Chestnut, Pepper was back in her own house when the Buckmans, rising later than usual, came out of their houses to begin the days work. When John appeared, Pepper came bounding up to him for her anticipated patting and ear scratching that John always bestowed upon his little "cow dog." Vickie followed Tim as he joined his father on the short walk to the equipment barn to get the tractors.

Pepper's on-coming heat cycle had not gone unnoticed by John but she was always near enough to him in the daytime for close observation and was confined, he thought, to the enclosed porch on recent nights, so John was not concerned. Pepper's frequent squatting and swollen anterior made it obvious she was at the critical stage of estrus.

Had he known about Pepper mating with the big, dark-coated fox, John would have been very surprised. Both John and Tim, thinking the other had released Pepper from the enclosed porch, failed to comment on her being outdoors that morning.

They had been too preoccupied with work and the discovery of the further reduced calf carcass and the time spent with Ken Kella to notice Pepper's absence that morning.

When Vickie tried to follow Pepper to Chestnut's lay-up near the bull yard, Pepper sent Vickie ki-yieing toward the calf lot before joining Chestnut for further amorous activity. However, Pepper came running back at John's call when he, Tim and Ken Kella left the calf lot just before noon that day.

Chestnut rested on a convenient limb of his treetop lay-up watching Pepper, Vickie and the five busy people working to move the herd of calves. When the people went indoors, Chestnut came in search of Pepper. From the grove of trees behind the houses, Chestnut had called, in vain, for her.

Pepper only half tried to open the pet door for a few minutes, but the now securely latched door did not open. In fact, the little dog was too tired from the past eighteen hours of mating activity and calf-herding, hard work on the slushy-topped ice.

When Mary and Lora carried the bowls of warm food to them, Pepper and Vickie had emptied the containers, shared a pan of fresh water and settled into the big wooden -box for a much needed rest and sleep.

The more rested fox finally left the Buckmans' yard to go to the hay shed to catch mice. He spent the night on top of the rolls of hay, only occasionally yipping for Pepper.

All the animals in a two mile radius such as dogs, raccoon, opossum, coyotes, foxes, deer and many others had heard the staccato crash of the shotgun in the still air and understood its deadly meaning as the fearful sounds rolled over the hills.

All activity among the night denizens ceased for a brief time while they evaluated the possible threat to them. Satisfied that their safety was not endangered, the night dwellers resumed their lives of hunting, feeding, evading or mating as the moment required.

Dutch and her new mate, more than two miles away, heard only a faint whisper of sound several seconds after Tan and brother expired.

Only a little more than a mile north, slick headed Old Mossy at the sound of the gunshots, turned away from the alfalfa hay he was stealing from the shed behind Grant's barn, to look south toward the gunshots point of origin. In a few moments he resumed his feeding, unaware that his jumping the fence into the calf lot had resulted in the ending of two of his enemies' lives rather than his own.

Ken parked his truck in front of the garage as the four Buckmans approached. They listened to Ken's explanation of his short, but decisive period in the blind where he had awaited the calf killers.

The pair of big lifeless predators lay on an old rug that covered the floor of the truck bed. As feral animals, Tan's and brothers remains were destined for the lab, to be used as research specimens along with the two coyotes killed the previous night.

Before leaving to start home, Ken told the Buckmans that he believed there was another dog still unaccounted. One with larger feet and jaws than any of the predators killed in the past two nights, but that he didn't think the larger animal would try to attack the cattle by itself.

With mutual thanks and farewells, Ken and the Buckmans parted to seek their own homes for the night.

~

Dutch came once more to the calf lot, seeking her missing offspring. She and her untiring new companion-mate had been fulfilling the second most powerful influence in their existence for the past forty-eight hours. At times the mating drive exceeded the dominant one, consuming food.

Her ten-month-old pups, companions and pack members, had been part of her being from the moment the big silver greyhound had been painfully separated from his union with her, so long ago.

The calf body was gone, but the scent of her beloved family's blood was still apparent in the thin layer of ice where they had died.

The big red dog raised her head toward the stars and cried her anguish and loss long, long into the night across the big blue hills.

~

After the first hectic week of February, things settled down to more normal routines for the four Buckmans. The weather had changed for the better and predators in the area limited their pursuit of prey to the much more available, smaller creatures of forest and field.

Pepper found and took advantage of opportunities to mate with Chestnut for another week or so before rejecting his attention when her heat cycle ceased.

Dutch and the Alaskan Malamute were almost inseparable, even after the many days of courtship ended. There would be a new litter whelped in the coming spring. Dutch now had near normal vision and hearing with her wounds healed and strength recovered.

Ken Kella made a practice of stopping by the farm once or twice each week. He also visited the park picnic area where the big red dog had been seen the winter before, and more recently by a park employee doing repair work at another site half a mile north of the old stone watering trough.

Henry Grant had stopped by Ken's office to report his sighting of "Big Red" and a large black and white dog near his farm.

Timber crews on private lands also saw and reported Big Red and the wolf-like dog hunting along a stream. They started calling the black and white dog "Bruiser" because of his rugged, massive appearance.

One Saturday morning, Ken and his fourteen year old son stopped to give the Buckmans a rundown on a report from the State Lab about the four carcass' Ken had taken there for autopsy.

Howie Kella, now legally Ken's son, was a bright, intelligent young man with a quiet disposition much like Ken's. This and other qualities on the part of Howie gave Ken a new and rewarding feeling of pride for his son as he entered into the lengthy conversation with the Buckmans.

Howie was an avid student of agriculture. He now attended the local high school and was a member of the Future Farmers of America, a group to which Tim had also belonged. Vickie seemed to like Howie from the minute she came up to sniff his legs. She and Howie were soon good friends.

The two long legged colts reached over the fence to nicker for attention as John, Tim, Ken and Howie came walking up to the horse pasture fence. Tim took two apples from his jacket, handed them to Howie and pointed toward the colts. Howie used his pocket knife to section the apples, then fed

136

them to the colts by holding out his hands, palm up, with two apple sections on each hand. The gentle, velvet nosed, little horses carefully picked up and ate the pieces of apple then nodded their heads pleadingly for more.

As the group left the horse pasture to walk back toward the Kella car, Howie's newfound friends put on a show of equestrian acrobatics that caused all the men to laugh with enjoyment. Their display of running, jumping, bucking, wheeling and snorting soon had the four older horses imitating the youngsters. Howie fell in love with horses, then and there. He then determined to have his own horse someday.

~

Big Red, as Dutch was sometimes called, and Bruiser were ranging far and wide to the north and east of the Buckman farm. Dutch sheltered in hollow tree trunks, fallen logs or under large, overhanging rocks when she chose to rest or sleep. Bruiser, with his dense double layer of long, course and fine, thick hair could curl up and sleep anywhere except in heavy rain.

For varying periods of time the striking pair of dogs would stay away from the cavern, but periodically came back for a night or two. On these long trips afield, they often left the public lands and hunted on private tracts of equally wild and primitive nature. Some huge sections were owned and maintained by a European Corporation who harvested the timber and loaded it on barges for transport down the Ohio and Mississippi Rivers for transshipment to the lumber starved continental markets.

Bruiser's first attempts to find and catch prey were futile. His noisy approach and premature charges alerted prey far in advance of his intended ambush. Except for the skill and ability of his mate, he would have become a very hungry dog.

Bruiser would never become a fleet footed pursuer of deer by himself, but he slowly learned to catch the less nimble denizens of the hills and valleys where Big Red led him on her perambulations of the Little Smokies.

Bruiser was far from starving, but he had become much leaner than when he first found his freedom. It had been almost a week since he had his last real fill of meat. All he had eaten one day was some watercress he found growing by a sheltered spring of clear water. He even learned to eat some of the first shoots of grass just starting to appear.

~

Throughout the foothill part of the state it was still common practice for people to raise their own meat. Many people raised pigs to the desired size and weight, then butchered the hogs for home consumption.

Some pigs managed to escape from pens or buildings and make their way into the woodlands where a few avoided recapture or getting shot by hunters or poachers. Of the ones who made it to the woods, a very few matured and reproduced. By the second generation the pigs reverted totally to feral, omnivorous bandits.

The dogs met the young sow and the lean, spotted boar hog as they ran along a tall wire fence, then turned away to investigate some muskrat houses along the edge of a pond.

A few yards from the pond was a mound of earth where long ago some one had built a root cellar. The door was missing but a heavily timbered doorframe remained in place on the north side of the mound. Behind the opening, a slab topped, stone walled room held up the insulating earth.

Bruiser saw Dutch crouch down in the familiar stance

she usually assumed when she spotted prey. He stopped also, but didn't detect anything until the hogs charged right at him.

The boar had been living wild for nearly two years, having escaped from his pen when he was only a little more than one year old.

Continual running, rooting and raiding had caused his shoulders to develop to grotesque proportions in comparison to his hindquarters. In order to identify the boar if the need arose, his owner had notched his big, ugly ears. Long, ivory colored tusks protruded from both upper and lower jaw and his gimlet eyes seemed to be bright red as he came screaming at the totally surprised dog.

Bruiser leaped straight up in the air as the boar lowered his head to hook Bruiser with his long, sharp pointed tusk. He landed on the rock-like shoulders of the stinking boar, which had stopped abruptly near the spot Bruiser had just vacated.

Bruiser was momentarily stunned by the combined effects of falling, and the hog's speed impacting on his rib cage. The boar was so tall, Bruiser's legs were all off the ground at the same time.

Surprised and further angered by the apparent attack on his back, the ugly porcine beast spun around trying to get his teeth into the dog. The boar's spin had sent the burden on his shoulders flying off to one side. The boar made another rush at Bruiser but ran into something he didn't expect.

Bruiser had had enough. He met the hog with a charge of his own and had the boar by the nose, in his long, sharp teeth, before the boar could do any damage to him.

The sow had turned and made off for the open door of the root cellar the moment the fracas began. That was all it took for the big red, and very hungry, dog to enter the contest. The three hundred-pound female hog beat Dutch to the cellar. Once in the cellar she changed from a frightened, exposed, prey animal into a feral defender of her den.

Dutch made some unsuccessful attempts to get past the hog's fierce, efficient defense, but the sow's courage and size made Dutch back off her attack. The excruciating agony caused by Bruiser's powerful jaws and long sharp teeth locked into his nose paralyzed the boar's fighting instincts and weakened him physically, at the same time. Only the hog's voice box and lungs seemed to be going at full strength. His screams were so shrill and loud Bruiser was almost deafened.

Dutch abandoned her hopeless efforts to get at the sow. She came sailing back over the dead grass like a racer to grab the male hog by the left rear leg. The skin and heavy muscles almost defied her crushing, ripping canines and incisors, but she continued to grind and chew until she cut and tore through the thick skin and fiber to reach the tendon.

Despite the terrific pain in his nose and leg, the spotted hog did not give up. With renewed violence, he suddenly shook his massive head and began lunging toward the opening of the old root cellar. The boar's strength was too much for Bruiser's and Dutch's combined weight to stop. When the boar gained some forward momentum, Bruiser was dragged back under the feet of the hog and stepped on by his iron hard hooves with such force that Bruiser released the grip he had on the hog's snout.

Free of the pain in his snout, the weight of the dog on his leg only a minor deterrent to his escape, the four hundred-pound hog managed to gain speed quickly and plunged into the cellar.

As the hog entered the open cellar doorway, Bruiser sank his teeth into the hog's tail and bit it off near the top. Dutch realized the battle was lost and surrendered her grip on his leg as she was pulled through the opening.

With both of the hogs now facing them in the protective doorway, Dutch and Bruiser backed away from the victorious hogs, turned and trotted off to seek less dangerous prey.

140

~

All four of the farm ponds were full of water by the middle of March. The water in the three smaller ones was almost clear but the large pond was a yellowish-tan color from the runoff of soil-mixed water rushing over the bulldozed land around the site.

Bob and Clyde had been busy for several days putting strips of cut sod, trucked in from the south, on the water-eroded slopes along the sides and above the pond. They had already seeded and applied new straw mulch to larger areas slightly damaged by an early spring rainstorm.

Fortunately, the small ponds had been constructed without much disturbance of the land around them and had not required any repairs to drainage areas supplying them with water.

At the Buckmans' invitation, Ken and Howie rode out with Tim and Lora to see the ponds and other scenic points on the farm one mild Sunday afternoon.

Howie and Ken rode the mares, followed, by the colts, while Tim and Lora rode the geldings. Pepper and Vickie ranged out ahead of the party as if scouting the way. At times the free-running colts darted away to join the dogs in a frolic of playful races. The colts always came back at Tim's call because he gave each one a large slice of apple from a supply he carried in a saddlebag.

When the group dismounted by one of the new dams, Howie asked for and received permission to give all the horses some pieces of the sweet apples. Tim unsnapped and removed the bits from the horses' mouths so they could eat the remainder of the apples in the saddlebag.

Ken admired the well-made dams and the irrigation piping systems built into the concrete. He also volunteered to assist with the fish-stocking plan Lora mentioned to him. He recommended stocking the small ponds soon, but waiting another year before putting game fish in the large, lake-sized pond.

Ken agreed with the Buckmans' thinking about the commercial potential of the large number of acres of water for fish growing or aqua farming. He said he would secure and supply them with some very successful operations reports from within the state.

Howie surprised all of the adults with his knowledge of the subject of aqua farming. His Ag teacher had introduced the subject and Howie had taken more than a passing interest in what he learned and had read several pamphlets and books by experts in the business. Lora, only half-serious at the time, told Howie he could be the fish-farming adviser to the "Buckman Fish Ranch."

Later, back at the horse stables, Howie expressed a real interest in working for the Buckmans, in any capacity, especially with the fish stocking and fish care activity and caring for the horses. Tim and Lora promised to discuss his request with John and Mary, then give him an answer, adding "If it meets with the approval of your parents."

When the horses had been groomed and fed, Ken and Howie left for home, a very happy father and son.

~

Chestnut was just beginning his third year of life. Pepper was four years of age and Vickie just one year old when Pepper should have had her second litter of pups. The mating of Pepper and Chestnut had not produced offspring. Some minute differences in their chemical or genetic makeup may have been the cause of failure. Even the erratic times of mating could have missed the critical period necessary for conception. John merely thought he had been successful in keeping Pepper isolated from any visiting male dogs and would have been surprised had Pepper whelped.

Early one morning, the first week of April, Chestnut carried a freshly killed muskrat up and dropped it in front of Pepper's house. Chestnut's built in calendar had told him it was time to bring food to the den. Pepper nosed the carcass a few times before picking it up in her teeth, carrying it to the garden, digging a hole and burying it in the soft black soil.

For the next ten days or so, Chestnut brought small mammals of several kinds to the yard, only to have them interred in the garden or by the little creek in the horse pasture. Chestnut eventually learned his gifts weren't needed and quit bringing them.

In the fifteen months since their friendship began, Pepper and Chestnut had become so accustomed to each other's daily routines that they knew when to expect a visit from the other.

Chestnut continued his play periods with Vickie each evening. Chestnut now had to work hard to keep Vickie from catching him in the brief races. She seldom lost sight of him when he tried to hide among the trees, and soon tracked him down when he did manage to hide from her. Her sense of smell was extremely sharp, permitting her to track him at her best speed. Vickie had learned when to anticipate the fox's quick turns and circles. She often cut across his trail to save distance and surprise the fox.

Pepper seldom took part in these mad scrambles. Chestnut and Vickie were too fast for her now that Vickie was nearly grown and ran much faster than Pepper.

Pepper and Chestnut often went for runs together without Vickie, in the fields and in the forest to the west of the feeding lots. Both little animals enjoyed their rodent hunts around the barn, sheds and piles of materials stored outdoors. They worked together on these rodent hunts to the detriment of the rats and mice, catching many times the number either would have caught by themselves.

When the groundhogs started feeding on the early peas, spinach, asparagus, radishes and cabbage in Mary's garden, she called Pepper to chase them every time she saw one near the garden. Naturally Chestnut entered into this activity.

Soon Vickie had joined Pepper and Chestnut in their stalks of the voracious, garden raiding 'chucks. By the time her regular garden was due to be started, the three little hunters had wiped out the garden robbers. Rabbits ceased to be a problem, also. After a few chases the rabbits sought safer places to meet and raise their young.

Later in the spring, moles began making runways and dirt mounds in the Buckman yards. Mary tried to get Pepper and Vickie to catch them for her. The dogs thought Mary was playing some new game and were puzzled at her digging and pointing at the humps in the grass. Vickie was waiting for Chestnut to appear one evening, when a mole started to push dirt up very near her.

About that time Chestnut showed up on the other side of the erupting little cone-of earth. Chestnut cocked his eye at the molehill and then quickly started digging in the mole tunnel, about two feet behind the molehill and the mole.

In just seconds, Chestnut had torn the top off the tunnel and continued to dig toward the mole, trapped in the end of the runway under the cone of dirt. As Chestnut's digging feet neared the molehill, the little yard wrecker decided to vacate his underground haven to make his escape. The mole popped out of the dirt, inches from Vickie. Vickie bit the head off the big-toothed, little yard wrecker in the blink of an eye.

From then on, Vickie did lots of mole digging before

catching on to Chestnut's trapping technique. After Chestnut caught two more moles, Vickie copied him and became more successful. For awhile, Mary wasn't sure which was worse, the mole tunnels or the four-inch deep ditches Vickie dug.

In time, Vickie mastered the method Chestnut used and made only short excavations. The mole problem ended finally, but there were visible differences in the yard where all the new dirt was added to repair mole and dog damage. Mary told John that Vickie had become a "real" yard dog.

~

One night, Dutch gave birth to four pups in the cave behind the cavern. Bruiser stayed in the area close by the den, watching over the strange acting Dutch.

He had learned to hunt and kill small mammals in the nine weeks spent with the big red Doberman. In the last two weeks Dutch had been very slow and inefficient, but Bruiser made enough kills to feed them both. He kept on hunting while Dutch stayed in the den for two days after whelping. Bringing food to her seemed to be a natural function of their pairing.

At first Dutch didn't let him touch the babies, but on the third day she abruptly gave him the "guard" signal and departed the cave. Returning after a very brief absence, Dutch checked the well-being of each pup, then proceeded to lick Bruiser's face and to nose his neck as if in thanks for his service. In fact, Bruiser had stayed at the cave opening all the time Dutch had been gone, not daring to go near the sleeping pups. Dutch's domination overrode his natural curiosity.

From the time of her first trip away from her babies, Dutch felt no concern over Bruiser's hesitant but increasing attention to the fat, furry little whelps. She resumed her own hunting trips without feeling the anxiety she felt with her first litter, the previous year. With Bruiser sharing their guardian-ship, the pups were never alone in the den.

On one of her longer journeys from the cave, Dutch came across the scent trail of Pepper and Chestnut. She followed the scent a short distance to a small open meadow in the woods, a quarter of a mile west of the Buckman farm.

Pausing in the woods, she watched the pair of familiar animals in their casual investigation among the clumps of veg-etation in the meadow. With a soft bark of friendliness, the big red dog walked forward to renew acquaintance with Pepper.

Chestnut did not follow Pepper when she trotted over to touch noses with her outsized friend. He sat down on the ground in the middle of the treeless area and waited until the strange dog and Pepper completed their ritual of greetings consisting of much sniffing, nosing and circling each other. The dogs parted at last, Dutch to continue her search for food, Pepper to return to Chestnut waiting impatiently among the dead grass and shrubs of the small prairie.

Pepper returned home in the faint light of early dawn. The scent of milk and puppies on Dutch had intrigued her, causing vague feelings of emptiness. When Vickie came out to join her, Pepper spent some time licking and grooming her pup, much as she had done in bygone days.

Chapter six

Chapter Six ~

With typical variations in weather, winter eased into spring-like days only to return with a day or two of arctic snow flurries or rain that felt colder than ice. By the time the calves started arriving, there had been enough warm sun-shiny days to drive the frost from the earth and start grass to greening in sheltered places.

Mary drafted Clyde to help get her early garden planted and her new flock of six-week old chickens, one hundred fifty this year, installed in her spotless brooder house.

Two new colts would be coming soon. The big-bellied mares required frequent visits to assure Mary they were not in discomfort or needing her attention.

John, Lora and Tim were busy with cattle activities of moving the feed bunks to new locations and putting the herd of yearlings and two year old heifers through a special inspection to see how many really top quality breeders there were. The culling out process of the entire herd always created mild disagreements about some animals. Lora usually waited until John and Tim had made their arguments then chipped in with the decision-making statement. In the end, only one load of market animals was shipped out to the commercial meat packers.

Tim and Lora discussed the possibility of increasing the numbers of cattle the farm could properly maintain. The high quality beef type breeders they produced on the farm were always in demand and quite profitable. If necessary, they could buy or rent some land if available and reasonably priced, for hay or pasture.

Casual inquiries turned up several small tracts of land in the immediate area, but none large enough to be worthwhile. The land just to the north of the Buckman farm would be ideal

Tim decided, but knew the owners, the Grants, were locked into a soil conservation program that would be costly to interrupt so no offer was made.

When the subject of expanding was discussed with John and Mary, they were interested, but hesitant because of the total amount of money the increase would involve. As the sorting, culling and calving work progressed, all of them had the matter in the back of their minds.

The final new calf count was one hundred thirty with seventy-two being heifers. Nine sets of twins more than offset a few calves that didn't survive, their mothers culled out for commercial sale. Four calves rejected by their mothers had to be moved to a convenient stall in the barn where they were bucket-fed a special formula of milk substitute. The rejecting cows were culled and shipped to market.

The haymaking started earlier than usual due to almost ideal weather with plenty of rain and few cold periods causing frost. Nearly two hundred cows, bulls and heifers were put on pasture by the middle of May. This reduced the amount of work required to feed them during a very busy time of the year.

Howie had his sixteenth birthday and secured his drivers' license the same day as a result of the driver training class at high school. He and his best friend had already rebuilt an older model car in the mechanical training shop at school. Ken had also been involved with both activities and was impressed with Howie's methodical and thorough attention to details.

Howie carried a big load of subjects in school. He was on the track team and did very well in long distance runs, beating most juniors and seniors in the cross-country events while he was still in his sophomore year. Each evening he had track practice and then a lot of homework. His crowded schedule prevented him taking a part-time job at the Buckman farm, but he made many visits to pet the horses, take short horseback rides and play with Vickie and Pepper.

Chestnut became accustomed to Howie and began approaching to within a few feet as time went on. By the time school ended, Chestnut was taking part in the romping play of Vickie, Pepper and Howie.

The new colts were born on a Saturday. When the labor began on Friday evening, an anxious Mary called the Vet. She remembered Howie's request to be present for the foaling, so she called him also. Fifteen minutes later, he showed up for the long session of waiting and watching the mares. The first colt came just after midnight and the second one on Saturday afternoon.

Howie, the vet, and all four Buckmans took turns in the long vigil, with all of them present at the actual births. Both miniature stallions were up nursing in less than half an hour after delivery.

Howie came more often after their birth to watch the colts learn to run and play as the anxious mothers followed them around the pasture. At first they were separated from the older horses, then became part of "Howie's remuda," as Mary called them. Now eight horses of different ages grazed together, even the newest ones nibbling at the tender young grass between nursings.

After school ended, Howie fed, groomed, and gave the horses treats at every opportunity. He became a regular participant in the daily activities on the Buckman "ranch," as he half seriously called the farm.

~

The Buckmans and the Grants had been friends and neighbors for many years. The Grant farm had been passed along, generation to generation, from the pioneer Grant who had settled on it in the first decade of the eighteen hundreds.

The Buckman family had been one of the Grant's first neighbors, taking up property only a couple of miles south. Over the years, there had been a few marriages between the two families resulting in the current families being distant cousins.

Henry and Melba had no children or living brothers and sisters. They had many distant "kin" living in other states, but the Buckmans were the only ones they considered family. The Grants, after long and careful consideration, had made a decision to sell their farm and take life easy. With a plan in mind, Henry and Melba arranged to be invited over for one of Mary Buckmans dinners, one Saturday in May.

After eating and clearing up, the six contented and relaxed members of the "family" sat down in Mary's spacious living room for a long visit. When all the current events had been discussed, Henry and Melba informed the Buckmans of their decision to retire, selling the farm to free them of daily work, hoping to sell by land contract to minimize taxes.

The Grant's decision to sell coincided with Tim and Lora's desire to add more hay and pastureland to the Buckman farm.

This desire was well known to John and Mary, but they lacked the funds to purchase land and did not want to go in debt for it at this time. The Grant's statement about selling by land contract changed the situation.

The younger Buckmans' position was completely different than John and Mary's. Lora had inherited a sizeable number of government bonds that matured at intervals providing a considerable amount of non-farm income.

After several semi-private discussions among the members of the group, a verbal agreement was made whereby the Buckmans would pay the Grant's one fourth of the agreed price

152

in cash, and the remainder in annual payments over the succeeding years. The details were to be finalized in a legal contract.

One major provision Lora insisted on was supported by Tim, John and Mary. The Grant's retained the right to occupy their home for the full life of either or both of the loved and respected couple.

With the verbal arrangements concluded, Henry went out to his car, returning with a gallon jug of mild, homemade, wild cherry wine. With many happy "toasts", the three couples spent the rest of the day reminiscing about the past and plans for the future

Tim and Lora absented themselves from the group long enough to do the evening chores and to privately share their happiness over the day's good fortune. When they returned to the house, Lora expressed her happiness by hugging and kissing all four of the older people and then telling them how much she appreciated being a member of their family.

Lora's actions and words caused Henry to sponsor another toast from the dwindling supply of wine. By nine o'clock it was obvious to all but the exuberant Henry, that he should not try to drive home, so Mary made sandwiches and coffee for all, then, with help from Melba, prevailed on Henry to spend the night in one of the Buckmans' bedrooms.

The next morning, after a late awakening, they all gathered in Lora's kitchen for breakfast. Both John and Henry had red-tinged eyes from their long evening's assault on the now empty wine jug, the two old friends having stayed up to talk for hours after the other four had gone to their beds.

It was ten o'clock that morning when the Grant's left to go home to dress for church. Henry remarked as he got in his car, "Well, better late than never."

~

Most of the Grant's property drained into the stream leading to the "lake" as the large pond was now called. With the acquisition of the nine hundred plus acres of Grant's farm, the Buckman family now owned the entire watershed for the lake. With this fact established, some possible problems with operating a "private" lake when fish production plans became a reality in the future were eliminated. Except for spring freshets, the entire outflow dissipated into an area of gravel, rock, and underground leeching in the little stream's wide, shallow channel. Thus, the lake was totally contained on private land.

About half of the Grant tract was still in carefully maintained woodlands. The balance, except for a small plot for tobacco, was planted with a mixture of grasses and legumes for erosion control. The Buckmans withdrew from the government programs to which Henry had been committed, but would continue the actual practice of conservation by careful use of the fields for pasture and hay production.

Another condition of the land contract was for Henry to sell the six thousand-pound tobacco allotment for the farm, to other tobacco growers in the county. The Buckmans had no need or desire to be involved with the year round, time consuming crop. Now even that small tobacco field would be planted in alfalfa or clover. Henry and Melba contracted the sale so they would get annual payments of one thousand dollars per year, until the full amount was paid.

This completed their divestment of saleable property, so the Grant's did something they had dreamed of all their lives. They flew to the South Sea Islands, Australia and Hawaii, spending more money in one month than they had ever spent in an entire year of their lives.

When the Grant's returned home, Melba spent a lot of

time with Mary telling her all about the wonderful trip, especially about all those beautiful, brown skinned people and how she had persuaded "staid old Henry" to put on a grass skirt and dance with the hula girls.

~

Dutch led her pack of four playful pups to the edge of the woods by the open fields where she had hunted ground-hogs, partridge, rabbits and other small game the first year. She was surprised to find a new woven wire fence stretched north along the boundary. The new fence began at the corner of an older one that was anchored to three huge locust posts with heavy metal pipe braces. The older fence ran south along the edge of the wooded area, and an intersecting fence ran east through the open fields that abutted the old property line between the Grant-Buckman properties.

The new fence had only one strand of barbed wire at the top, but was too high for cattle to reach over or get across by jumping. The bottom strand of number nine wire was several inches above the clean, fresh dirt path left by a six foot wide 'dozer blade used to clear out the old posts, wire and brush from the fence line.

Dutch led her little band of trim-footed, long-legged pups north along the new wire to a small depression where the fence was more than a foot above the ground. She and the pups slid under the fence and started east on the old dirt farm road, which now showed signs of recent use, toward a place where she had caught several of the, less wary, young 'chucks the previous year. Concealed from the adjacent fields by the eroded depth of the road and a fringe of grass and weeds on each side of it, Dutch came to a full stop and went into her "stalk" mode.

The pups mimicked their mother, to a lesser degree, as

she began to creep up to the place she had been seeking. When she left the road to pass through the roadside fringe, the four followers formed a single line, prompted by some direct eye signals from the big red dog.

While still in the weedy fringe, Dutch stopped again. She was somewhat puzzled at another change to the land in front of her. The fields had been mowed and the hay rolled into big round bales that lay scattered all over the area. The large number of dirt mounds in front of groundhog burrows, that she remembered, had been scraped level by a tractor-mounted scraper blade. Signaling her student pups to "stay," Dutch eased out into the open field to investigate the bare patches of earth where "chuck holes" should have been. The new earth had a strange repugnant odor that made her eyes and nose water. Dutch quickly dropped her investigation of the plugged and treated dens to move over to a shallow uncut waterway where a few normal-smelling, active burrows remained.

Later, Dutch guided her pups across the road into a smaller field of tall grass and clover, where she gave them their first lesson in "how to catch a wary woodchuck". Afterward she carried the ten-pound carcass back under the fence into the woods where the four fierce, little wolf-like predators worried and battled the kill.

Now hungry herself, Dutch opened the 'chuck's belly to expose the viscera which the hungry pups soon ate. The five of them consumed the rest of the delicious meat, then the young dogs curled up to sleep under a thick clump of elderberry stalks. While they slept, Dutch caught and brought another 'chuck back to the sleeping place.

While the four pups under the elderberry plants dreamed and gave chase to rabbits in their sleep, a very lean female of another kind also led her litter of fourteen thin, hungry offspring on a search for food. Her fourteen nipples were sore from the rough nursing of the constantly hungry pigs. The sow frequently made a quick turn to flip one or more of the long nosed, sharp toothed sucklings away from her almost empty dugs.

Her apparent lack of concern for her babies was belied anytime the feral boar came near her pigs. With a fury he could not overcome despite his great size and deadly tusks, the sow attacked the gimpy-legged, would be killer of his own progeny and drove him away, squealing in pain and frustration.

The sow was the benefactor of the two dog's battle with the boar several weeks before the birth of the pigs. The damage done to his back leg made it easier for the sow to fight off his three legged attempts to kill the young pigs. The dragging left leg gave audible warning when he tried to stalk them in the woods or overgrown fields of the abandoned farm.

The porcine family had a stroke of good fortune when the big boar left the root cellar to pursue other fertile females in the dense tract of land owned by the lumber company. His coming and going was through one of the many deep ditches over which the fence was built. When he returned seeking the sow, the pigs were already big enough to run like rabbits, avoiding his first uncertain attacks.

The black sow had moved her brood out of the root cellar to enable her to find food and teach the young pigs to forage for themselves. The pigs proved to be quick learners and saved their own lives by becoming very efficient at finding and consuming acorns, bulbs, roots, bugs, grubs, worms and every kind of green plant from hog weeds to clover.

Also in abundance were wild flowers and berries of all kinds, still green but palatable, except for the sweet, sugary strawberries that grew in profusion and caused the young pigs to race madly about to get a full share of the tiny red jewels.

By the time they were a month old, the sow was able to fend them off and completely wean them by increasing the severity of the rejecting tosses of her nose and by occasional nips from her teeth. Although the skinny pigs only weighed about twenty pounds each their frames were large enough to easily carry forty pounds.

Unlike her truly wild ancestors who stayed with their young for several months, the domestic sow was ready to leave her brood and mate again only a few days after weaning her current litter.

Fortunately, or unfortunately, the gimpy "Spots" had tried to steal a sow away from another boar, older wiser and much more skilled in the arts of porcine contest than was Spots. His antagonist was an old Tamworth boar that had spent seven years in the forest feeding himself, fighting, killing and eating most of the other escaped hogs that came within the range he defended. On rare occasions, he accepted a willing female. More often than not, he managed to kill and consume the resulting offspring and the defensive sow when the slaughtered pigs were not sufficient to satisfy the hunger of the six hundred pound, seven foot long, red coated monster.

The Tamworth had killed Spots in a one-sided, short battle. He tore the guts out of Spots with his first pass. His five-inch long, razor-like tusks opened the smaller boar's belly from front to back. He continued to rip apart the squealing Spots as he tried to flee, and sealed his fate by severing the muscles and tendons in the right rear leg before Spots got a good start. The old Tamworth fed on the big carcass for several days, even driving his harem of three away when they came along after smelling the ripening meat.

The black sow did not miss Spots and did not mate for several months. She did put on a lot of weight and grew much larger before she met the huge Tamworth.

~

The busy hay making season was underway when work began on the Grant homestead, or Grant place, as it would always be thought of by the Buckman family. A fence builder was employed to clear out the old and construct new fences around the fields to be used for pasture this year. Other fencing of woods and hay land would be done later.

The work needing to be done was more than their present equipment and manpower could possibly handle, so another set of cutting, conditioning and baling machines were leased from a local equipment dealer. Additional help was needed. John made a few trips around the neighborhood and arranged for several local farmers to run the new rigs and drive the hay-transporter tractors on a two-shift basis during the peak of the season.

Pepper and Vickie hopped in the truck to ride with John every chance they got. As usual, they tried to get out to visit with other farm dogs where John stopped on his help-hunting expeditions.

Stopping by Paul Cross's home one day, John left his truck window open as he walked toward a small field where Paul was working some dogs. John stopped and waited for Paul to finish the lesson he was giving to one dog, then walked on to where Paul was praising his ecstatic pupil.

Four other young dogs bounced up and down, trying to get some of the lavish praise the one dog was getting, but stayed where Paul had left them. Paul motioned to the dog at his feet, directing her to line up with the other four already in line by the fence. Almost before his directions were completed, his pupil carried out the signal commands.

All at once Pepper and Vickie arrived, rushed up to the five dogs by the fence and began sniffing and nosing at the recumbent pupils. John called to Pepper and Vickie to "come back," a command they both knew well. Vickie responded at once, coming to John, then following his order to "heel". Pepper stopped her sniffing and nosing to stand in a trance-like, rigid position. Her memory and senses were calling back the presence of the young dogs whose scents were almost replicas of Vickie's familiar smell.

John and Paul suddenly realized they were witnessing a poignant time and set of emotional reactions by Pepper. Shaking all over now, Pepper began to give out with flute-like sounds, rising and falling in pitch, then dying away to a soft whispering moan.

Struck by the little black dog's distressed recognition of her family, John and Paul remained silent as Pepper began moving along the row of immobile dogs, licking and crooning her way along the line. As she caressed them with her tongue, most of her pups rolled to their backs or crouched in a humble manner, thus showing their submission to the dominate authority of her motherhood.

As if on signal, all the young dogs broke ranks to tear around Pepper in a demonstration of total delight. Vickie hesitantly joined in, then acted as delirious as the other five pretty animals. John and Paul walked back to the truck in complete silence, each avoiding the other man's damp eyes.

The two men talked casually for a few minutes, then mutually agreed it was time to call in the dogs to allow John to proceed with his trip to find help for the Buckman farm.

Paul used a whistle, he kept on a chain around his neck, to signal his five dogs. They came running as soon as they heard the sound, which was almost inaudible to John. Pepper and Vickie scampered up on the heels of Paul's dogs, all, seven in a stage of excitement.

John had to pick up Pepper in his arms and place her in the truck. Vickie jumped in at his command. He held Pepper away from the door with one hand while entering the truck and closing the door. He closed his window and quickly left Paul's place in order to reduce the stress on Pepper as soon as possible.

Pepper settled down, accepting the kind but firm way John spoke to her, calming and reassuring her as they drove home, rather than to his planned destination when he left home earlier that day.

~

The fields first mowed and baled at the Grant homestead were the fields planned for long term pasturing. The mowing and scraping operations were necessary parts of a series of steps required to prepare them for grazing. The old growth was detrimental to young grass and legumes on which cattle grew and liked best, so it was removed and stacked outdoors under inexpensive but adequate tarps. The groundhog holes had to be plugged and treated to prevent the 'chucks from reopening the holes posing danger to cattle and horses which would graze the land.

As soon as possible after the fields were prepared, lime and fertilizer were put on and seed sown where needed, to improve the quality and variety of the vegetation. The "regular" hay lands would receive the same general treatment to produce the large volume of high quality hay the Buckmans would need for the larger numbers of cattle they planned to raise on the increased acreage of the farm.

Earlier in the spring, Tim, John, and Lora had spent several days sorting the young breeding animals in order to keep more of their own heifers for the future herd requirements. As a result, forty more of the best yearling heifers were retained that would have been sold in prior years. Another group of two-year-old heifers was graded, saving twenty-five additional breeding animals.

With the four hundred fifty acres of new hay and pastureland, the Buckmans planned to have two hundred or more cows producing calves each spring.

More oats and barley, and less hay, would be raised on the "home" farm to balance the total amounts of feed and hay required for all seasons of the year. Yearling and two-year-old heifers would be wintered on the Grant place while all young calves, bulls and bred cows would be wintered in the feed lots on the home place.

When Howie Kella's school closed for summer vacation, he became everyone's right hand man. He went from tending gardens and horses, to nursing orphan calves and operating tractors. When the tank truckload of mixed bass, blue gill and pike arrived, he became the head honcho of the fishponds. Despite his methodical pace, he accomplished a tremendous amount of results in every task he was given to do. His memory was so good it was never necessary to tell him how to do a job more than once. "He's the best darn thing that ever came here," John claimed.

John went to Portsmouth one morning, returning home in the afternoon with a twelve foot fishing skiff, a five horse-power motor, fishing tackle, life vest and several kinds of rods, reels and cane poles, all piled in the bed of his truck.

When Mary asked, "Just when do you think you'll take time to use all that stuff?"

John replied, "That stuff, as you call it, is for Howie. How else would he be able to keep his eyes on all those fish in the ponds?" John turned his head and winked at Lora as he started unloading "all that stuff."

John's uncanny ability to forecast rain seemed to be extremely good, as the hay harvest and field fertilization work went forward. Rain, only occasionally, fell on new mown forage before it could be baled and stored under sheltering roofs.

The first hay harvest produced over five hundred of the big round bales, including that made on the Grant place. The additional manpower supplied by the area farmers made for an easier, less tiring, schedule for John and Tim, than in former years. One of the young farmers helping with haymaking elected to take his pay in the form of young calves. John and Tim thought it a good choice, giving him some extra days of work to help him receive more "pay calves."

~

Dutch gave up hunting completely in any of the fenced fields when she found her old "'chuck pantry" occupied with the herds of young heifers. The memory of Tan's and Brother's deaths caused her to be leery of, rather than attracted to the big smelly animals. Bruiser had gone under the fence to get an upclose look at a group of the largest heifers, which caused them to bellow and charge at him in real anger. He barely made it back under the fence before the bawling, snorting, ground-shaking herd could trample him. From that day forward, the dogs shied away from any place containing bovine residents.

The four young pups were learning more and becoming more skilled each day. Their baby fur was giving way to shorter, smooth coats of summer hair. It was already evident they would be more like Bruiser, but would have long legs and slimmer bodies, inherited from Dutch. The net result of their mixture was more wolf-like than either progenitor.

What humans call luck, but considered a normal part of life if thought of at all by Dutch, continued to be a major factor of her existence. Bad luck and good luck pushed and followed her from the time of her birth to the day she came across Bruiser. Since that time she had been more in control of her destiny than ever before. She had chosen to accept him, to trust him and to teach him her way of life.

In normal circumstances, dogs do not pair like their wild cousins. Dutch and Bruiser were two of the exception proving facts of life. They were mated for life in the total meaning of the words.

The pairing was proven when both Bruiser and Dutch fought and drove off or killed other feral dogs daring to intrude on the range of forest and fields chosen as home. Both dogs began to scent-mark the boundaries and to patrol them periodically. For her own reasons, Dutch chose to leave the stray and pet dogs that were encountered on the edges of their territory, strictly alone.

Most of the trash barrels in the parking areas of the parks had been replaced with large hoppers. These could not be turned over by dogs or deer. This almost eliminated one source of food, but some of the careless visitors threw some edible items on the ground. Dutch still avoided the site where she had been shot with bird pellets, but sometimes led her pack to other picnic areas in the park sections of the huge forest only at night when few humans were there.

Bruiser had been fed hamburgers, cooked or raw, by the bird watching sisters dozens of times during the period he had served as their protector. He had developed a liking for the rich meat and searched for it each time he was in one of the picnic sites.

One night in July, all six of the dog pack came to a county-owned, nature study and picnic area, just a few miles off the main highway through the county. The area was equipped to serve some of the nature lovers with disabilities attracted to the little smoky hills.

A very wealthy couple who used wheelchairs had donated the land and a large amount of money for improvements. They had found it almost impossible to find places where they could enjoy the outdoors.

In this unusual wildlife sanctuary, neat concrete sidewalks, convenient accessible restrooms and many other accommodations had been installed for people who used crutches, wheelchairs or other mobility aids. Bus loads of visitors from distant points were invited and assisted by a group of local citizens who felt rewarded by their efforts to support equal rights for people with disabilities and to help them enjoy real nature.

Much care and skill was employed to attract and protect the wildlife the special visitors came to see. The natural habitat was guarded to reduce the amount of changes that could be caused by human sponsors and visitors alike. Visitors used the walks and rest stations between the viewing shelters, where they could look out through screens at birds, animals, wildflowers and all the other natural inhabitants of the sanctuary.

Ken Kella was among the group waiting to welcome and assist an especially equipped busload of visitors from Cincinnati. The tour bus guide had called to advise them to expect the group at seven A.M. that morning.

Standing by the broad smooth parking lot, Ken looked around in appreciation of the pretty little hills, streams and woodlands of the sanctuary. The only thing that seemed out of place was a big picnic table sitting by a large metal refuse hopper at the west end of the parking lot. The table had been made without benches for wheelchair users.

A group of cyclists had moved the table there, and left the heavy lid of the hopper open when they left.

The night before, the dogs had searched all around the small picnic and parking area but found very little to eat. The four young dogs arrived at the open hopper in a group. Many interested odors wafted down to them from the top of the container. They could reach the top by standing up on their back feet, but couldn't get a good enough purchase with their front feet to pull themselves up and into it. As if with one mind, they scrambled up on the table and peered into the open bin.

The hopper was only about half filled with refuse from picnics and car trash boxes. The hoppers were washed and sterilized each day, so the smells coming out of this one were mostly good food smells. The big metal bin was deep and made the pups cautious about jumping into it, but try as they would, they couldn't reach any of the tantalizing food.

Two of the pups crowded on top of the hopper in search of a way down in. One pup just sat down on the picnic table as if waiting for the problem to be solved. The most persistent of the lot kept trying to reach down with his mouth, over-balanced and fell into the bin.

The two on top heard the pup in the bin crunching up a dried out bun and tried to go over the top of the vertical lid. The lid fell over and down with a loud clang, leaving the pups on top standing with their front feet on the lid. The lone pup on the table just sat there with ears up, eyes wide open, and a "what happened?" look on his face. This all happened in the brief time it took Dutch and Bruiser to trot the length of the two-acre parking lot.

The pup inside began to howl in panic as Dutch and Bruiser reached the scene of entrapment. Bruiser began biting and barking at the container in his anger at the metal box. The big red dog made her way to the top, clawing and scratching at the lid. The three pups jumped down and ran to cower under a nearby tree. The only visible evidence of the older dog's attack on the hopper was some scratch marks in the green paint.

The heavy metal lid fit the hopper well, but not perfectly, allowing some air to enter. The little prisoner gradually quieted down and then started hunting through the refuse for scraps to eat. He even found an unopened paper carton of coffee cream, which he tore open and lapped at with his long tongue.

The trapped pup whined and was answered by one or both of the perplexed parents on the outside. The pup tried everything he could do to get out of the bin. By standing on his rear feet he could just touch his nose to the small crack between lid and rim of the hopper. Jumping only banged his head against the thick steel cover. Dutch stood to put her nose to the crack and tried to lick the pup's nose only a quarter of an inch away.

All night long the pup struggled to get out, exhausting himself until even his voice almost failed him. Dutch, Bruiser and the other three pups kept watch over him but were helpless to do anything but wait.

At seven A.M., people started parking cars at the far end of the lot. At the sound of the first motor, the dogs had hidden in a circle of shrubs, thirty yards away. They were still hidden when Ken came near the hopper, walking by the side of the wheelchair of a lady who was talking excitedly as she propelled the chair with her hands.

She was telling Ken how much she had missed the birds, rabbits and squirrels that she had fed as a child on her dad's farm. Both Ken and Wilma heard the sound of an animal coming from the large, green trash container they were just passing.

Ken said, "Please excuse me, while I check to see what that sound is," pointing to the hopper.

"Please do. It sounds like it's in pain," said Wilma.

Ken walked over and raised the lid on the hopper, pushing it all the way open. He saw a mustard, ketchup, and cream smeared young dog, crouching fearfully down in the litter at the bottom of the bin. He moved back a step or two to tell the lady what he had just seen.

When Ken stepped away, the pup gave a weak sounding bark and sprang up, hooking his front feet over the lip of the, hopper. His rear feet scraped at the inside of the- bin but he couldn't get traction to push his body higher. Ken stepped back over to the hopper to give the dog some help getting out, but the pup shrieked in fear of his reaching hand.

Wilma, looking past Ken, saw a red blur of streaking animal coming across a strip of grass toward them. Without thinking, She rolled the wheelchair a few feet past Ken, stopped in amazement, and started shouting at the big red dog, teeth bared now, racing at them.

Ken had already made a quick grab and caught the young dog by the back of its neck and in the same motion, lifted it out of the trash bin.

Suddenly he became aware of the lady shouting and the red dog's snarling approach. Wilma screamed, "Dutch! You stop!" and then shouted, "Down, Dutch, down!"

The scared pup ran past the lady in the wheelchair just as Wilma gave her last shouted "Down." The oversize, red dog came to a stop, only feet in front of Wilma, and sank to the ground. The small gray and the big red dog jumped up and ran several steps away. The red dog stopped, turned around and looked at her old friend, Wilma, before she went out of sight behind a cluster of shrubs about a hundred feet from the amazed couple by the refuse container.

Neither Ken nor Wilma had realized the serious danger they had been in when Dutch charged them. The moment of action was so brief, and the pup's high pitched wails had masked the infuriated sounds the big red dog made as she rushed to the defense of her offspring. Past experiences had made Dutch think her pup was being harmed by the couple near the pup's prison.

Ken had been too occupied by the pup's struggles to escape and by his hoarse voiced cries of panic to comprehend the meaning of Wilma's shouted commands to Dutch. Ken first saw Dutch when the just released pup ran toward her.

Dutch recognized Wilma's voice and responded to her

commands of "stop" and "down" from years of ingrained habit. If not for the sight of her released pup, she would have pressed her attack to the end. The slight morning breeze wafted to her the remembered scent of flowers and dry sweet grass exuded by Wilma. The soft memories weakened Dutch's anger and helped enforce the power of Wilma's shouted commands.

Ken spent two hours with his charming lady guest, talking about Dutch at first, telling each other what they knew about the big red dog, but changing to the topics of nature surrounding them as they moved about the small sanctuary. The colorful birds and small animals thrilled Wilma, which made Ken more than glad he had been her guide for the day.

When the allotted time ended for the touring group, Ken and Wilma exchanged addresses and phone numbers so they could keep in touch. Wilma was anxious to hear news about her old companion Dutch, and asked Ken to call her with any information he might learn.

Wilma promised to send Ken a letter with all the background information she could recall or gather about Dutch. As the bus drove away, Wilma was still waving her hand out the window at the tall, kind man she would always associate with Dutch and her day in the beautiful smoky hills.

Chapter seven

Chapter seven

Chapter Seven~

During the spring and summer, John and Howie made numerous plantings of what John called "quail food." The once plentiful numbers of the little songsters had dwindled down to only a few coveys some years earlier. Thanks to people like the Buckmans, the quail were again common to the grassy fields and brushy hills of the region.

Buckwheat, millet, maize and hegari were seeded in places where soil, sunshine and moisture were present to germinate and nourish the plantings. Located in areas the cattle couldn't get into, the seeded areas would produce the tiny grains necessary to the survival of grouse, quail, partridge and the beautiful but rare pheasant. Some strips, field corners and drainways were not cut when the large grain crops of wheat, oats and barley were harvested which added to a bountiful and varied diet for wildlife all year long.

Over the years, John and later Tim, had created or left in it's natural state many nesting and cover areas for the small-winged, or furry four-footed creatures on their land. Even snakes, except poisonous ones, were welcomed and protected by the conservation practices on the Buckman farm. One glorious Saturday morning in early October, cars, pick-up trucks and vans began arriving at the farm. The Grants, Kellas, Crosses, Clyde and Bob with their families, and other friends and relatives had accepted invitations to come for a picnic at the Buckmans. By noon, twenty vehicles carrying fifty some people had arrived.

The picnic took place at one of the new, small ponds where groves of trees and open grassy areas had been raked or mowed and prepared for this special day. Howie and his sister, Nancy, had both brought special friends with them. Ken and his wife, Alana, brought Ken's mother. Paul Cross came with his wife and his father. Clyde and Bob brought their wives and five children. The last car - a new especially equipped sedan - was driven by Wilma who had just passed the test for operating the car. She showed her special license to Ken with a great deal of happiness and pride.

By the time the picnic was laid out on plank covered, sawhorse tables, everyone was ready to begin on the feast of special dishes each group had brought with them. The day was planned, weather permitting, to include an evening meal, a fireside sing-along and fishing anytime for the children.

The crude, strong tables were loaded with an incredible amount and variety of dishes, baskets, pots, pans and platters of delicious smelling food. Baked ham, turkey, meatloaf, duck, roast beef, baked chicken, pork, fried chicken, steak and chops, plus squirrel from Clyde's own woods. John and Tim loved squirrel but lacked the heart to shoot them. Potato, ham, egg, vegetable and fruit salads shared the table with beans prepared three ways, macaroni and cheese and scalloped potatoes. Homemade breads, buns, rolls, pies, cakes and cookies shared another table with milk, cream, coffee, cider, iced tea, lemonade and four kinds of homemade fruit juices. Tubs under the tables contained ice packed reserves of all liquids on the table, plus some quart bottles of homemade wine, homebrew beer and a gallon jug of clear liquid called "thunder" by the users.

Jars, cans, bottles and bowls of preserves, jelly, jam, pickles, onions, olives, mustard, catsup, horseradish, piccalilli, butter, applesauce, apple butter, wild grape marmalade, sauerkraut, tomato slices and plates of cheese, some homemade, were displayed on another long table.

The meal was ready but the Buckmans were waiting for one more guest. Dean Hitch, the young farmer who took his pay in calves, was a student minister at a small, local church. Dean and his family were coming from a wedding and were due at one o'clock. They arrived at the picnic grounds right on time. Dean said a prayer of thanks and asked a blessing on the food and all those present. At his "Amen" the children flocked to the tables, where the adults were waiting to fill their plates and hand out glasses of the beverages on top of the table.

To Ken's surprise, Wilma had emerged from her car wearing a set of leg braces and supporting herself on a set of arm crutches. Ken and Alana assisted Wilma through the line to select her meal and beverage, a glass of wine and one of cider.

Dean Hitch had brought out a number of folding tables and chairs early that morning which he had borrowed from his church. These were lined up along the pond ready for the hungry guests to use for eating, visiting, resting or playing games later in the day.

Mary and Lora supplied all the table service and silverware for the group. Mary didn't like plastic, paper or styrofoam tableware, so even the napkins were bright colored cloth. Her only concession was the disposable, linen-like tablecloths, which she used on all the tables. When she and Lora were satisfied that all the guests were well supplied with food and drinks, they allowed John and Tim to fill plates for the four of them and escort the two ladies to seats among their friends and relatives.

By two o'clock that sunny afternoon, most of the appetites had been satiated. The vast quantities of food fulfilled even the most dedicated food lovers in the group. The clearing of the tables and washing of tableware was simplified by having each person file past the garbage can, to the tubs of hot water resting on cement blocks over low fires by the shore of the pond, then to a stack of towels for drying everything. Mary and Lora had everything organized so everyone could enjoy the entire day.

Mary appointed Henry and Paul as inspectors and stackers of the cleanup crew. They sent some children and Tim

175

back through the washing line to "do it again" when food particles were found on their table service.

In less than half an hour the dishes were clean and all the tables covered with clean cloths. Now it was time to visit and play, and the children were ready to go fishing.

John and Tim took charge of this. Asking several adults to help, they assigned a "guide" to each child wanting to fish. From an open-topped barrel, John handed each pair a set of bamboo poles equipped with line, sinker, hook and a can of worms from a wooden box on the ground by the barrel.

Tim sent the fishing partners to places around the small, three-acre pond with instructions to stay at least fifty feet apart. He also told them he would blow a whistle every ten minutes. At the sound of the whistle, all fishing pairs were to take ten steps in a clockwise direction. This would give each angler a fair opportunity to fish all "good or bad" spots.

Howie was not considered a child, but he was given the honor of casting the first line and hook. Accompanied by his pretty, petite friend-both dressed in cutoff jeans and short sleeved shirts. Howie baited the hook and walked to the shore near the group of laughing, joking kibitzers who were giving him all kinds of advice on how to catch the "whale" awaiting his pleasure in the pond.

Howie swung the line out over the water and eased in the baited hook down to the red and white float but the float didn't float, it sank right out of sight. He gave a slight tug on the line, but the line only tightened and the thin, cane pole bent slightly.

The jibes and jokes ceased abruptly, when the line started moving rapidly away from Howie. He raised the grip of the pole to a vertical position, but the limber bamboo only bent more as the opposing forces combined. Howie was getting worried and unsure what to do, when the tension eased allowing the pole to straighten a few degrees. All at once the line

176

went slack, the pole straightened all the way, and the float popped to the surface of the water.

In quick reflex actions, Howie snapped the pole over his shoulder and stepped back from the shore. His alert responses set the "whale" into a series of runs that almost broke the line and pole. The contest continued for three or four minutes. The onlooker's were very quiet until finally, the fish was pulled to the edge of the pond.

John had known what to expect shortly after the fish was hooked. He ran to his truck to grab up the long handled landing net that he had purchased earlier, and rushed back to the shore in time to reach in and scoop up the fish.

All the former jokesters congratulated Howie. Tim, Ken and John exchanged happy, knowing grins and winks. They had contrived to get a few dozen large bass and put them in the pond, without revealing their trick to anyone else. Howie got a kiss on the cheek from the pretty girl, who looked at but refused to hold the fish while pictures were taken. The fish was estimated at four to five pounds by the "experts." The example set by the "head honcho of the fish ponds" was enough to stimulate some of the "older" kids to fish also.

Ken's wife, Alana, and her daughter Nancy were almost identical in appearance, coloring and expression. Their dark brown eyes and oval faces were framed in glossy, soft curls of blue-black hair. Nancy, at age fourteen, was only a little smaller than Alana, but could have been a younger sister from the similarities to her mother. Both had perfectly smooth, glowing, copper-tinted skin, well-balanced features, smiling eyes and pretty faces.

Nancy and her bubbling, blond-haired girl friend were having a great time at the picnic. They had met some new friends, and walked all around the place talking, laughing and whispering as young girls love to do. They made sure that they got into the pictures when cameras were brought out to photo

Howie and his "whale."

The enlarged and constantly changing group of fishing persons caught a number of keeper-sized bass by the time the limited amount of bait was used up. The fish were dressed and filleted for the evening meal, so their companions of the day could share in the first fish harvest at the Buckman farm.

Ken and Alana were glad they had received Mary's happy approval to include Wilma in the outing. They had exchanged phone calls and letters over recent weeks. On a trip to Cincinnati, the Kellas had made a short visit to Wilma's home and were shown many pictures of Dutch, taken over the years.

Lana, as Ken called his wife, was the person who gave Wilma the inspiration to begin her driving lessons and purchase of a car. Wilma had partial use of her legs, and had kept her-self in good physical shape using special exercise equipment, installed in her single story home.

During the day, Paul Cross' father Willard, called Bill, had assisted Wilma at the picnic. Bill escorted Wilma to a nearby grove of gum, oak, and maple trees that were in full autumn colors. The leaves were so many shades, tints and combinations of color they stretched the mind to find adequate words to describe them. Brilliant reds, yellows, and browns, mixed with still dark green leaves, seemed to float among the blue-cast spruces scattered among the hardwood trees.

As far as the eye could see, the smoky hills were shrouded in the riotous splendor of early fall. Bright, warm sunshine caused some leaves to glow like embers in a fire, and others to take on purple, amber and orange casts. Between the hills, the haze appeared to be violet or soft gray where huge stands of cedar, pine and hemlock trees dominated the forest.

When the scattered cotton balls of high-riding clouds passed over, their shadows caused almost all the colors to change. Some leaves darkened but the yellows and oranges of poplar and maples seemed to brighten in the reduced sunshine.

When Wilma appeared to tire from the unaccustomed exercise, Bill unfolded two camp stools he had been carrying- and placed them where the two could sit with their backs against smooth barked trees and relax while they talked and enjoyed the scenery and each others presence.

Bill was fifteen years older than Wilma, but the two of them had so much in common that conversation came easy for them. Both had lost their spouses and had lived alone for ten years. Her husband had been a successful realtor. Bill had been a horse breeder and real estate salesman before retiring at age fifty-five. Both of their Scotch-Irish ancestors had migrated to southern Ohio from North Carolina when each was only a child. Bill had one son, Paul, but Wilma had lost her husband, her unborn child, and her mobility in the same car crash, ten years previously. In only an hours time, Bill and Wilma established the basis for continued association and slowly made their way back to the group by the pond.

When the sun started sinking behind the hills, the group was treated to another spectacle of glory. The reddish-orange sun was framed between two nearby tall, cone-shaped hills that cast shadows of purple, violet and indigo into the valleys. The last bright rays of light focused on the long ridge of little mountains to the east of the farm, bathing them in iridescent splendor that brought tears to the eyes of some members of the silent, watching group.

As the approaching shadows came across the picnic ground, Ken watched his family of Alana, Howie and Nancy link arms to stand and gaze west over the hills. Their coppery tinted faces glowed with beauty and health when the last beam of sunshine winked out, leaving a rosy afterglow of luminescence about the lovely Wyandot woman and her striking children.

A fire was built within a circle of flat rocks that John and Howie had arranged for the evening "sing." The fish were fried and eaten by the entire group, each one getting at least a small piece. The food on the tables had also been much reduced by the continual return of snackers to the tables for "another taste of this, or a little piece of that." Most of them avoided the use of dishes by making sandwiches or taking pieces of pie and cake in their napkins or bare hands.

A number of the group had brought musical instruments with them. Henry, Bill and John had often played together in other places over the years. Dean Hitch played his guitar and sang occasionally for the young people's group of his church and had become a favorite of their biweekly social meetings. Clyde had his harmonica and Bob set up his washtub-broom handle-baling twine bass fiddle. John tuned up his banjo, Henry his fiddle, and Bill joined in with the mandolin.

Henry led off with a lively tune about mountain dew, switched to one about his grandpa's mule and then one about a long-tall woman with long "yeller" hair. By the time he was into the second song, all the musicians and most of the adults had joined in to play or sing.

The youngster's soon came back from their games of hide and seek, run-sheep-run and fox and hounds. By the time it was truly dark, all the chairs, blankets and small rugs had been arranged in a semi-circle in front of the "band" and the "old songs" were being recalled.

As the fun-filled evening progressed, it became apparent to most of them that the Kellas had done a lot of singing together. Ken's bass, Lana's soprano, matched by Nancy's alto, and Howie's baritone, in beautiful harmony and tonal clarity was pleasing to the ear. Tim had a good clear tenor voice and Wilma's high, flute-like, trained soprano voice blended well with the Kellas.

For a time, some of the young singers took the lead doing school songs and pop tunes to the enjoyment of everyone. Many of the adults had attended the same schools as did most of the youngsters.

During the evening, most of the empty food containers and personal items had been stowed back into the vehicles, and the picnic area cleaned spotless by various members of the group. By nine o'clock, some of the youngest children were sleepy and most everyone, young and old, growing tired.

John, Mary, Tim and Lora stood to sing a rehearsed song about good friends, good neighbors, and "goodnight", for the final song. Everyone applauded their singing and started saying goodnights, thank yous, come and see us, and farewells. Wilma left to spend the night at the Kellas and Bill to spend the night with Paul and his wife.

When the last container, chair, table and stool had been loaded, Tim doused the fire with water from the pond and walked back to where Lora and his parents waited by the two remaining vehicles.

The moon rode across the clear, dark blue sky, shining down on the four of them, making them pause to look around the soft hills and valleys. On mutual impulse, they drew together in an arm-hugging circle of reverent happiness. Two little dogs, exhausted by a long day of play, sat on the ground to look up at their strange acting, human friends.

~

The young female coyote's injured tail had been painful and slow to heal. When the shotgun blazed and crashed in the dark, she had just summoned up the nerve to go under the fence to feed by her mother at the rear of the kill. She was turning to flee the noise, when the flattened ricochet pellet struck her tail about three inches behind her hips.

When Tim's final shot was fired at her running form she was already moving at top speed and far enough away for the pellets spread to miss her, even though she saw the puffs of snow and ice they made around her.

Arriving back at the old den, she dove into the hole under the rocks and hid in fear, expecting her mother to be close behind her. All night she cringed in the den, licking away the oozing blood from her wound. She was hungry, tired and scared, but at dawn she curled up and slept for a time, waking frequently in anticipation of the old coyote's return. At noon, she left the den to slip down to a rill of melting snow for a drink.

Far away, she heard the sounds of dogs barking as Pepper and Vickie helped drive the stubborn calves from the lot. Much closer, the little coyote heard the sound of a squirrel digging in the leaves under an uprooted pine tree. Ghosting through the brush and young trees, on the softened snow, she caught the swift little streak of red and buff fur as he raced for the safety of the nearest standing tree. She took her kill back under the fallen pine to feed and then sleep again, not returning to the den until night came.

From then on, the young, lonely coyote fared well on a diet of rabbits, squirrels, grouse, quail and small rodents she found in increasing numbers among the streams and open woodlands as the snow and ice melted away. She also found a vine-covered cliff-like hill where clusters of wild grapes had dried on vines close enough to the ground for her to reach. She ate as many of them as she could hold, from time to time.

In a few short months the memory, and need for her mother, diminished. The nearly grown, little wolf ranged over an increasingly larger area as spring then summer came to the hills. She grew and put on weight as a result of her skill finding and catching food of all kinds. Eating berries, fruit, and many kinds of vegetation as the seasons progressed, she was preparing her body to fulfill her real purpose in life, which was motherhood.

~

Pepper and Vickie had become expert in their roles of working cattle. From early spring they had been getting more training and working time than ever before. John, Mary and Tim were careful to use the same verbal commands and hand signals when directing the little "cow dogs" to prevent confusing them.

As Vickie matured, her longer legs and faster pace made it possible for her to take on the wider range position, while Pepper worked close in to the person in charge of the cattle moves sorting or holding them in one spot, for any reason. Vickie was larger than Pepper by a few inches and several pounds heavier. She did not hesitate now to take on the most belligerent cow on the farm.

On one occasion when Lora was out on horseback checking the herds, she found a calf mired in soft mud below a small spring. When she dismounted to help the calf, he began bawling and a group of cows ran at Lora as if to trample or butt her. Vickie dashed in to bark and snap at the cow in the front of the bunch. The old cow charged right on over Vickie and sent her rolling on the ground.

Unhurt, Vickie streaked up to the cow's head and fastened her teeth in the cow's tender nose, stopping the cow long enough for Lora to scramble back into her saddle.

The cow swung herself around in a tight circle trying to dislodge her furious attacker, but Vickie held her jaw grip on the cow's nose until Lora called her off. The calf had extricated himself during the short minute of the incident and had fled the frightening scene. Lora praised Vickie as she rode off a short distance, dismounted, then hugged and petted the bristling dog until both of them quit shaking.

The leaves were just about gone from the trees when the major work projects of the year were finished. Mary, Howie, and Clyde had all the garden crops stored and the big garden covered with compost from the stables and bull yard worked in and planted with winter wheat for ground cover.

Mary had put fifty hens in the laying house this year. She wanted to be sure everybody had plenty of the big, brown-shelled eggs. At her suggestion, John took three hogs to the butcher, one more than last year. Clyde, Bob and now Dean Hitch, were going to be well supplied in the coming winter, especially when two beef animals were also shared with them.

When it came time to pick the late apples and pears, Tim put the entire crew on the project one Saturday. It seemed almost accidental when the Grants, Kellas and Crosses dropped in to help with the pleasant task "to beat the frost." They had to use every crate, basket, and box they could find on the place to hold all the fruit. The bed of John's pickup was still piled to the top with apples to take to the cider mill. When the hired crew and guest pickers left, Mary made sure each family took baskets of fruit home with them.

~

The older colts were now one and a half years old. They had been gentle and easy to train from birth. The time and attention Mary had spent on them from day old babies, and all the attention Lora, Tim and Howie gave them as they grew larger, had resulted in two fine, future cow horses. The stallion had been gelded and had become as calm and easy to handle as the docile, little filly.

Now the two youngest colts were being treated in much the same way the first pair had been, and were just as comical in their pasture games. The difference was a larger group of

184

followers racing, kicking and bucking along with the little black stallions.

Tim and Lora had been giving some thought to buying a pair of trained cutting horses to work the growing herd of cattle, but the cost was going to be very high for really good horses. Now they were considering the possibility of having to have the oldest colts trained as cutting horses, but that also posed problems. The colts should be three years old before the rigorous training started, would take at least a year or more, and would still cost a lot of money for transportation, feed and training.

One day in November while at lunch with John and Mary, they asked for the advice of the older couple hoping for a less costly solution to the problem. All of them had seen real cutting horses perform at rodeos and knew the horses they now had on the farm could not be compared to the western version of cutting horse.

The size of the problem would grow along with the increasing cattle herd. At certain times within the coming year, the total number of cattle on the place could be as many as six hundred and fifty head. With the many cows, heifers, bulls and calves to work, it was neither safe nor practical to do much on foot, especially around some of the belligerent old cows and bulls.

Tim and Lora didn't forget the importance of Pepper and Vickie in working the cattle, but the dogs physical limits were taxed at times with the present herd and could not be expected to do even more.

Tim's parents, having previously discussed the situation themselves, made several suggestions after hearing Tim and Lora out. The first suggestion was to run ads in newspapers for one or more trained horses. A second idea was to call some of the people they had bought breeding stock from in Missouri and Kansas. The third, and actual recommendation, was for Lora and Tim to take a trip west through the big ranch states and buy some horses at one of the winter horse auctions. The last suggestion offered the benefit of seeing many horses and actually riding and testing them for performance, ride ability, gentleness and personality traits before buying anything.

Lora really liked the last idea. She had to convince Tim they could take time away from the farm, but John and Mary assured him that with all the qualified help available, everything could be done easily and properly without anyone being over worked while they were gone. Satisfied at last, Tim agreed since this was the season of least work during the year.

The next day John made some long distance calls getting information about horse auctions, made a list of names, addresses, and phone numbers, then walked across to leave the list on Lora's kitchen table. He also placed an envelope containing an anniversary card and twenty one-hundred-dollar bills on top of the list.

A couple of days later, Tim and Lora left in the well-packed station wagon for Missouri, Kansas, Oklahoma and Texas. Pepper and Vickie had tried to get in the wagon also, but John and Mary picked them up in their arms to console them, John saying "He couldn't snare four cowhands at the same time."

In the spirit of the occasion, both young people had dressed in western style clothes that morning. Lora had also packed one suitcase with her prettiest nightgowns, lingerie and perfume for her second honeymoon. Lora still looked like a college girl, but had the maturity and common sense of a much older person. Tim looked his actual age but was such a happy, satisfied man that he seemed to be younger in spirit than Lora. He was actually a serious thinking, tenderhearted person who always gave more than he expected to get from those he loved. For that and other personal reasons, the young Buckmans were extremely well matched and enjoyed a good marriage.

Holding the squirming dogs, John and Mary waved them out of sight. Happy as a pair of newlyweds, they took turns driving, checking maps, eating when they pleased and stopping when they felt like it. The route and reservations had been easy to decide and arrange for the trip to Missouri. From there on they would make reservations each night for the following night, or nights, as circumstances required.

Now that the trip was underway, Tim relaxed and set a leisurely pace. They took some side trips to see points of interest or to eat in some of the well-recommended restaurants in out of the way places.

Lora did some shopping and actually bought a few things in St. Louis and Springfield. Most of what she purchased were gifts for Mom and Dad, friends and neighbors. Tim took her into a fur store but the first coat she saw, a blue fox, reminded Lora of Chestnut and she left the store almost in tears. Tim changed his plans right then about what he would get her for Christmas.

They spent four days in Missouri and Kansas, then doubled back on the way to Oklahoma for a second look at some horses that were very good but decided to do more looking and test riding before buying. They liked almost all the horse and cow people they met, making them glad again for taking the trip.

In Oklahoma, they saw dozens of horses and rode a number of them. The best and most desirable one was at a small sale barn along their route. In talking to some people with trucks and trailers full of horses, in the parking lot of a restaurant where they had stopped for lunch, Tim was told he should inquire at the sale barn and received directions for finding the place.

They parked by cattle pens behind the sale barn and walked along the pens toward the sale ring. A man riding a chunky, short, coupled gelding was driving cattle and horses into the sale ring.

They stopped and stared in amazement at the way the horse handled the work. The horse appeared to know exactly what to do in every instance without any guidance from his rider. His performance was flawless as he separated pens of calves, singled out individual cattle, or pranced sideways to bodily force some small groups to go a certain place.

Once the rider was obviously pointing the cutting horse at a gray horse in a small group of other horses, intending to drive it up the alleyway by itself. The gray refused to leave the other horses and kept darting among them to avoid the cutting horse's persistent moves. Patiently at first, the gelding pursued the gray back and forth across the end of the very large pen trying to separate and head the recalcitrant animal into the alleyway. He had no success until suddenly, he lunged forward and gave the gray a couple of hard bites on his side and neck. Slowly he forced and crowded the gray horse toward the open gate of the runway and then drove him to the sale ring.

When the chunky gelding and his rider came near Lora and Tim a short time later, Tim engaged the man in conversation, first telling him how much he admired the action just seen and then inquiring if the horse was for sale. Both the Buckmans assumed the man was a regular employee of the sales operation, but learned from his responses that he was the owner and used the sales operation as a training school for cutting horses. Lora asked how much he would take for the "pupil" he was riding.

The man hesitated, then answered, "It would take a heap of money to buy this ole' horse, lady. I use him on the circuit," meaning rodeo and horse show circuit. He added, "One year this pony earned over thirty thousand in prize money and never even worked up a sweat."

They were shown some other horses he was training, but none of them were "settled" the man's term for fully trained and reliable for other than "workin' hands." The man first took Tim and Lora to be tourists making the usual remarks about the horse he was riding, but was pleased to learn they were serious about buying horses for their own cattle work. He invited them to his office and showed them a wall full of pictures, newspaper and magazine articles about himself and his horses.

Over cups of coffee they exchanged information with Gant, the name he preferred, then waited while he used the phone to call an "ole' buddy in Texas."

Surprised at Gant's hospitality, they spent two pleasant hours with him touring his operation and listening to his talk about good horses and good "hands" he had ridden with all over the country on his circuit of rodeo shows and exhibitions. When Lora and Tim left, they had some good feelings about Gant, and a small list of horse breeders to visit in west Texas.

The prior years, Tim had made other trips to cattle breeders to buy registered bulls and brood stock. He had seen many cow horses working cattle, but never anything that came close, to the horse Gant had ridden that day.

Lora had been equally impressed and said, "If we had a pair of horses like that one, we could put them out with Pepper and Vickie while we sit on the fence and watch."

Tim chuckled and said, "Or just give them a list of instructions each day. I think that horse is smart enough to read."

Every two or three evenings Tim would call home to let his parents know how the trip was progressing and to satisfy himself about conditions on the farm. Lora knew Tim was concerned his dad would do something to hurt his back again.

He didn't have reason to worry though. Mary watched him and privately instructed Clyde, Bob, Dean and Howie to "keep John out of trouble and don't let him lift anything." Bob and Clyde were working full time and Howie and Dean came in the evenings and on weekends so John needed only to supervise, and check cattle "from inside the truck," as Mary firmly instructed him.

Howie had become a good rider and went out almost every evening to ride among the cattle or to inspect fences. John and Mary had complete confidence in him and listened closely to his reports each evening before going home. On Saturdays, Howie rode horseback while John drove his truck to pen up any animal requiring doctoring. Pepper and Vickie had learned to separate an indicated cow from a herd. This greatly reduced the time and effort it had taken earlier to isolate an animal for treatment. John and Mary always emphasized these facts when they talked to Tim on the phone.

When Tim and Lora arrived at Gant's old friends ranch in Texas, they were welcomed and treated like family, Gant having spoken so well of them in a second call made after the couple left, driving west. They insisted on "putting them up" in their own home and even called the motel to cancel their reservations. Their hosts, the Tylers, assured them that they liked having "folks in" so they had a chance to make more good friends.

Within two days the Tyler's had shown them over a hundred horses that were good cow ponies and had helped them to reduce their choices from a dozen down to just four. They kept test riding the four and then picked two six-year-old geldings as the best natured for final workouts with cattle of all ages and sexes.

The two couples got down to discussing prices. Mrs. Tyler was the business head, or so her husband claimed, in the partnership horse-ranch operation, which also raised calves for sale to feedlot operators. The Tylers had become very interested and curious about the Buckman farm and it's high quality beef cattle business.

The Texas couple was working to improve their cattle herd by slowly upgrading with prime breeding stock from time to time. They were in need of a few top bulls to put with their cows.

The discussion about prices changed to "working us out a little swap" in Tyler's words, with no money mentioned, which was met with an agreeable response from the Buckmans.

Several bulls were bought and sold by the Buckmans every two years. This practice was followed to prevent any chance of inbreeding on the farm. They now had a dozen good three and four year old bulls to sell or trade.

With these facts before them, the two couples worked out a tentative plan for an equitable exchange of horses and bulls. After the deal was sealed with handshakes, Lora and Ida Mae, as Mrs. Tyler had become, left Tim and C.B. alone in the corral, to walk to the house. As they walked along together, Lora made deal of her own, to be kept secret until the Tyler's delivered the horses to the Buckman farm in a few days. After reaching the ranch house, she made out a check and handed it to Ida Mae, who gave her a bill of sale in exchange.

Among the many horses they had inspected, ridden, and tested, Lora had liked a large number but had helped make the final decision based on the performance, strength and personality of the two best animals for the work on the farm.

Her secret deal was for the other two finalists, a big bay horse for Howie plus a slender, beautiful, young sorrel mare for Nancy. Nancy had become like a young sister to Lora, coming over to visit while Howie did his evening stint on the farm, or on Saturday to ride with Lora on one of the two "mother horses," as Nancy called the mares.

With sincere regrets Lora kissed the Tyler's good-bye, which made C. B. turn bright red and Ida Mae laugh at him with glee as she gave Tim a hug. The time to leave had arrived. The men shook hands and gripped shoulders in genuine friendship while standing by the station wagon, under the portico at the side of the adobe ranch house.

Somewhat heavier loaded by the two saddles the Tyler's had put in the luggage space earlier that same morning, the wagon was pulled out and headed east for the roundabout trip home. Lora and Ida Mae kept waving at each other until a turn in the road blocked their view. In two seconds, Lora had slid across the seat, put her arm around Tim and snuggled up tight against his side.

The temperature had been an even eighty degrees with bright clear skies when they arose at seven-thirty that morning. Lora had poked her head out the window to sniff at the sagebrush and greasewood scented air, and then decided they would dress in shorts and sleeveless shirts for the drive to Abilene, Texas that day. Both of them preferred open windows to air conditioning and it was obviously going to be a gorgeous, warm day.

As Tim drove along at fifty-five miles an hour, Lora squirmed closer to him and asked, "Don't you just love these beautiful Texas nights?"

Tim slapped her lightly on a bare leg and replied, "If you get any closer, you'll be on the other side of me, or the Ranger's will arrest us for having two drivers under the steering wheel."

Lora just laughed and wiggled away about half an inch. They found the saddles under blankets and luggage when they reached their motel in Abilene that evening. A note taped to one read "These hulls have been on the backs of some good old ponies. We hope our new friends find them comfortable and easy to sit on. They were made for cutting horse work and are lighter than some rigs. See you very soon, C.B. and Ida Mae."

Lora rushed to the motel, picked up the phone and called the Tylers. She thanked them through her sniffles, then gave the phone to Tim. He talked a few minutes, also thanking the kind couple before saying goodnight. He hung up the phone and gave Lora a big hug.

They swam in the glass covered pool, tried the margaritas, and ate Mexican style beef for a late supper, strolled through a cactus garden in the moonlight and then retired to their room for showers and a TV show while laying on the king sized bed.

Lora had spent one complete day in Dallas, shopping like mad, spending like crazy and laughing like a bride.

Tim had warned her to "straighten up or Mom and Dad will think I'm bringing a new woman home."

Lora only laughed more and replied, "Maybe you are," then added, "I sure feel like one. We should do this more often." She grabbed Tim and gave him a big, warm kiss right in the middle of the huge, crowded store.

Fort Worth, Dallas, Little Rock, Memphis, Nashville and Cincinnati fell behind the wagon's wheels to finally bring them back to Rockhill, their old home town, on the last day of November.

Mary came running out to meet them in the garage as soon as they got home. She almost smothered Lora while trying to get her arms around Tim at the same time. John and Howie had been tending the horses, so John left the job for Howie to finish while he rushed up to the garage to welcome "his kids" back home. He was even more exuberant than Mary was, so Lora just squeezed him back with all her might while smooching him all over his cheeks and lips.

John jumped back in mock alarm to say, "Tim, what on earth happened to the shy girl you left with?" Then added, "This must be one of those Wild West cowgirls you found out there."

Lora wouldn't let anyone help unload the car. She handed out their traveling bags, then locked the doors, saying she would finish later. Howie came up just as they started to leave the garage.

He shook hands with Tim and also got kissed by Lora, who said, "I've missed you, little brother."

This made him smile and give her a hug while saying, "Me, too," then "See you later," as he walked to his car.

A few flakes of snow were falling when they walked out of the garage. The dogs came running up the back road followed by Dean on a tractor, who waved as he went by Pepper and Vickie who had caught Lora and Tim's scent which caused them to run up barking and jumping for joy. Lora picked Vickie up in her arms then reached down to get Pepper. Tim petted and talked to both dogs as they wiggled in Lora's arms for a minute before she put them back on the ground.

Mary whipped up extra food for the travelers and kept their plates full until Tim and Lora were stuffed. Over coffee the proposed trade of bulls for horses was explained and then discussed with the older couple. John and Mary only asked a few questions before urging them to call the Tylers and tell them to bring the horses as soon as it was convenient, adding their own invitation for the Tyler's to stay at the farm when they arrived.

Lora placed the call, talked to Ida Mae for a couple of minutes then gave the phone to Tim. C. B. and Tim worked out the timetable for transporting the horses, a visit with the Buckmans and a time to take a look at the little Smokies, now getting the first snow of the year. Tim reminded them to bring warm clothes.

After hanging up the phone, he asked Lora to tell them about the temperature in southwest Texas and her bikini costume on the day they started home. This brought a blush to her face and caused Mary and John to laugh in fun.

~

The light dusting of snow melted like frost the first day of December, while Lora and Tim rode out to check the cattle. The ride took them north along the east line to the Grant place, then west to the feed lots where two year old and yearling heifers were feeding on baled hay and grass that was stored there.

The young animals had access to the bales of low quality hay harvested in the first cleanup of the fields and bales of prime alfalfa in other hay bunks. They seemed to eat both kinds of hay with equal appetite. This pleased the pair of riders because the clean-up hay could be fully utilized and thus save the prime hay for later use on the farm or to be sold after the first of the coming year.

After inspecting the grain kept in metal bins in the Grant barns they walked up to the back door of the Grant house to knock, then join them in their kitchen for a cup of coffee and a retelling of the events of their trip.

It was hard to get away from the nice old couple, but they finally did, leaving Henry still talking as they rode away south on the horses.

When they stopped to look over a small herd of young bulls near the lake Lora said, "Tim, we must find a way to give Henry something to do. Did you notice he only talked about being tired of TV, reading and sitting around?"

"I sure did," Tim answered. "That's why I was in a hurry to leave."

"Henry is a good man with all kinds of tools," Lora said. "Could we use him to build or repair any of the hay bunks or grain feeders?" she asked in the same breath.

"That's a good idea, Lora," Tim replied.

"Could he do the work there at his place?" Lora asked.

"I don't know why not. He has the tools, power and plenty of space to work in. He even has a big heater in the tobacco stripping room. If it gets cold he can do all the cutting of lumber in where it's warm, then do the assembly or repairs in the barn on good warm days," Tim replied.

"How will we handle paying the old darling?" Lora queried.

"I'm not sure how to answer that. Knowing Henry, he'll probably try to pay us for letting him do the work, but Mom and Dad can decide how to outfox the rascal," Tim replied, smiling.

"In fact, let's just turn the whole thing over to Dad and Mom. They like to spend time with Henry and Velma. This will give them a good reason to get together more this winter. It might even keep Dad out of the cold more, as well. He can do all the running for material and keep Henry supplied," Tim finished.

"Sounds good to me, Tim. Now if I can find away to keep you in by the fire with me this winter, we'll all be warm and happy," she said. She reined her horse over against Tim, leaned over and planted a kiss on his cheek, adding "You old softie."

They finished their rounds on the horses then groomed and put them into their stalls which Howie had just cleaned and stocked with hay and a dipper of grain for each gelding. Looking down the line of eight stalls, Lora was suddenly struck by the realization that in less than a week they would have twelve horses to house, groom, feed, clean up after and exercise. Tim and John would be more than surprised when the Tyler's showed up with four, not two, horses. She had heard them say stables for two more horses could be squeezed into the barn, but what about the other two? She decided she'd better confide in Mary and get her advice.

When Lora revealed her secret to Mary she expected

her to be surprised, but not dumbfounded. For a moment, Lora thought she had made a major mistake buying the horses and another mistake telling Mary about them.

All at once Mary cracked up. At first, what Lora said just didn't register. Then the idea of someone, anyone, coming home from a vacation of three weeks with "two horses worth" of four bulls was overwhelming by itself. Now she learned two more horses are coming as a complete surprise to everybody. Here she was, trying to help keep the secret.

The look on Lora's face was too much for Mary. She thought her laughter had offended her daughter-in-law, which was something Mary would not intentionally do under any circumstance. Then Lora, seeing and understanding the very confused look on Mary's face broke up with laughter herself.

The two women, so much alike in their personalities, habits and traits, stood in Mary's kitchen laughing 'til they gasped for breath. Finally, the mirth reduced to a controllable level, Mary made a suggestion that Lora thought was fine. When the new horses arrived, she would have no serious problem explaining to Tim where to house the extra horses.

~

The Tyler's arrived on schedule, the opening day of deer season. They had driven most of the night, taking turns at the wheel of the horse-van, a large bus-like vehicle with space for up to eight horses in the back and space for the people up front. Two bunks, a table, refrigerator and propane stove made it possible for two or three people to travel, delivering horses in comfort while saving both time and cost for everyone.

When C. B. and Ida Mae stepped out of the horse-van, they could hear distant gunshots and echoes reverberating across the rolling countryside. It took all the Buckmans to convince them the sounds were actually deer hunters. The Tyler's had no prior knowledge there were many deer in the state.

As soon as the greetings and introductions were completed, C.B. said, "Well, we better get these horses unloaded so they can stretch their legs."

Tim said, "You're right. The stalls are ready. Let's bring them out for a short walk and then put them in the horse barn."

C.B. opened a sliding door at the side of the van, led out one of the cutting horses and gave the halter rope to John, went back in the van, came right back out with the other cutting horse and gave the halter rope to Tim. Then both C.B. and Ida Mae went into the van, not saying a word. They just came back out with the third cutting horse and the sorrel mare. At this time, Tim merely thought the last two were for other customers of the Tyler's and were just unloaded so they could be exercised. Then, Tim noticed some peculiar looks on the faces of Lora and his mother. Even the Tyler's were acting amused about something.

All at once Tim became suspicious and said, "Will somebody tell me what's going on here?"

At that, Mary and Lora had to tell Tim and John about the two extra horses. The men were sure surprised but not upset by the secret purchase, and very pleased for the reasons Lora gave.

The men were just happy that the Kella kids were going to have horses of their own to ride and enjoy. As for a place to stable them, John beat Lora to suggesting that a few big round bales be moved, out of the hay, barn to make room for the four young colts, leaving room to keep all the trained horses in the larger, individual stalls.

The four new horses were led up and down the road by the hay storage sheds, then seeing them interested in the thick bluegrass still growing green on the roadside, John suggested putting the horses in the pasture for a time before they were stabled for the night. This was done, and the horses put on a small show of delight by running once around the little field and then stopping to roll on their backs in the dusty area near the gate.

With the dust on their sides and backs, the winter hair on the horses was more noticeable than before. C.B. told them even Texas horses put on a warmer coat in winter in preparation for the cold north winds that are common in their part of the state.

Lora cautioned everyone to keep her secret until Christmas. When Howie came to start the chores, he was just told where to put the new horses for the night and encouraged to spend extra time grooming and talking with the big bay and the sorrel mare, since they seemed to be a little bit upset from the trip.

They didn't look upset to Howie, but he did pay them attention and found them to be as tame and quiet as a pair of house cats. He then told his sister Nancy. She wanted to go over right then to see the new animals, despite being dark outside.

Nancy met the Tylers and saw the new horses the next afternoon, after she and her brother had deliberately finished school early for the day.

When the Kella kids got there a little after two o'clock, they found all the Buckmans, the Tylers and six saddled horses at the stables. The day was very pleasant but cool as expected, and everyone had jackets on when the afternoon ride began.

Nancy was told to ride the slender sorrel mare and Howie to ride the bay cutting horse. The Tyler's were given Tim and Lora's old geldings, while they rode the new gelding cutting horses. The first stop on the ride was at the calf lot to see how the new horses worked the newly weaned, young stock. First Tim, then Lora, showed off their "ponies," as C.B. always called them. They were very quick moving and agile in their actions.

Howie was warned to hang on when it came his turn to "cut out" a calf. He picked an easy to find bob tailed heifer so he wouldn't get mixed up, and pointed his bay horse at the calf. As long as the bob tailed calf went in the general direction of the holding point, (the place chosen to drive the calves), the bay-horse just wove left and right in smooth acting side steps to block any change in the calf's direction. The calf tried to run back past the horse to escape. In order to cut off the calf's escape, the big bay cutter swooped in so fast that Howie found himself hanging sideways in the saddle, both hands gripped tightly on the saddle horn. The horse's next movement was a direct reversal of the one that unseated Howie, actually aiding him in recovering his seat in the saddle.

Like many well-trained horses, this one would stay after the cut, the animal being driven without the rider, unless called off. This test of Howie's horse was completed with the bobtail forced to the holding point in only a couple of minutes.

Nancy insisted on penning a calf also, and at Ida Mae's suggestion, let her mare take charge. The calf she selected was very determined to stay in one herd and kept dodging behind other calves. The sorrel mare took her time, walking it out to the edge of the herd, then out-maneuvered the calf to the holding point without dumping Nancy in the process.

C.B. put on a demonstration of calf roping and tying that was done in a manner that did not hurt the calves. He used all four of the new horses to show they all had rope savvy, keeping the rope taut as he began to tie the calf. Tim and Howie watched the roping and tying with keen interest, picking up points of information as the demonstration went on.

As C.B. finished showing how well the four Texas horses did in his roping act, he commented, "On a working ranch you need a horse that can do anything that comes along in the days work. You don't have time to change to a different horse for each job. You just take a good cutting horse and let him relax while he does the easy things," he chuckled.

The six people at the calf lot heard a horse whinny nearby. When they looked up, on the hill above the lot, John and Mary were there on the brood mares with Pepper and Vickie at their feet. To reduce distractions during the test or demonstrations, Pepper and Vickie had been kept at the horse barn with John and Mary when the riders left the stables. They had followed in time to see the Kella kids try out their (unknown to them), Christmas gifts and applaud their performance in a quiet way.

John and Mary surprised the other riders when they came to the calf lot riding the gentle mares. They had been good riding partners for most of their adult lives, but because of John's back injury had been reluctant to get on horses until recently.

John had said, "Come on Mary. It's time to hit the saddle again."

He quickly saddled the two mares and led them out of the barn door to the old mounting block by the garages. Mary had run to the house to put on riding clothes and boots, coming back just as John came out with the horses. When he saw her in her tight pants and snug-fitting jacket, John gave Mary a low whistle of admiration for her trim, smart look and generous curves.

Riding toward the cattle pens, John motioned the dogs to "seek away." The dogs ran to the little hill by the road and came back with Chestnut behind them. Mary laughed at the funny look this brought to John's face.

After C.B.'s roping demonstration, all eight of the riders went to the bullpen, while first C.B. and then Tim and Lora test rode the cutting horses with the big, placid bulls. The two youngsters hadn't asked to "cut out" and drive the bulls; they knew the older people hadn't overlooked them. They accepted the cautious acts of safety whereby the more capable riders made the more dangerous rides, knowing their own examples would in time make them the "testers" of the future.

The entire group was pleased with the horses. All four horses performed well with all three riders. The Buckmans were more than satisfied with the deal that was about to be concluded, as the Tylers rode among the bulls selecting the animals they would load in the van and take to Texas in a few days.

Their attention was drawn to the sound of guns being fired in the forest to the southwest of the farm, the easiest area for hunters to get into. Occasional shots could be heard to the northwest also. More experienced hunters had penetrated that remote area to escape the dangers of novice hunters in the easy to find spots, where temerity held them by the scores.

Ida Mae said, "I've heard more shots fired today than in all my thirty-two years of living in Texas. Who would believe there could be that many hunters in this little ole' state? Why, I'd be surprised if there were any deer in those pretty woods anyway," she said, pointing her hand toward the encircling, smoky little mountains.

She still had her hand out when she saw a young deer run along the fence at the back end of the horse pasture and disappear into a stand of cedars, pines and poplar trees on a hillside to the southwest. Other deer followed the same trail in small groups of does, fawns and an occasional buck. All day this little migration had been taking place. The shy, clever deer had learned to seek this haven when the shots boomed out in the forest each year.

John told Ida Mae, "There may be over a hundred deer hiding on this farm right now. They're smart and know where to find safety."

She was more inclined to think he was understating the number of deer from what she had seen in only a few minutes.

The group of riders headed back to the barn. As he rode alongside Ida Mae Tyler, John decided to go back to riding horses again, now that his back was in such good shape and so many good horses were available. Lora was riding in the back of the group with C.B. by her side. In front were Tim and Nancy, followed by John and Ida Mae, with Mary and Howie third in line.

As they rode along together, the joy and satisfaction of seeing this rare spectacle in the foothills of the Appalachian Mountains was overwhelming to Lora.

It made her catch her breath as she wondered, "How could anyone be so lucky to be part of a family scene, time, place and life drawn together in this space I occupy? How is it possible to live a life of such joy, while the news hawks report their disasters night after night, as regular as sundown?"

These pensive thoughts were in her mind as she heard and responded to C.B.'s pleasant and sincere compliments. He appreciated the farm and family, as well as the two dark-eyed, softly smiling kids on the "gift horses" they rode with such skill and natural talent. Laura wondered why she was so favored that she should have such intelligent young people become part of her life.

She retraced the series of events that resulted in such good fortune. Was it mere chance that led Tim to speak to the people in the parking lot, sending them to Gant who introduced them to the Tylers? Was it fate for the Tylers to become fond of the Buckmans? As these thoughts trailed through Lora's mind, her feelings settled on her open face and misted her blue eyes. C.B. empathized with Lora's reaction to this privileged happening with bowed head and affectionate pats for his horse. They both knew the goods and gifts brought into the beautiful rolling hills of Ohio symbolized true wealth, that being friendship. Young and old, all were friends riding together on this cool, bright day in December.

Howie rode along by Mary, his big bay whickering softly to Mary's mare and to the horse in front of him. Howie had enjoyed the day and had not been embarrassed when the gelding's agile moves almost dumped him to the ground. He had learned to accept knowledge any way it came. He would be more alert in the future, never coming that close to losing his seat again.

The small cavalcade of riders was back at the horse barn as dusk began blending out the day. The sounds of gunshots thinning, then ending, as night drew near. C.B. was squatted down petting Vickie. Ida Mae was seated on a bale of straw with Pepper at her side. John and Mary came back from the hay barn where they had just fed and watered the four colts.

Tim, Lora, Nancy and Howie were brushing and combing the last of the horses in the stables. All of the horses were crunching noisily away at grain in their feed boxes. Lora had regained her happy frame of mind after her pensive mood. Nancy and Howie kept chatting about the new horses they had ridden that day. Each thought about how great the new horses had performed, but also felt slightly disloyal to the nice old mother horses they usually rode.

~

In the few days the Tyler's had left, Lora and Mary took them on drives all over the county and along the great Ohio River to see the beauty of the hills, forest and small canyons of the Little Smokies.

One morning nature put on a display neither of the Tylers had ever seen before. When they arose at sunup to walk from Lora's to Mary's for breakfast, every blade of grass, shrub, tree, fence and wire was coated with heavy jewels of pure white frost. The rising ember colored sun cast a copper tinted glow on the crystals of ice and splintered into rainbows of blue, gold, pink, and silver. As far as the eye could see, the winter day was aglow in the changing luster of sun and frost.

The Tyler's had spent almost their entire lives in the dry, warm plains of Texas where it rarely frosted; the humidity so low it seldom produced enough ice crystals to draw attention.

All through breakfast, C.B. would get up from the table, walk to a window, look out and make comments about the "fairy land" or "those pretty little snowy hills". He was further amazed to find how quickly the frost disappeared between his trips to the window.

A warm current of air from the southwest had combined forces with the climbing sun to quickly increase the temperature from thirty to forty degrees, changing the frost to huge diamond like drops of clear water hanging from every twig, blade of grass, or wire.

Ida Mae and C.B. had taken lots of pictures to bring back home to show friends "what pretty winter weather they have in Ohio." Lora just hoped the weather didn't make an unseasonable change to show the Tyler's what "real winter" could be like in Ohio.

She consoled herself by thinking, "We usually have real winter in January and February, not December."

She was glad they had nice weather with lots of sun and occasional light rain for an hour or two at night while the Tylers visited.

~

The Tylers became fond of the Buckmans and all the Kella family members in one short week. They were reluctant to leave, but had other horses to deliver by Christmas, so had to load the bulls and leave for home, just about the time they started to be familiar and comfortable with all their new friends.

They had been fascinated with the way Pepper and Vickie worked cattle. Also, the two little dogs had liked the Tylers, showing them rare friendliness and even coming to them for praise and treats from time to time right from the first day of their visit.

Several times they jokingly said they were going to take the dogs rather than the bulls "in the swap". The Tylers got their own surprise when Paul Cross, waiting on them by the road, waved them down and led a carbon copy of Pepper into the open door of the van.

John had alerted Paul as the Tylers prepared to leave. Paul had the little female, he had been perfecting for field trial work, ready to hand over when the van came in sight. He had agreed to give up his favorite one of Pepper's offspring only when John had promised to let Pepper have another litter of the same parentage as soon as nature permitted.

The Tyler's left Ohio feeling "like a million" and lucky to know all those good ole' Buckeyes so well. Lora felt relieved for the good weather, but sad when they pulled out to begin the trip home through the smoky hills in the bright sunlight.

The surprise of Pepper's grown pup, resulted from the Tyler's love shown for all animals and the way the Buckmans felt about the slow talking Texan's. The gift would stand out as the best one of their lives, but that would be learned much later by the happy Tyler's on their way home with "Little Bit" between them in the van.

The little female dog became calm and relaxed in a few hours. When they stopped for the first meal, C.B. took her for a walk while Ida Mae fixed lunch in the tiny kitchen. She gave Little Bit a bowl of ground beef, raw egg and some small pieces of cheese all stirred together.

When they started down the road again after watering the four big bulls, Little Bit came to lie on the rug between the big chair seats in the front of the van. By the time they reached home, Little Bit had become one of the Tyler family.

~

Nancy and Howie could hardly believe their ears when they were told the horses they had been riding for the last three weeks were Christmas gifts from the Buckmans. The youngsters had become very attached to "Sugar," Nancy's mare, and "Blaze," Howie's gelding. They had traded horses at times so both had the pleasure of learning each animal's gait and habits, while also giving each horse different riders to learn about.

The new horses taught all their riders more about cowwork in a few weeks than the riders had learned in several years on the backs of pleasure horses. Now Barney and Charlie, the two original geldings, were being taught some of what the Buckmans and Kella youngsters had learned.

Lora and Tim made good use of the Kella kids liking for their horses and for working stock on the big farm. Nancy on Sugar, quickly became a real hand at sorting and moving animals. When the cattle buyers came on Saturdays or other days when school was closed, the two young Kellas were almost always on hand to "cowboy" in real life situations such as helping sort, drive and weigh the animals.

Tim and Lora rode their new cow-horses for any of the work where horse training and cow-sense helped save time or trouble, but still used the old faithful geldings for fence riding and other routine work. A few times Mary and John rode the old geldings to join the other four riders moving large groups of cattle from one place to another.

Pepper and Vickie learned to work with the new horses to make the work of separating the cattle much easier than ever before. Howie and Nancy learned to give the little cow-dogs proper directions by voice and by hand signals, but the dogs soon learned to tell by watching the horses which animal was being singled out for attention.

The four horses obtained from the Tyler's had made a tremendous change in the farm operation from the day they were delivered. John and Mary found it easy to resume riding and did from horseback much of the work John had been doing afoot before the trained cutters were acquired.

The combination of trained cow-horses, Howie, Nancy, and at times John and Mary, with the ever-present pair of dogs made the "work" more like fun than labor for all of them.

Chapter eight

Chapter Eight ~

The gunshots in the morning air again warned the animals of the woods, fields and streams that the two-legged predators were back. After the first few hours, the shots were less numerous. The wary deer quickly learned to stay hidden from the prowling gunners. However, the young deer were not as wary or wise as the mature bucks and does with many years of experience. Many of the young paid a high price to learn fear, stealth and patience.

The three-day, "buck only" season and the weather forecast of rain had reduced the number of casual and novice shooters in the woods. Because of the three-day limit, most of the dedicated hunters were out all three days.

This set of unique circumstances resulted in a different kind of hunt than the previous year. The hunters were spread over a large area, with fewer gun-carrying hopeful's staying close to the roads. The mid-week opening day and more seasoned hunters capable of making clean kills greatly reduced the number of people firing into the woods from vehicles parked on roadsides or moving along like portable hunting blinds on the back roads.

Fewer deer were wounded to suffer slow death, but still some died after being shot and running some distance through the forest. Part of these deer were not found by the gunners and became food for the predators who had given up daytime hunting as soon as the first shots were heard.

Dutch had become alarmed before the gun season opened. Some hunters were out scouting for likely spots before the brief season began. Practice shots were fired giving early warning to those familiar with the ways of the two-legged hunters. She kept her band of wolf-like pups in the rock house on the cliff, except at night, for nearly two weeks before the gun season opened. Her black and white mate was always near and often on the hilltop behind the cavern, which was Bruiser's personal "on watch" location.

The first evening after the last day of heavy shooting, there were dead deer only a mile or so from the den. The first one they found had already been opened and smelled of coyote, but had not been fouled with urine. The big red dog passed it by with only a cursory sniff. She kept going and found a small spike buck only a few hundred yards away. The six dogs fed on the tender meat and then found a place in a dense deadfall nearby to spend the rest of the night and the next day.

During that day, Dutch lay hidden while watching a man follow the blood trail left by the dying spike buck. The drops of blood disappeared at the western edge of a small stream about fifty feet from the partially consumed carcass of the spike horn. The deer trail ended at the creek because the dying deer heart had quit pumping blood as he ran up the rocky east bank of the stream. There were no hoof or blood marks leading to the small carcass concealed by the fallen treetops and brush.

When the wind shifted momentarily, the man raised his head to sniff the air and gaze about the area. He seemed to smell something, but failed to identify what it was. He turned to walk back the way he had come, stopping once more to look directly at the deadfall tree tops where Dutch and her pack were hidden.

The hunter had felt sure he would find the deer because the blood trail had been bright in plain sight the evening before as the last light of day faded away. He had marked the spot where night had caught up with him by the creek and returned at first light. He was determined to save the meat he was sure he would quickly find, but the trail ended right where he stopped tracking the night before.

Vic searched around the creek in vain for a sign to follow. He circled about the banks of the stream but finally turned

212

away. The peculiar scent on the almost still air made him apprehensive, and gave him a strong desire to be gone from the feel of hidden eyes at his back. The hunter left, unaware the meat he was seeking especially for his big seal-brown dog would be fed upon again that night. His dog's mother and half-grown siblings would eat heartily but were now all watching him from the shadows deep within the deadfall.

The man's scent had disturbed Dutch more than any human scent normally did when she came across it in the forest. This scent contained an overlay of familiarity and deep significance to the big dog's questing memory. Signaling her band to stay, Dutch cautiously went to the place where the man had gone down on his knees to study the rocky streambed. Dutch inhaled the fresh man-scent and at once the memory of her pup, chained to a tree near the old stone trough came clear in her memory.

No gunshots were heard in the forest this morning. Even the man she trailed had no gun that Dutch could see. He was traveling in a nearly straight line back to the place his friend, Art, waited with the campsite all cleaned up and the seal colored dog on a fiber leash hooked to the truck bed.

It was almost noon when the two men put the seal-brown dog into the truck and prepared to leave. All at once Seal started barking and whining, while looking in the direction from which Vic had just come. Then the two men caught sight of a very large, red Doberman standing in the woods fifty or sixty feet away. She ignored the men and came close up to the stone trough where Seal had been tethered the past four nights.

Vic and Art, cautious but not really afraid, slid into the truck through the nearest door and sat silently watching the scar-headed red dog as she obviously communicated with her kin-fellow in the truck.

As they watched through the rear window of the cab, Seal pushed his nose through the space in the side racks and whuffed excitedly to the dog on the ground. Then the red dog trotted over, put her front feet on the truck's rear wheel and stood to touch noses with Seal.

In moments, the red dog dropped to the ground, turned and loped away. Seal walked up to the cab, lay down on his rug and remained unmoving. The truck pulled out of the forest and sped over the highway toward home.

~

The eighteen-month-old bear was surprised at how easy his mother caught and killed the animals that rooted up the dirt and leaves under the wild cherry trees. He was also surprised that the squealing pigs didn't climb over the heavy wire and run off in the night to some safe place in the woods.

One swipe of her front arm had silenced the first pig as it ran in panic about the woven wire trap. The trap partially enclosed the trunks of the six cherry trees by the boundary fence between the abandoned farm and the private timberlands to the north. One end of the long narrow pen-trap had a heavy wooden gate hinged at the top along a strong steel cable. The gate was held open in a parallel or horizontal position by a lighter cable at the bottom end, ready to drop and close the opening securely against anything trying to leave or enter the trap.

In addition to the heavy steel wire around the trees, a rusty quarter inch diameter cable was woven around and through the trees. This reinforced the wire against even the huge red Tamworth's efforts to walk through to reach the bait of ground corn sprinkled on the ground inside the compact pen trap. Long strong poles had been used at the top and bottom to increase the height and strength of the structure. Latch boards at the bottom of the opening kept the door from moving in any direction once the trip wire released the heavy door so it swung into the vertical position.

The trip wire or trigger could be set so the animals inside the pen released the gate, or for remote operation via a long wire to the hidden trigger-man in the grove behind the boundary fence. Steel posts, about a foot apart, had been driven into the ground across the opening. The cable had been laced around the post tops to keep them from spreading out when one of the large animals tried to force its way in. The trappers wanted only young hogs, not the big sows and boars at this particular trap.

The old female bear had found the little trail of cracked corn the pig trapper used to lure the pigs to his trap. At first the quarter-cup-sized mounds had been only a few feet apart. As they came closer to the pen, a few grains trickled on the ground led the hungry old bear thirty to fifty feet before finding enough grain for even a small mouth full. The trail of corn led right up to the wooden drop gate behind the hedge of steel posts. Corn spread inside lured the pigs through the trap gate.

The old female stood on her hind legs to push at the top of the barrier, but even her strength barely shook the reinforced structure, made to withstand a five or six hundred pound hog. Giving up on the trap end of the pen, she moved around to the side and crawled easily over the top. After smacking the sixty-pound pig to the earth with her front paw, she grabbed it in her teeth and shook it violently back and forth to end it's life. So energetic was she with her shaking that the hard-bodied little shoat slipped out of her mouth and flew over the fence to land twenty feet away on the grass.

When her big brown cub dashed over to pick up the dead pig and run, dragging the young porker away, the old female simply cornered and killed the other pig in the pen. She crawled back over the fence and followed her cub into the woods. Both pigs were long, lean, greyhound sized animals with tough, stringy flesh.

The old bear had caught a pig in the deep water of a wide stream earlier that week and had killed another when it separated from it's mating act with an older boar too late to avoid the bear's silent deadly rush and smashing front paws.

Several times the young male bear had tried to catch the pigs in the woods or along the stream where they spent much time in hot weather. They had a large area along one side of the creek worked into a mud bath that they used to coat themselves with a layer of blue-gray mud.

The heavy coating of mud had saved one of the long-nosed rooters from the young bear because the slick, heavy mud filled the young bears eyes, nose and mouth as he tried to bite into the shrieking pig while gripping it with his long, sharp claws. The mud didn't seem to affect the pig, but the hundred twenty pound bear lost the struggle with the lean, mean, sixty or seventy pound porker.

As cool weather came the old bear became cross and even vicious at times, biting and slapping the young male away. She refused to share her catches of ground squirrels, chipmunks, woodchucks, snakes looking for winter dens or the grubs found in old stumps or logs.

The year-and-a-half-old cub had been surprised his mother permitted him to keep the big pig. He ran as hard as he could with the pig flopping and dragging against his front legs. Quickly tiring from the unaccustomed exertion, he began tearing at the shoats stomach each time he paused to shift his grip on the kill. He came to a full stop in a stand of paw-paw trees along the side of a ravine. He listened for the sound of the old bear coming to take back the pig, but he couldn't hear a sound that he associated with pursuit. The smell of the pig's blood came to his nostrils causing him to tear anew at the porkers belly. He had it open and was holding it down with his front feet while he chewed away at the tender entrails.

All at once he became aware of a huge, hairy-headed monster with clashing teeth, slashing toward him through the paw-paw trees. The charging beast didn't slow down or dodge the two to four inch diameter tree trunks, but charged right through them. It was intent on one thing - - reaching the animal feeding intently on the pig carcass.

The huge boar was only ten or fifteen feet away running down hill at twenty-five miles an hour when the cub saw the open-mouthed, enraged glutton knocking his way through the shallow-rooted, banana-smelling, miniature forest.

The cub turned and lunged for the trunk of an ash tree, about a foot in diameter, growing up the edge of the ravine. He jumped, scampered up the tree five or six feet, then felt the pain of the hog's teeth in the skin on his rump. A frantic thrust of his muscles pulled him free from the teeth that had only gripped a small piece of skin, leaving a bare patch of hide but doing no real harm.

The cub worked higher up the soft-barked tree to a limb the size of his leg, some ten or so feet above the red boar's clashing yellow tusks.

It took the furious boar a minute or two to find the pig carcass. He had smelled it when the bear tore it open and came charging in to get it, he thought, from one of his own kind. The boar's total surprise at the cubs vertical escape route saved the cub from far more than a nip on the rump. If the cub had fled on the ground as the boar expected, he would have been killed at once.

The old female bear stopped just inside the woods to fill up on pork. She ate everything except the head and front quarters of the pig. Picking up the uneaten meat, she ambled along, looking for a place to hide her next meal. The smell of the pig she had been eating and the torn up carcass the red boar was feeding on camouflaged the rank smelling scent of the boar, until she was only a dozen feet from the evil-eyed

Tamworth.

The bear was at her prime. She was four hundred pounds of well-fed muscle, tendons and powerful bones. The red Tamworth had been lord over all in the forest for the past several years. His six hundred pounds of whipcord-tough and whale-bone strong muscle and bone were encased in a tough, thick-fitting hide that could turn the teeth of all but the most powerful jawed predator.

The bear reared up on her back legs, dropping the meat she had been carrying in her mouth, to roar a message of hate at the red hog eating the meat she had just killed for her cub.

The red boar gave out a sound of equal fury - - the squealing snarl of a blood lusting killer. Head up, nose even with his shoulders, the boar exploded to top speed in mere moments, determined to rip the black, roaring demon apart with one ripping scythe-like pass.

The speeding hog smacked the ash tree a glancing blow with his shoulder as he hurtled down the incline at the towering, arch-bodied bear. The blow on the tree terrified the trembling cub who caterwauled in treble-voiced terror, disrupting the pig's concentration.

The maddened boar was not accustomed to any opponent standing its ground when he charged and clashed his long tusks, but this hairy, black beast was a fighter from a different forest.

Before being live trapped and transported by some well intentioned sportsmen on vacation, the pregnant bear had fought and won battles in the iron ranges of Upper Michigan. She had, in fact, thrashed marauding male bears that looked bigger than this noisy boar.

Just as the boars tusks seemed to penetrate their target, the wary waiting bear hauled off and hit the stinking pig a powerful swat on the side of his nose with her right forearm. The incredible speed and power of the blow turned the hurtling hog head over heels on his bristling back breaking off two long yellow tusks at the same time. Then with her left arm, she smashed down on his neck with her three inch long hooked claws. As the boar rolled over to regain his feet, her claws tore deep furrows in his jowls, letting blood pour out in dark red dribbles on the yellow paw-paw leaves.

But this boar was made of stern stuff, not to be whipped by two swipes from a mere four-hundred-pound antagonist. He charged back again with his remaining tusks almost touching the ground to rear up and slash at the bear's lower belly as he ran under the flailing paws. The old bear sidestepped and smashed both her front feet on the red back under her nose. The boar sagged to his knees, and the bear bent over to bite into his right ear.

The boar tried, in vain, to jerk loose from the bear's excruciating teeth ripping through the tender ear. With her long-clawed rear feet she alternately ripped away at his exposed side and rear. Finally, the tough old red fighter tore free from the tougher old bear and ran off bleeding through the trees.

The bear cub stayed in the ash tree for a long time after his still mad, old mother went swinging off in her shuffling stride. He came down to follow her, hoping she would welcome him at her side again. She didn't. When he found her at the hog trap, the old sow bear drove him off, cuffing and biting him. He screeched in pain, running for his life over the hills.

~

A crew of timber cruisers and road builders moved through a section of forest studded with ancient oaks, beech, walnut, cherry, pine, maples, ash and poplar trees. The foreman, or woods' boss, of the crew and a helper used a transit to establish the road grades and colored tapes to mark the road sidelines. Men with spray cans of paint marked the trees with spots of paint on a buttress root and on the trunk, chest high, on the tree to be harvested. Other men and women measured, graded and recorded the yield and estimated value of the standing timber.

Some individual trees, (den trees, rare specimens, unique shapes or sizes), were banded with special ribbons to warn the cutters not to damage them in any way. Some strips of land along hillsides, streams and wildlife-breeding areas were surrounded by stakes. These had special tapes stretched head-high, completely around them, to keep men and equipment from causing any mechanical change to the "protected" sites.

Soon after the cruising and surveying work was completed, teams of chainsaw equipped trimmers cleared the small trees out of the roadways, then cut down and trimmed a number of hollow trees to be used making temporary crossings over ditches and narrow gullies. The hollow tree trunks were cut into lengths like wooden pipes to fill the ditches and gullies. They were covered with a layer of dirt, rocks and rubble to form a culvert-like bridge for the crawlers and skidders used to drag out the huge saleable tree trunks.

When the three hundred twenty acre, half section of privately owned forest was all prepared, the timber cutters began "felling" the trees and cutting away limbs and unsaleable "tops." The skillful cutters were able to drop most of the trees in such a way they did not harm the tape marked "keeper trees," but at times some leaning or top heavy, old giant had to be pulled over. This was done by a dozer using a cable fastened high up on the trunk while the cutter carefully sawed a "hinge" at the bottom of the tree to make it fall in a planned spot. The dozer operator and the cutter used hand signals to communicate due to the noise made by the chainsaw and the dozer engine.

When particular conditions made it necessary, a tree was "topped out" by a man equipped with cleated boots and climbing belts. He would scale the tree and cut off the crown of limbs at the very top with a light weight saw, which he pulled up after he was in a "safe" position, high up on the swaying tree top. When the "topper" started up a tree, "all hands" were kept away from the immediate area and all noise making equipment was shut down for absolute quiet.

The topper wore a small two-way radio on his left shoulder that was always turned "on" with the switch taped so it couldn't accidentally be turned off by bumping or scraping against the tree, or by tools the topper used. Another man on the ground - also an experienced topper - was equipped with a radio, climbing rig, emergency first aid kit and a light rescue outfit. If the "man in the sky" got into trouble of any kind, the backup or rescue man on the ground was ready to assist the topper at moments' notice. The two men were in constant communication by radio. The man on the ground kept watch over the topper with a pair of wide-range, ten-power binoculars, to warn the topper of anything that might endanger him during the hazardous operation.

The large company that owned the tract being harvested had thousands of acres of timberlands all over the country. When they had a "big stand" to "cut," they brought in a highly skilled crew of professional loggers to do the work. This was a big stand and the company's best crew was doing the harvesting in the cold of January, when the ground was most likely to stay frozen, causing the least amount of damage to the precious soil of the rolling hills.

The cutters and toppers were Oneida Indians from upstate New York. They were hard working, serious minded men of skill and intelligence with college education. They were also family men who much preferred the "mild Ohio winter" to the humid summer work in some places to which they traveled at the behest of "the company."

Toppers never climb when the trees are snow or ice covered, when the wind blows or rain falls. Lightning is feared above all else. When a storm threatens, the wise stay out of the woods. But even the most careful man can become a victim of an earlier storm when wind or lightning had caused hidden damage to a tall tree standing like a monarch above its lesser sentinels in a forest of hundred year old "virgin timber."

Two men in their late twenties stood at the foot of a five-foot diameter, hundred and twenty-foot tall "tulip" tree. It was a clear bright January morning with not a sign of wind to ripple the few leaves clinging to the otherwise bare limbs above their heads.

Other than a few dead stubs, the trunk was "clean" for seventy-five or eighty feet. Then four or five sets of small, leg-sized limbs grew horizontally from the trunk for another fifteen to twenty feet. At that point the tree became "double," in that two large central columns with many outreaching limbs formed the crown.

The taller of the two men tossed one end of his climbing rope around the tree, caught the free end when it whipped back around to him and secured it into the slip catch of the end he was holding in his other hand.

Both men had already "glassed" the tree and had agreed where it was to be topped at about ten feet below the double trunk. As the topper ascended the rescue man backed away from the tree, watching and "talking" the topper up the poplar trunk. This time, the man climbing had a small, Swedish steel, bow-saw attached to the light line uncoiling from the ground as he made his way up to the first small limbs. This man preferred the bow saw to a chainsaw for limb work. He would exchange the bow saw for a chainsaw when he would make the topping cut.

When the topper reached the first limb, he put his regular safety belt around the tree above the first set of limbs, then moved his climbing rope up above those same limbs. Setting his "spurs" firmly into the trunk, he began undercutting, then top cutting the limbs so they fell away from the tree when they broke free. He always positioned his feet so the falling limbs could not touch them. He cleaned the trunk all the way to the double columns then moved back down to the topping point, continually inspecting the trunk for signs of splits or bad spots as he descended.

Satisfied that all was as it should be, he lowered the bow saw to the ground where his partner switched saws on the "tool rope" and moved away from the tree to a safe distance. Secure in his rig, the topper started the chainsaw and notched the treetop on one side, then changed positions and started the other cut on the opposite side of the trunk, several inches above the notch cut.

The saw hummed smoothly as the sharp chain ate into the tree, throwing a steady stream of chips out to float down in the still, cool air. All at once, the topper "felt" a sound coming from the tree. He quickly killed the saw to listen for the sound. Then he "heard" a slight ripping through his feet. He spoke to the man on the ground to get a "binder cable" ready to send up, and at the same time lowering the chainsaw.

The binder cable was a half inch diameter super strong, woven steel wire rope, with a fast coupling rig used to draw the binder tightly around a tree trunk to keep it from splitting and trapping the topper in his own safety belt.

The rescue man moved quickly to send the binder aloft as the topper had instructed, but warned him to "fly down" if he heard another warning sound from the tree. In less than two minutes from the time he called for the binder, the topper had it in place and started retrieving the chainsaw to finish the job.

He again cut into the tree and had just passed center,

when all at once he heard and felt the trunk split above him. By the time he had the saw pulled free, one side of the top leaned out, broke free and started falling to the ground. Before he could kill and pitch the saw away, it was all over. The binder had done its job, keeping the tree from splitting down through the topper's belt, to squeeze him hard enough to injure or kill him.

The binder cable was buried in the bark of the tree as the split pushed down the trunk. It held until the heavy half of the top broke free, leaving the other half standing in place. Left exposed was the brown vertical scar of a lightning strike from the fork above his head, down to the fresh saw cut on the exposed top.

During the entire incident, both men remained calm and stoic in every way. The tall tree swayed for a few moments after the one side fell, then steadied back to the normal minute motion all trees have all the time. The topper finished the job, then casually descended to the ground.

Both men gathered up all the tools and walked down the hill to a small "cook shack" for a cup of hot coffee. The tall man took out his pipe and folded leather tobacco pouch. When he had the pipe going well, he slowly puffed smoke in all four directions of the compass before handing it to his partner who repeated the ceremonial act of the old ritual.

The shorter man said, "The father spirit is here in these little mountains, today."

Finished with the pipe and coffee, they went back up the hill and the taller man "talked" the other one up the second "tulip tower" only a couple hundred yards south of the first one.

~

Dutch, Bruiser and the four young "wolves" scented the hogs when they crossed over a low, oak and beech covered hill five miles northeast of the cavern. The floor of the forest had been stirred and trampled by the five members of the sow's litter still roaming the woods. Some of the original fourteen had fallen prey to the old bear, one to the young bear and the rest in the baited trap by the long, woven wire fence line on the south side of the company property.

Dutch moved her head around to meet the eyes of each of her followers. Bruiser stayed close to her side. Two pups moved off to her left and two to her right. The leaves and litter on the ground were damp from the melted snow, making very little sound as the six dogs spread out to begin the encircling stalk of the much larger and somewhat fatter shoats busy feeding on the mass now accessible since the snow had melted.

Bruiser spotted the sentinel pig and gave the signal to "freeze." All six animals became motionless until all of them located all of the hundred forty to hundred sixty pound beasts in the woods ahead. Like gray wraiths, the young wolf-like dogs slid around the now uneasy herd of pigs that began drawing together near the root mass of a fallen pin-oak tree.

Some sound or scent caused the young hogs to form a tight half-circle of defense against the earth-filled tilt of protective roots. Four of the shoats were females, and only one a small hammed black boar with a long, sharp nose, tiny gimlet eyes an unusually long, thin tail.

Knowing the time had come to close in, all the dogs walked slowly out into the open, advancing in a semi-circle facing the head swinging, tooth champing pigs. The pigs stood hip against hip, heads up, watching for an opening or an easy-to-grab, careless predator. The dogs came ever closer to the embattled, bristling hogs.

Bruiser had maneuvered to get directly in front of the long-tailed, black boar pig. They stood eye to eye, only feet apart, tension building and nerves causing muscles to bunch and quiver at the approaching deadly moments when one must attack or give way.

On a hill about a half-mile away, a well built, darkly tanned man made his way up the side of a mammoth poplar tree. A light, even breeze had begun moving through the woods, but only softly agitated the few leaves enough to wave them gently over his head, not enough to cause concern. The climber paused at a stubby, dead limb to knock it loose to clatter into the brush far below.

At eighty feet up the tree he stopped his ascent took out a small pair of three power "opera" glasses to study other tall trees standing to the south of the one he was climbing.

As his magnified vision passed over a gap in the canopy of oaks on a low hill, he lowered the sight line to look over a large oak laying on the ground with a plate-shaped fan of roots and dirt at it's base. Some movement there caught his eye. Refocusing the lenses, a rare sight came into clear view as he stared.

The soft southern breeze fanned a feather-like spruce top to partially block his vision, so he backed down the tree a short distance to get an unobstructed view of the heart-slowing scene on a small hill, just to the south and below him.

Without moving his eyes from the wolf like animals and the five frozen pigs he spoke into the radio to tell his partner to take the ten power binoculars and climb another tall, slender tree just to the east of his location. He kept up a low-voiced description of the action developing between the two groups of predators in the clearing by the supine pin oak.

Normally the pin-oak roots would have penetrated much deeper into the earth, but a solid layer of hard stone, only one or two feet deep on the hill, forced the growing tree roots to turn outward as they reached the impervious rock. Over the years, as other trees died or blew down in strong winds, the pin oak's branches and roots grew apace to occupy all the available space around it.

In time, the tree's roots began dying, their circle shrinking, to finally reduce the broad root base to only a twenty-foot long, ten-foot wide oval. When the wind storms power felled the old oak, the entire layer of loose rocks and soil went up with the roots, leaving only rock to wash clean in the rains and melting snow.

The thin layer of damp leaves on the smooth rock was slippery under the feet of the wary hogs as they shifted their feet nervously in preparation for the imminent battle. Dutch sensed this advantage and feinted a lunge at one of the young sows, causing her to jump and fall backward when her feet slipped, knocking the boar aside. The boar squealed in anger and fright, then made a dash for freedom as Bruiser shifted to the side, creating a tempting avenue of apparent escape.

The first thrust of his back legs propelled the young boar out to the shallow rim of the old root space where his hard hooves found purchase in solid earth. In a rush of panicked speed, the tough, young male hog sprinted across the clearing, followed by Bruiser and the two female, yearling dogs.

Dutch and the two male dogs quickly changed positions to contain the four remaining hogs for a short period of time, before turning to race after the rest of her pursuing family.

The two men in the trees were dumbfounded at the speed attained by the pig and the wolf-like dogs, pressing the young black beast, zigzagging through the almost bare woods. When the last group of dogs relinquished their holding action of the aggressive gilts by the fallen tree, the quartet of females fled like deer toward the root cellar where the remembered safe den assured their safety.

Bruiser ran up along the left side of the darting pig with one of the black-eared, gray females on the right side, the other behind, snapping at the foaming-mouthed creature's rear, trying for a grip on one of his thrusting legs.

The deadly race moved north, just east of the men in their safety harnessed perches high above the speeding stream of animals. Dutch and her two male pups were running in single file, cutting straight through the zigs and zags made by the gasping boar.

When Dutch drew along side her pup at the hogs rear, she gave a sharp-barked "attack" signal to Bruiser. He put on a burst of speed to get slightly in front of the tiring boar, then darted around to grasp him by the end of his long, tapered snout. At the same time, the young females darted ahead to sink their teeth into the boar's flopping ears. Dutch lunged in to grip the hog's left rear leg, above the knee joint.

The ensuing action was violent and final, ending in the normal tradition of predators and prey. The victors fed on the fallen beast, as he had on the lesser prey that came into his scope of life in the rolling blue hills.

The dogs fed on the nut-like, rich meat of the boar, while three hundred yards west of them, the men in the trees descended to the ground. The gentle breeze blew their scent north, away from the pack. Their careful movements going down the tree were unheard and out of sight.

Tools in hand, the pair of amazed toppers soft-footed their way back to the tool shed in the log yard, cleaned and stowed their gear, marked their time sheets and quit work at noon on that warm-feeling Saturday in January. They stopped by the combination office-cook shack to turn in their time sheets and tell the boss they were headed into Rockhill, where the company leased motel rooms.

As they turned to leave, the tall, coppery-skinned, dark-eyed man asked a question of a short, blonde man seated at the

228

desk, "Hey Chief. Would you like to hear a crazy Indian story about wolves 'running wild' in these woods?"

The boss replied, "You guy's better get out of here and go have some fun in town. I think this working in the woods is getting to you."

The shorter man, smiling, said "White Chief smart man. We go now. If we no come back Monday, you make big smoke signal." With that, the departing toppers winked at each other, and walked, chuckling, out the door.

~

After filling their bellies, the dogs drank from a clear pool of water where a spring bubbled to the surface, then lay down in the leaf-drifted lee of a cut-bank to doze and loaf the mild day through.

In the dusk of early night, the wind switched to come from the northwest. The rising wind carried the smells of oil, engines and fresh sawdust mixed with the smell of many men, to the lazing dogs.

The woods were dark and quiet, but the smells of men and equipment was strong enough to cause Dutch and her pack to move on, leaving the half-eaten hog carcass on the ground.

Later that night, small creatures began the cleanup process that would leave only a few bones to whiten in the sun and rain before turning into minerals to enrich the waiting soil.

~

In keeping with his promise to Paul Cross, John took Pepper over to his house at the first sign of Pepper's mating season.

Vickie was kept in the enclosed porch all the time, unless someone put her on a leash to walk around the homestead area or to run beside a horse while the rider made short trips near the house. Vicki's close observation and restriction of freedom was the result of Chestnut's amorous attention, one crisp January evening.

The handsome, dark-coated fox hung around the Buckman homes for a few nights following Pepper's absence and Vicki's confinement before setting forth on a new venture of significant implications and lasting results. Over the past three years, most of the area fox families had changed. Some had left, some had been killed, and others had moved in to fill territorial gaps or created new ones with overlapping boundaries.

The only foxes left in the immediate area were his overaged, mate-less mother and one half brother who seldom came to the scent post dividing points of Chestnut's very large, private home territory, in which his nine year old mother was permitted to share.

With game or prey of all kinds plentiful on his range of rolling hills, Chestnut made no attempt to keep other foxes from hunting food, but would not permit them to establish dens, lay-ups or "sunning grounds" in his territory. When the mating season came with the cold of January, Chestnut went in search of his permanent mate.

His size, agility and striking appearance were all factors in his favor among the contending males for the few available females of breeding age within the voice range radius of Chestnut's domain.

For several nights, Chestnut's clear, ringing love calls were sent out into the moon swept hills. Some responses from curious females resulted in occasional rendezvous where the young foxes played games of coy allurement, danced and yodeled in abandoned joy or play-mated in their mock courtships.

Chestnut met and frolicked with a number of young "belles," most of them followed by hopeful, jealous young males already smitten by the flirtatious, selective vixens they pursued.

For two weeks, he continued to seek out the female of his undefined ideal. Then "she" found "him." She came silently up to him on the long, tree-covered slope along the side of the smallest pond. He heard her coming in a start and stop series of movements, quite common in young females seeking first mates.

The long, silvery guard hairs overlaying her blue-black coat and blending with her almost white feet reflected flecks of moonlight as she danced toward him through the park-like setting of tree clusters, back-dropped by moon bathed water of the pond.

The two delicate, but strong and agile, little animals were dressed in their luxurious winter coats, sleek with good health and excited with the joy of life and their first meeting.

Chestnut performed all the ingrained rites of courtship of posing, cavorting, dancing and whirling to show his splendor and physical ability to his prospective mate.

She had already chosen him when she touched his nose and pressed her head against his shoulder. The rest of the night was a routine prescribed by her ancestors carried to her in their transmitted genes. The ritual called for the displays and demonstrations as proof for each other of the capability and interest to fulfill and maintain their pairing.

By the dawn of the first morning of their meeting, Chestnut drove away all contenders and paid continuous court to his playful new bride. They made the hills ring with their yipping-yodeling songs and shrieks of bliss for many nights and frequently in daylight as well.

Chestnut became a responsible adult, almost over night.

He also became part of the proper wildlife of the Little Smokies from his first meeting with the beautiful vixen.

Pepper came home after more than two weeks of time spent with the perky Australian Blue Heeler. She had been lonely and anxious to come home for two days before Paul put her in his van and brought her home. Vickie was outside, unrestrained for the first time in many days. The two females acted like a pair of kids in their joy over the reunion.

Howie and Nancy took them along on a quick trip to the ponds and then to the calf lot, bull yard and back to the barns. They didn't find Chestnut's fresh scent on any of the places they had expected it to be. The pleasure of the long run with the horses kept both dogs occupied long enough for them to find other interest-holding activities and new things to do.

Vickie would be two years old in just two months. It had been almost exactly two years since Pepper had gone for her first run by the feed lots with Chestnut. He would be three years old in a few weeks. Pepper was a sedate, six-year-old "cow dog." As far as Pepper knew, Chestnut was a lusty, young bachelor just looking for fun and freedom. She had yet to learn of Chestnut's overnight maturation while she was away from the farm.

~

The nocturnal wail of a coyote could be heard between the yipping and yodeling of foxes. At first the calls were like inquiries for any voice speaking a common language, but changed to more direct questing when some faint howls from far points made clear her message was received and understood.

She ran her territorial borders every night calling for any creature of her kind, not begging, but making sure her howls and wails were plain and invited response from some ambitious bachelor or virile novice. Time passed as she drew close to the peak of her mating season, when a slim, gray dog with size and shape very much like her own began coming close to her in search of the passionate voiced female.

The young dog was one of two males whelped by Dutch the previous year. He was dark gray on his back shading to lighter gray mixed with rufous red on his flanks and hips, and sharp pointed, black tipped ears. To most untrained eyes, he could have been dog, wolf or coyote or a mixture of the three canines so similar in many cases.

The young, wolf-like dog made plain his amorous interest in the female coyote with the side-pointing tail. She was afraid of him at first, her memory of the fight that killed her siblings still alive in the back of her instincts or mind. Nature aided the female coyote to overcome her anxiety enough to approach the dog for nosing and coy turns around each other. The urge to mate was much stronger than her natural timidity and fear of the friendly acting dog.

Her many nights spent calling had not been heard by an eligible male. Those of proper age already had mates of their own, leaving no other suitable swain for Crooked Tail. When the excited young dog demonstrated his willingness to be that swain, she led him on a playful round of the scent post and food caches she maintained on her home ground.

Before the night ended, Crooked Tail accepted the virile dog as her mate and then led him to a secluded place near the center of her home territory for the three week long honeymoon. The food caches were nature's way of providing for the mating period. Crooked Tail had instinctively made the kills and stored the food at some ingrained traits message. The coyote seldom ate during the cycle, but the dog cleaned out all the cached meat and hunted occasionally to satisfy the increased demands on his body.

Dutch and her pack stayed away from the crooked tailed coyotes' area. Both she and Bruiser were occupied by nature's demands. Left alone for the first time, her remaining three pups found plenty of food. They contented themselves with the skill sharpening games they habitually played when not hunting or dozing in the dry, warm nook. The two females were too young to be in season, as the three pups played in perfect companionship until Dutch and Bruiser returned to take them on a longer journey through the forest than they had ever taken before.

The journey was for a reason the young dogs did not understand and required nearly a month to carry out. Dutch wanted the young dogs to find their own home areas and make their own way in life. Her pairing with Bruiser made it imperative for the offspring to move out of "her" home ground. Taking or sending the young dogs away assured them of unrelated mates and also reduced the drain on the food supply in the home territory.

Dutch led her band out one cold night, going mostly east but swung north or south to visit or investigate anything attracting interest on the journey. They found plenty of food as they moved unhurriedly, for several days, across the rolling hills. Passing downwind from a small set of farm buildings, the pack all scented the female hound confined on a chain by the barn. The lone male pup in her group left, not to return, in response to the blue-tick female's keening call.

Two nights later, both female pups took up the chase of a young smooth-headed buck and did not return that night to the hollow sycamore where Dutch lay sleeping.

The old dogs took a wide swing to the north, which lasted more than a week as they cautiously passed under or over the highways encountered on the circuitous route back to the rock cavern on the cliff.

They had to make one detour when only a few miles from home. The wire fence along the south line of the private timberlands had been extended almost a mile further west than before. This fence ran beside the section of land the timber company was harvesting at this time.

The west end of the tall fence was almost due north of the ravine that passed in front of the cavern den. All the trees had been cut that were scheduled for harvest. Two dozen or so mammoth walnut trees had been left for last, so the large, valuable trees could be topped and then dropped onto the discarded limbs and tops from many other trees that covered the ground. This method cushioned the fall of the walnut boles, worth many thousands of dollars, if undamaged by striking large rocks, stumps or humps in hard ground.

To keep the trees from splitting when they crashed to earth, cables were stretched from high up on a nearby anchor tree. It ran down to the base of a second tree, providing a slide-like arrangement to slow the descent of the huge, black wooded treasures.

Nathan Snow and Jonathan Whitewater, the two Onieda toppers, were about to finish up their work in this "stand" and were then planning to go home for a ten day "break" in their nerve-stretching, six or seven day work week schedules.

The walnut trees were clustered together in a basin of fertile black loam north of the new fence. When Nate and Jon finished topping and dropping them, they were chained to the top of special sleds or skids to protect them as they were dragged from the woods to a log yard, loaded on long-bed trailers and hauled to a barge on the river for shipment to Belgium.

Before the trees were sawed off at the bottom, a small "backhoe" digging rig was brought in to clear the earth away from the trees. Going down to the first main roots, some times in deep rich soil, an excavation of six to ten feet might be made to get all the straight portion of the precious walnut wood. As much as a thousand dollars worth of top quality wood could be saved with this method.

Some of the massive forest monarchs had been growing in this small, secluded bowl for well over a hundred' years. As they grew, soil washed down from the hills and valleys above to settle in the ground clutter of limbs, brush and leaves. It was left to accumulate around the walnut trees as they grew larger and taller. A bed of gravel under the soil provided good drainage and the new soil and humus created a continuous supply of nourishment for fast growth and good health. When the decision was made to harvest the valuable nut trees, orders came down from "the old man," president of the forest products division. His orders were to have the best men supervise the operation on those particular trees, from start to finish.

The president gave further instructions that several bushels of nuts from the trees were to be collected and planted, to start thousands of new walnut trees from the outstanding parent stock. The young trees in the same grove were to be protected in every way to prevent any damage to them, and the soil was to be restored to the original level and condition.

The smallest trees in the group to be cut were four feet in diameter at a point three feet above ground. The largest ones were well over five feet thick. The least value of any tree was estimated at sixty-five hundred dollars and the tree of most worth would be in excess of twenty thousand dollars. The estimated total value of all twenty-seven trees was two hundred fifty-six thousand dollars. The future worth of the young trees to be left would exceed a million dollars.

When "the old man" called he talked to the woods boss, to Nate, and to Jon, before the work started to reiterate his orders for caution and care for all the walnuts.

When the first tree base was excavated, the "hole" was fourteen feet deep. The solid round trunk at that depth looked perfect in every way. At the cry of "Timber!" from Jon as he scooted up the escape ramp in the side of the hole, the chocolate colored pillar leaned against the guide cable and slid down to the cushion of limbs and cull tree tops. The prostrate giant was measured, appraised, marked and then cut into two lengths. The butt log was forty-five feet long and the top log was thirty-eight feet long.

The first two logs were rolled onto a pair of bogey skids and pulled away by a four hundred horsepower "crawler." It took over two hours to "snake" the first "pull" from the "stump to the truck." The stump was in a hole fourteen feet in the ground.

It took sixteen days for five men to remove what nature spent from one to two hundred years to produce. Left alone, the trees could have lasted for another great number of years, or could have died, been blown apart by a tornado or burned up in a fire in only a month or a year. As it was, the harvest was made without loss or permanent damage to the environment and thousands of new trees would be raised to replace them.

When the last basement sized hole had been leveled and mulched with shredded bark and slashings, Nathan Snow and Jonathan Whitewater walked through the saucer shaped glen of trees. They walked to the rim of shaley earth around the sides of the stand and stopped to fill and light Nate's red stone pipe. He puffed, turned and puffed again until he completed the old custom, then handed the pipe to his partner who did the ritual for himself before passing the pipe back to its owner.

As they walked up the skid road, the tall man put his hand on the arm of the shorter one and said, "There are some real nice spirits in these woods, cousin."

The other man walked on a few steps, turned his head and replied, "There may be some pretty smart spirits up in the main office also. The old man sure wants us to take care of these woods. He said this is the best timber in these hills and he wants to keep it that way, or help make it better."

They stopped again at the top of an eleven-hundred-foot-high ridge to gaze around on that last day on the job. The smoky haze was blue-gray, shading to lavender in places. Jonathan pointed out over the "Little Smokies " and said, "I think, someday I'd like to live here. This is my kind of country."

As they walked down the long hill, a coyote wailed the first call of late afternoon from her place near the freshly dug birthing den. The sound made both men smile at the same time as they remembered tales passed down through the years from ancestral times about the "little gray brothers." An afternoon coyote call was a sure sign of good news before sundown.

Their jackets were slung over shoulders, shirts unbuttoned almost to belts, showing the lightweight insulated, thermal tops both wore. The air was moist and warm, much different than the early mornings' weather when even the jackets were on and zipped up as the sun came over the eastern hills. February was almost gone and the worst cold weather with it.

The partners reached the landing, or log yard, before the sunset. A long, tan maxi-van was parked by the mobile office cook-shack. They both knew who would be waiting inside, by the presence of the company vehicle parked there.

Entering the cook-shack dining room, they were hailed by a small red faced man with a fringe of white hair around his bald head and a close cropped, white strip beard running from ear to ear around his chin and cheeks.

"The old man" hopped out of his chair and trotted over to them with outstretched hand and a big grin on his face. He greeted both men and shook hands while smiling in, plain to see, liking for both. He offered both men a cup of coffee and ushered them to the little table where the blond haired, young woods boss was grinning and motioning them to chairs. Seated, they sipped at the coffee while the "old man" poured himself a warm-up and joined them at the table.

Enos Hanson, the old man, had started his career in the

238

forest of northern Wisconsin at age sixteen. He had done everything from cooks' helper to topping trees by the time he was twenty years old. He did all the jobs with a smile, a laugh or a joke on his lips. The timber-man he worked for took a fatherly interest in him and talked him into spending two years in college to learn how to manage a business, and keep the books. He had been back to school at various times since to increase his knowledge and improve his mind.

Now, at sixty-four, he was the top dog in one of the largest timber, mining and transportation companies in the world. He earned his title, President-Forest Products, by hard work, good sense, and his unfailing good humor. He made the people in his organization proud of the company, of him, and themselves as a result of his tremendous leadership qualities and fair treatment.

Seated at the table, he started talking. "I flew over the stand this morning to see how things looked from the air. The whole job looks well done with very little damage to standing trees and the roads are in good shape, just a little bit of dressing to do after the cleanup crew finishes."

He took a sip from his cup then continued, "I've seen a lot of timber work done in the past fifty years, even before I started in the woods. But, that job you fellas did on that stand of walnut looks as good from the air, as anything I ever had the pleasure of being part of, or even seeing."

Pausing again for a moment, he looked around the table at each man, then added, "I was down at the river to see the walnut going on the barge. There wasn't a bad mark on any of those beautiful 'sticks'. Why even the crane operator handled them like fresh eggs."

Everyone at the table smiled at this, knowing how particular the "crane jockey" was with the expensive, veneer quality logs.

The old man hadn't finished. He said, "When that load

of walnut gets to the factory in Belgium, they will turn those big sticks into more than two million dollars worth of fine "skins" for furniture and high priced paneling. You three especially, and the other people also, deserve more than thanks and a pat on the back. All of you will get bonuses and some extra time off this spring."

"Nate, Jon. Both of you have Bachelor Degrees in Forestry from good schools. Yet, both of you are out here in the woods working at the most dangerous jobs you can find. Now, you're headed home for a well-deserved rest. I want you to take a month, not ten days to think over and discuss with your families a proposition the company wants to make you."

The young Indian men looked at each other, but didn't comment, as none was required at this point. They finished their coffee and waited for Hanson to resume his serious words, given with a friendly smile.

"I'll be up in your neck of the woods in a few days, and since things will be slow around here for a while, you can take a month off with no problem, while the ground dries out from the spring rains. When I get up there we'll talk about an offer for you to take on more responsibility and still be able to work in the woods, which you seem to like," he said. "Oh! Another thing," he added, "The jobs you'll be offered will mean you and your families will be together."

Hanson's last statement piqued both young men's interest enough to make them start to ask questions, but Hanson wouldn't give them anymore details at that time. He would only say, I have to clear up some points with the company," meaning the other major partners on the board of directors, "Then I'll be up to tell you all about it."

They were on the way back to the motel soon after. Nate and Jon drove out of the log yard just as the sun's last rays dimmed in the west. The hills were bathed in rosy luminance, while the haze of evening blurred the deep alleys and canyon-like ravines all around.

"That coyote we heard must keep in touch with the big spirits," Jon said.

"In the words of our great grandfather," Nate replied, "The spirits are in the minds of all creatures."

"All creatures are children of the spirits," Jon responded, grinning at Nate.

"If that's true, the coyote knows many things he doesn't tell," Nate said half seriously.

Some of the other men had the keys turned in and the luggage packed, ready to load, the minute Jon and Nate reached the motel. In five minutes, the two loads of young Indian men were on the road, headed back to their homes in the forested mountains of northern New York. Except for "pit stops", they would drive all night, each man, taking turns at the wheel while the others napped or talked softly to keep the driver alert as they sped through the night.

~

Enos Hanson flew into Watertown in a company plane, then rented a car for the drive east to the small village where twenty-odd men lived who worked for the company. The village was in a high valley of a range of small mountains that had been all Indian lands up to the time of the Revolutionary War. The village land was part of a section purchased by ancestors of the present inhabitants.

Nathan Snow and Jonathan Whitewater were waiting for Enos at the restaurant-tavern that served the community as a post-office, bus station and social center.

With his usual good humor, "the old man" greeted the two young Oneida men with handshakes and sincere expressions of happiness to see them again. Enos had come to renew his friendship with the wives, children and other family members of Jon, Nate and the other company employees.

He left his car parked at the big log and stone "center," and the three of them rode in Nate's car to Jon's home. The families of both men were gathered in the Whitewater's large modern home, setting in the midst of a birch grove with a snow-topped mountain rising behind.

Enos knew everyone's name from previous visits and from his habit of sending presents at weddings or births. He was well respected because he was truly interested in their lives and for his fair treatment of all employees.

After spending an hour or so visiting with the families, Enos brought up the main subject of his coming to their homes. He wanted the wives and children to hear what he had to say.

First he gave Nate and Jon the bonus checks he had promised them, then explained the promotions he had hinted at when he last saw them in Ohio.

What he had in mind was for Nate and Jon to take charge of a large operation he had been developing for more than twenty years. This was the timberland owned by the company in southern Ohio, the acquisition of a large amount of additional property and the rehabilitation-reforestation of all present and future wilderness property.

Enos offered Nate the position of Timber Land Manager, and Jon, the position of Reclamation and Purchasing Manager. New homes would be built for the managers and an assistant for each of them. Their utilities, a business vehicle of their choice, and salaries of gradually increasing amounts were proposed. In addition, any person or family moving permanently to Ohio would be guaranteed a fair price for their present homes, and have all expenses related to relocating paid by the company.

Since the company already owned over twenty thousand acres and would acquire four or five times that amount, as it became available, they would need several good men on a permanent basis in addition to the four management persons. Only one other person would be appointed by Enos, an Office Manager-accountant, who would make up the staff of five salaried persons living "on location" at the new department of the company. Nate and Jon would select the people for the many tasks to be performed and have suitable homes built or renovated, as necessary, for their needs.

Enos added another facet to the plans for the operation. He said, "As soon as we get organized and can find the right person, we will hire a full time naturalist to take charge of restoring natural wildlife and preserving it forever. While I'm on the subject, everyone on the property is to help preserve and improve all aspects of habitation and conservation, at all times."

Jon and Nate nodded their heads in agreement with this very emphatic statement. They shared the old man's love of nature and had frequently bypassed timber to leave places for the little creatures of the forest.

Enos sat talking with the two families for about an hour, then told them to talk over the proposal while he walked over to an old friend's house to visit. The old friend was a man Enos had worked with off and on, for forty years. He always spent a night with him when he came to the Oneida village, if time permitted.

Albert Pereau was a tall, lean, half-French, Half Indian, who had been born in Canada some seventy years ago. His white hair, gray eyes and deep red skin made him an eye-catching person in any circumstance.

When Enos knocked on his door, he was thinking about the first time he had seen Albert at logging camp in Minnesota over forty years before. Enos was working as an errand boy-cooks helper at the time. At age sixteen, weighing a scant one hundred twenty pounds, Enos was the butt of many pranks and tricks by the gang of timber-jacks, teamsters, and truckers who ate in the company operated mess hall.

One hulking giant of a man delighted in causing the young "roustabout" embarrassment or even pain with his crude tricks and vile mouthed humor. One night while Enos was clearing tables and carrying big trays of dishes to the kitchen, his tormentor had tripped Enos, causing him to strike his head against one of the heating stoves in the room.

Enos, fed up with the man's dirty tricks, had jumped up, a stick of wood in his hand, and knocked the sneering man off his chair. Not badly hurt, the red faced giant got up, grabbed Enos and started crushing him in a "bear hug" that cracked two of the youngster's ribs.

Albert Pereau, the foreman on the job, told the giant to let Enos go at once. When the man refused to release the boy, Albert pried his hands apart and pushed the boy to the side. The infuriated logger made a big fisted swing at Albert and started calling him names like "dirty half-breed," mixed with filthy swearing about the "punk kid."

Seeing that he couldn't avoid a fight, Albert took the initiative, knocking the loud-mouthed bully out cold with a few expert blows to the midsection and chin. When the bully revived, Albert fired him, paid him off and sent him into town with one of the trucker's hauling logs.

For a time, the men in camp called Enos "stove wood" as a good-natured way of expressing their respect for his spunk in taking on his tormentor. The owner of the logging business heard all about the "ruckus" and assigned Enos to work with Albert, learning to be a good "jack." The friendship between the pair grew over the years. When Enos became a manager in the large company he now served, he made sure Albert had a choice assignment any time he wanted to work.

At his second knock, Albert came, yawning, to the door. He had been taking an afternoon nap and hadn't heard Enos knock the first time. Standing in the doorway, his snowy hair almost touching the top, Albert just gave a small grin and held out his hand. He had been expecting his old friend and knew it would be a long and pleasant night. He prepared himself by taking a nap and "fasting" since his five o'clock breakfast that morning.

Enos could smell the aroma of roasting meat when they entered the long kitchen-dining room at the hand-hewn log house. He got a big surprise when Albert introduced a slender, good-looking woman as "my wife, Alma." She was about a foot shorter than Albert, a blue-eyed, brown haired beauty in slacks and loose hanging shirt. She clasped hands with Enos and welcomed him to their home, saying she had heard much good about him in the past few months.

Enos spent a pleasant evening with Albert and his, obviously, happy wife, who served up a real fine supper then set out a bottle of Albert's homemade wild grape wine. While the men reminisced and talked about the new operation in Ohio, Alma did the dishes, then left to go to the local school where she taught classes two evenings each week. She left the men sipping wine by the fireplace at the end of the room.

Enos spent two more days "on vacation," visiting all the other employees homes, then left to drive to the airport for the flight to his home in a suburb of Detroit. He had completed his mission to his satisfaction by having both Jon and Nate agree to take him up on his proposal. Six other top woodsmen and their families, plus some single employees agreed to make the move. Nate and Jon would be the first to make the trip to get the groundwork underway for the relocation of families at the end of the school year.

Enos was very pleased when the "new managers" suggested that all the homes be built from "native materials" for all the families moving to Ohio. Some of the smaller "old houses" on company lands could be used as temporary quarters for some of the homebuilders while constructing the log, stone, slate and glass, permanent homes.

Albert and Alma capped his final evening with them by an offer Enos was more than happy to accept. Alma was a professional architect and Albert was a skilled craftsman with much experience building rustic homes. They offered to spend "a year or so" helping with the new homes. They would use their almost new thirty-foot camping trailer to live in until a house could be renovated for their use.

The enthused managers and a crew of ten people left New York for Ohio a few days after Enos flew home. Albert and Alma were to follow in a couple of weeks when Alma's evening classes ended for the year. Nate and Jon wanted to get a large supply of logs cut before the sap rose when warm weather came to the little blue mountains of their new home.

The caravan of trucks, vans, station-wagons and four-wheelers, some pulling campers and some with heavy utility type trailers hitched behind, arrived at a pre-selected, temporary base of operations at noon, one snowy March day.

The temporary base was a large rambling house that had belonged to an organized group of small businessmen in Dayton. They used the house, barns and several other buildings for vacations, hunting, horseback riding, fishing and weekend outings for several years. The group had dissolved, putting the five hundred-acre resort up for sale.

Enos had purchased the property and put a middle-aged couple, Ora and Betty Wells, in as caretakers some years earlier. They occupied a small house just behind the "lodge," as they called the larger house. They kept watch over the property as well as doing some yard and building maintenance work for a small salary, garden space, free rent and free firewood.

The lodge was located several miles from the main properties the company owned, but was close enough for convenience and large enough for the first group of people to be comfortable in for some time.

The vehicles were unloaded, beds set up and clothing put away before dark, that first day. The caretaker had built a fire in the big, old fashioned, wood burning boiler-furnace, a day earlier so the old lodge was warm and comfortably dry for the new "guests."

The lodge had a big, well-equipped kitchen and a dining room with space and tables for at least forty people. The previous owners had removed some of the walls and put in a beamed ceiling to create another large room called "the great room" across one end of the first floor. An open fireplace and chimney of gray limestone occupied a twenty foot section of the outside wall of the great room making an eye-catching compliment to the old, weathered barn siding used to line the rest of that wall. The other walls were covered with rough-sawn boards stained in earth tones making the, otherwise, bare room seem warm and cheerful. An area in front of the fireplace was made of one huge slab of split granite. The rest of the floor, four inches lower, was covered with two-foot square pieces of red, brown, green and gray slate that blended harmoniously across the twenty by forty-foot floor space.

The second day, Nate and Jon drove into Rockhill to get some chainsaw oil, gas and other supplies. They asked the store owner, a man they had dealt with while working in the area the previous two months, for help finding two or three people to cook, keep house and do the laundry for ten to twenty persons for eight to twelve months time. Mr. Kechan, the storeowner, took the phone number of the lodge and said he would call them in a day or so to pass on some names of people for them to talk with about the "jobs."

On the way out of Rockhill, Jon and Nate stopped at a grocery store to pick up a list of "get me's" for other members of the group at the lodge. Their lack of familiarity with the store was apparent to a couple behind them in the aisles, who offered to help them find some items on the list. In a few minutes mutual introductions were made, with the Kella's offering to help the Snows and Whitewaters with any of the many problems newcomers have when moving.

Both Jon and Nate recognized the name Kella, having heard it mentioned by various people at the motel and restaurants earlier that winter. They invited the Kella's to come to the lodge some evening to meet the rest of the crew, and discuss common interest in the field of wildlife conservation. The invitation was accepted but no date was set that day. Ken and Lana invited Jon and Nate to their homes, also, before they parted in the store. None of them knew how closely they would be associated in the years ahead.

~

Crooked Tail dug the new burrow under the lip of a flat layer of limestone on the east side of a vine and brush clad dry wash, high up on the hill. The dry wash, or gully, sloped off to the south to end in an open prairie surrounded with an unusual variety of vegetation. Hazelnut bushes, wild currant, raspberry, blackberry and dewberry vines grew among the cedars, sassafras trees and paw-paw thickets. Grape vines and honey-suckle twined up persimmon and wild crabapple trees near the wide mouth of the dry wash. Wild plum and mock cranberry bushes thrived where a seep of underground water emerged to keep a small area damp and spongy, at the foot of a head-high rock shelf on the west side of the tiny prairie.

There were many springs and small creeks within a mile of the new den. Some of the creeks were homes for muskrats, marsh rats and other water loving, small animals. The hills and valleys all around the birthing site teemed with more than fifty species of the creatures making up the coyote's natural diet.

The female coyote was sleek and fat, her belly starting to swell with the new life she carried. She worked at enlarging a chamber at the back end of the long, curving burrow, making a three foot diameter, two foot high, domed birthing place. When the den was finished to her exacting instincts, she carried in mouthfuls of dry grass and packed it down with her nose to blanket the entire bottom of the space.

At night she sat on the hilltop or lay among the rocks on its steep eastern slope to wait for her mate, if he was not already there when she loped up the hill.

Recently, the young wolf-looking dog had begun bringing small kills to the hilltop. Sometimes she ate them completely and sometimes she ate only the vicar, burying the rest. Sometimes she preferred the green plants and roots she found by the springs and sheltered streams of the small valleys. She also searched out dried persimmons and crab apples buried in leaves, left from the year before.

Early in March, she spent more time in and around the den at times, pulling the dense loosening fur from her back and sides, adding it to the bed of grass in the snug den. During the last two weeks, she made other partial dens in nearby areas.

~

Chestnut and his mate had, also, made a new home den by enlarging a groundhog burrow by the north side of the middle pond. The den was inside the fence built to keep stock out of the pond area where young trees had been set out by Clyde and Bob the year before. The enclosure also contained many older trees and shrubs that provided seclusion for the busy pair of bright-eyed, beautiful, little foxes. Silver Feet worked out all the nooks and side shoots of the main tunnel and made two new openings in the maze of passageways for reasons she didn't comprehend but felt compelled to create. Chestnut worked at the den in a haphazard manner that seemed to upset his mate, so he gave up his digging in favor of hunting and supplying her with food.

At times, Chestnut tried to get the pretty female to follow him into the grove of trees behind the Buckman homes, but she always stopped some distance away then trotted off by herself when the two small dogs appeared. He would stay only a brief time with Vickie and Pepper, before trailing his bride back to the north end of the farm where she waited.

Silver Feet had, knowingly or unknowingly, dug one of the new openings below the old tunnels, and one at the top of the knoll where it came out under an ancient tree stump more than five feet wide on its flat top. The openings created a natural flow of air up the maze of passageways and out through the hole under the stump.

She liked to lay curled up on the stump in the sun to snooze and loaf during the daytime. Lora and Nancy saw her there one day in early March as they rode their horses over the hills, checking pastures and fences in the area. The fox was asleep but scented the horses and riders on the wind, causing her to sit up and look around for the intruders to her home grounds. The little silver-black fox was not frightened but became nervous as the riders went by several hundred feet to the east of her den.

Both Nancy and Lora were surprised at the rare silver-cross fox's presence on the farm. When they got back to the house after stabling the horses, Lora brought out a book on canines of the country to read up on the whole subject of foxes. The book explained the color variations of the red fox and had pictures of red, brown, silver, blue, and black and various combinations that occurred in the species.

When she told Tim about the newcomer to the farm, he immediately made a connection with the new fox and Chestnut, saying, "Lora, that just might explain why Chestnut is seldom seen around here lately."

Lora agreed with his assumption and said, "We should set up a camera with a long range lens and make a picture study of them, if they are denning where we can get good shots."

Tim, Lora, Howie and Nancy all began secretly scanning the north fields and woods for the den. They found it at last, by using the field glasses from hilltops near the ponds.

None of the openings were apparent to the naked eye, but were easy to see with a pair of ten power binoculars. The men made a near replica of the blind built in the calf lot when the young bull was killed over a year before, but with a straw covered top. They set up a camera with telephoto lens to film the new family when the time came for filming to begin.

~

A few weeks before they spotted Chestnut's mate, Lora had been sick to her stomach in the mornings and hadn't done much riding for a few days. Thinking she had caught a touch of flu, she stopped by to see her old family doctor. He was a seventy-year-old friend, adviser, father figure and doctor to the whole community.

He took her temperature, pulse and blood pressure, checked her eyes, nose and throat, then told her she was "fit as a fiddle." He gave her some liquid to settle her stomach. He suggested she drink lots of juice, water and herbal tea but no coffee. He sent her off with a pat on her shoulder in fond concern for the pretty lady he had helped into the world thirty-odd years ago.

Lora followed his instructions and took her medicine and felt better for a week or so. She began getting nauseated all over again as soon as she got out of bed each morning.

Mary became aware of Lora's distress and asked her some motherly questions with a knowing look in her eyes. Then, at Lora's replies said, "My dear Lora, you need to go see a good obstetrician. I think, from all the evidence and your answers, that you are going to have a baby!"

Lora, somewhat suspicious in a hopeful way, had not said anything to Tim about her secret thoughts, but she was instantly sure Mary was right. She grabbed Mary, hugged and kissed her, then went looking for Tim.

He was just leaving the workshop to come to the house when Lora ran up to him, and gave him a kiss, hugs, and more kisses, before saying to Tim,

"You've just been smooched by your child's mother."

Tim didn't understand at first, but when she took his hand and pressed it against her mid-section, he had started to grin and hug her back. Arm in arm, they went back into the shop to tell John, who was as delighted as Tim was when they told him the news.

When all three started walking to the house, John pulled off his jacket and put it over Lora's shoulders, saying, "You keep this on till we get inside. We mustn't take any chances on you getting a chill."

After Lora's and Tim's second trip to the obstetrician, they further astounded Mary and John with the news that there would be a set of "twins" coming along in less than six months.

Mary and John went around trying their best not to look too proud as they "casually" dropped in on the Grants, Crosses, Kellas, and other close friends to visit or pass the time of day with them. However, they did manage to impart the real reason for their visit by including the announcement about "our twins" which are due this August or early September.

Lora 's morning sickness ended and she felt great. Her doctor said it was all right to ride as long as she was careful and felt no ill effects from sitting the saddle. Lora's doctor said she was a horsewoman herself and had six children who had been prenatally exercised on horseback without harm.

~

In late January the Tyler's called to tell Tim and Lora they would be passing through Ohio in April. They would be on their way to New York to deliver a load of ponies to a buyer and would like to visit the Buckmans at that time. This good news helped Lora, who hadn't been feeling well, to perk up and take renewed interest in more of the outdoor activity.

The planned visit turned into two visits when the Tyler's trip took place. By phone, C.B. arranged the trip to include a three-day rest stop for the horses at the farm on the way to New York and a weeks visit on their return to Texas.

Ida Mae and C.B. rode Barney and Charlie, each day, to work them for their host. The Texan's used the time to "school" the geldings, teaching them quite a lot in a short time. The Tyler's said both Barney and Charlie had good cow savvy and were fast to learn. They also gave their riding companions many "pointers" by demonstration and verbal instruction that helped everyone improve their horse teaching capabilities.

Howie and Nancy were able to spend three days in a row with the group due to a teacher's conference that closed school on Thursday and Friday while the Tyler's were there. Nancy carried a notebook and pen in her jacket to take copious notes on everything the Tyler's said about how to "work and teach" the "ponies."

Tim and Howie took advantage of both Tyler's skill with a lariat to learn some basic "throws" and how to rope and release an animal without harming it. They did their practice roping on cull cows and calves, developing some skill, aided by the good ropes the Tyler's gave them from a supply they kept in the horse van.

While the Tyler's were there, C.B. offered to take the big two-year-old colts back to Texas and train them for the Buckmans. He also expressed an interest in buying some of the best young heifers the Buckmans were planning to sell that spring.

When the Tyler's left for the trip home, they had the two colts and six prime yearling heifers in their van. The final arrangements called for twelve more breeder heifers to be picked up later, when the Tyler's made a second delivery of horses to their New York buyer in May.

During the visit, the Tyler's told how well "Little Bit," their gift dog, had adapted to their home and ranch. She had become a valuable part of the Tylers' cattle working crew.

Ida Mae said, "Our ranch foreman would give up one of his best cow ponies before he would Little Bit. He thinks she's smarter than most people." She chuckled and added, "That ornery old cuss wouldn't even let us bring her on this trip."

C.B. had told John he wanted two more of Pepper's next litter, trained by Paul Cross, and that he would even train the two colts in exchange for the two best dogs.

"That is, if you and Mary will carry them down and spend some time with us when the little cow dogs are ready."

Mary had packed up some extra nice apples and pears for the Tylers, and also stocked up the van refrigerator with meat, butter and eggs, jams and preserves from the homemade supply of country food she always had available.

The final parting took nearly an hour, with none of them wanting to say "goodbye," but knowing they would see each other soon made it easier. The sun was "hand high" in the east when the van pulled out the drive to go west. Howie and Nancy followed them as far as Rockhill, where they went to high school, barely in time for their first class of the day.

~

Pepper had become irritable with Vickie when she persisted in her efforts to lure the older female to play games with her. Chestnut came by only occasionally to touch noses and nuzzle the shoulders and sides of the two little cow dogs. Vickie did everything to entice either Chestnut or Pepper to run and frolic as they did before when they were together at dusk and early nights, but they seemed to be withdrawn and occupied with their own lives, leaving her to amuse herself most of the time. Fortunately, the cow work increased about that time and Vickie was tired enough in the evenings to appreciate the additional rest and sleep.

Dutch and Bruiser were both getting slick and filled out with plenty of food and the easiest period of their life together since pairing more than a year ago.

Bruiser was now as sharp in all his senses as any of his wild, arctic ancestors had ever been. He was tireless in pursuit and canny in his ambushing of predators. He and Dutch were so tuned to each other's abilities and strengths that they rarely failed to finish a chase or stalk successfully.

As her whelping time drew near, Dutch moved her home den to one of the huge piles of tree tops in the harvested woodlands north of the new fence at the head of the ravine which passed in front of the cavern. The place she chose was created when several cull logs and discarded treetops were pushed over a rocky knoll to clear a road for the huge walnut logs. The resulting mass of material covered a hollow in the side of the knoll but left an open passage to the center from both north and south sides. Dutch dug, scraped and nosed out a snug, dry space the size of a small room and prepared it for the new litter's arrival.

Bruiser resumed his lone hunting a couple of weeks

before the whelps were due. Dutch spent most of her leisure hours rearranging her "nest" and dozing in the sun, waiting her time.

~

The big, rusty colored Tamworth had become fat and lazy from eating the bountiful crop of acorns, nuts, dried wild fruit, and cured marsh hay, which he chomped up in great quantities. When the, now big, black sow hog came looking for a mate, the old tyrant had been on his best behavior - very rare for him. His regular harem of three feral females had kept him sexually busy for three weeks, then wisely departed to hide their massive birthing nest far away from the old cannibal's regular range.

When the four-hundred-pound, black sow found him he had been alone for many days and welcomed her like the lothario he was. Perhaps the memory of a deadly conflict with another four hundred pound black female made him cautious, for over the next two weeks he had even permitted the black sow to eat anything they found as they alternately mated, fed and slept as they moved about the woods. Possibly the loss of two of his great tusks in the battle with the bear, and the breaking of another one on the other side, had reduced his deadly capability to the point of caution.

A large, misshapen lump just behind his massive shoulders, a memento of his battle with the bear, made him slow in mounting but did not impair his ability to perform the required function the amorous sow desired. The sow had chosen him as a result of his sole availability after weeks of disappointing searches during previous, unfulfilled, cycles.

Now finished with him, she left him to make a long, circuitous return to the old root cellar. Her roundabout journey lasted three months and brought her "home" in early March. The four shoats that remained after Dutch's pack caught the young boar had stayed near the old cellar for safety. The nearby trap had been blocked open and frequently baited with shelled corn for a couple of weeks. When the greedy pigs became accustomed to finding the corn in the trap-pen, they all began to go in together to be assured of a fair share of the "bait.

On a bright moonlit night, the trappers, concealed behind a brush blind on the hill behind the boundary fence, jerked on the trip wire and caught all four of the young sows in the trap. The trappers came back the next morning leading a horse, which pulled a long, narrow, boxed-over sled.

With a syringe of tranquilizer solution fastened to a long pole, the two lean, dark men jabbed the long needle into the sides or hips of the angry porkers then waited a few minutes for them to fall asleep on their feet, fall to the ground and lie perfectly still. They dragged the four gilts into the escape-proof box on the sled, closed and locked the gates on both ends of the box. They stopped to roll cigarettes before reaching through the slats to inject the hogs in their necks with a second shot of fluid.

After locking the trap shut, the quiet-voiced, methodical trappers started off with their load of live, but sleeping, young sows. The sled slipped easily over the frosty grass and leaves, permitting them to make good time back to their indestructible, log and stone, pig barns near a small village at the end of a gravel road two miles from the hog trap.

~

As always, spring came at last with redbud, dogwood, wild plum and crab apple trees creating a soft, colorful blanket of incredible colors for the newly awakened woods.

The earth itself was a garland of violets, trillium, phlox, anemone, columbine, buttercup, kitten britches, larkspur and many other bright faced flowers. The grass greened, and trees budded out in tiny feathers of every shade of green. Frequent, warm showers washed and freshened every growing thing. Warm sun urged every plant and creature to multiply and grow.

Nest, dens, burrows, caves, hollow trees, even thickets, sheltered young of every size, shape and description. Mares foaled. Cows calved. Foxes, coyotes and dogs whelped, and a myriad of small, four legged creatures brought forth their young to join thousands of birds hatched in trees shrubs, and on the ground.

Chestnut and Bruiser both hunted to feed hungry mates and their whimpering whelps. Howie and Nancy petted, groomed, and slipped treats to two new colts in the mare stalls.

Pepper now nursed her new litter of seven demanding babies, while Vickie watched in obvious delight as her prospective play- mate brothers and sisters tumbled over each other to be the first to find the chosen fountain of delicious liquid Pepper provided.

The three small ponds teemed with spawn, and the "big pond" was stocked with catfish and a special, fast growing, crossbred perch for Howie's future fish marketing.

~

John and Mary took Lora and Tim for a ride in the two-seater buggy John had purchased from an Amish carriage maker near Cleveland. They drove by the smallest pond to see if they could spot the family of young, multi-colored pups chestnut and Silver Feet were raising there.

The silver-blue-black female had become accustomed to the quiet voiced, careful, human visitors. They merely watched in a concerned way when they came on the side of the pond nearest her home grounds. She would send her gangly group of four underground when she felt their safety threatened.

Both adult foxes accepted the occasional fish Howie or Nancy placed on the log between the pond and the den, but only after they retreated to a proper distance.

Silver Feet vaguely remembered a gentle, young, woman who once gave her bits of dried fish, handing them through the heavy netting around her pen at the fox farm where she was born. The rosy-skinned, young girl who now left the fish for her had a coaxing voice like the girl in her babyhood. At times, the silver fox felt almost compelled to approach her when Nancy talked her way to the feeding log.

John parked the buggy and tied the horse some distance from the small pond. Tim helped Lora, despite her protest, down to the grassy meadow. Mary took John's hand and stepped down to link her arms with her handsome, gray-haired mate of so many wonderful years. They walked over to the grove of trees and checked the outdoor grill Dean Hitch had just built of stone and slabs of slate.

Tim led Lora up to the top of the hill overlooking the entire farm. When they neared the crest of the hill, a doe and her two spotted fawns trotted off to the side, stopped, and watched the young couple walk past on the way up to the three old pine trees at the very top.

A trio of tiny rabbits - no larger than the palm of her hand - were half hidden in a clump of orchard grass by their nest. Lora saw them just in time to prevent Tim from stepping quite near the ear flattened, crouching, little gray puffs of fur. She knelt to stroke one with a finger, causing it to close its eyes as if for additional concealment. Tim lifted her up and they walked the last few steps to the pines.

At their feet the earth seemed to explode as a covey of

quail burst from the tall, dead grass still standing from the previous year. Lora gave a little shriek of mock fear and whirled about to throw her arms around Tim's neck.

Since she was so handy, Tim used one hand to tip her face up, hold her tight against him with the other and give her a long, slow kiss. Lora liked his idea so well she wiggled closer, pushed her little rounded tummy against him even harder, and kissed him right back.

After the kiss Tim whispered in her ear, "If you get any closer, our kids are going to be behind me."

"Well, we're not on the Texas highway. At least we won't get a traffic ticket," Lora replied.

They stayed on top of the hill for long minutes, looking at the tranquil scene all around them. With slow steps and frequent stops, the young couple made their way back down the hill.

Chestnut stood watching them go from the side of one of the smoky, blue hills beyond the ponds. A large, dark-coated, leggy pup stood just behind him, waiting for the big fox to continue the interrupted hunt for mice that darted through miniature grass tunnels in the turf of the hillside meadow.

Mary and John were waiting by the buggy when Lora and Tim came back to them. Lora looked at her wristwatch, then said, "We better hurry. The Tyler's will be here in an hour or two. I'm anxious to tell them about the "double surprise.""

"You're right, Lora. As soon as they hear about our twins, they'll want to start training a pair of ponies for them," replied John.

"That should work out perfectly. We'll let them help us pick out some real little ones next week, so the twins and the ponies can grow up together. That way, in five years, we can have two more sets of cow-hands on this place," Lora said with a big smile.

fin ~

Glossary ~

auger – a screw-like device in a tube. the screw rotates to move material up the tube.

barren – heifer or cow that did not breed to produce a calf.

beef herd – consists of cows, bulls, heifers, calves and steer.

blind – a hunter's shelter which conceals and protects.

Blue heeler – a breed of medium-sized dogs developed to herd domestic livestock.

boar - a male pig of reproductive age.

bole – the stem or trunk of a tree.

brood mare – any female horse that produces young.

buttress root – a tree trunk with a widening base.

chunky – refers to the well-formed muscles on a working horse.

colt – any young male horse.

colts – (plural). all young horses.

coupled gelding – a well proportioned, castrated male horse.

covey – a small group of partridge or quail.

cull – any animal below the standard for the herd.

disk – to make rows in the soil with farm machinery.

downwind – all things behind you when you face into the wind. to approach an animal from downwind so he doesn't detect your scent, walk toward the animal with your face into the wind.

dug-heavy – the breast or nipple of a female mammal swollen with milk.

escarpment - a long, steep cliff-like ridge of land.

estrus – when a female mammal is receptive to mating and able to reproduce.

farrier – a blacksmith.

feral – having reverted to the wild state.

filly – female horse under four years of age.

foal – any baby horse or pony.

fryers – a young chicken suitable for frying.

gelding – a castrated male horse, making the horse gentler in nature.

gimlet eyes – piercing eyes, like that of a pig.

grouse – a member of the order of gallinaceous game birds, such as pheasant and turkey.

hay – edible grass, clover, alfalfa, etc., used to feed cattle and horses.

hegari – a grass crop with a large, loose head of small, round seeds at the top. this grain is used for animal feed and bird food.

heifer – a young female cow before she bears her first calf.

horse colt – male horse under four years of age.

in heat – a female's signs of her breeding readiness.

imbued – to inspire or to infuse with.

kibitzers – a gossiping group.

lay-up – a secluded place to rest or hide.

lee – the side or part that is sheltered or turned away from the wind.

litter – three or more baby animals in a family group.

Lothario – a charming man who seduces and deceives women.

maize – an undomesticated form of corn.

mare – any female horse four years or older.

millet – a cereal grass used to feed chickens.

omnivores – eating all types of food, both plant and animal.

partridge – a gallinaceous game bird, also known as a ruffled grouse.

paw-paw tree – an unexplained variety of papaya tree found in Midwest and southern forests.

perambulations – to walk about in order to examine or inspect.

pheasant – a gallinaceous game bird with long tail feathers and bright plumage.

placenta – the afterbirth, consumed by dogs, cats or other mammals.

porcine – of or related to pigs or swine.

portico – a porch with pillars.

pullets – young hens less than one year old.

progeny – offspring or descendants.

promulgate – to put laws or rules into action.

quail – a gallinaceous game bird, such as the bobwhite.

recalcitrant – hard to deal with, manage or operate.

recumbent - lying down or reclining.

remuda – In the Southwest, a group of extra saddle horses kept as a supply of remounts.

rufous red – a brownish red color.

satiated – satisfied to the full.

shoat – a young weaned pig, not yet of reproductive age.

short coupled horse – a horse whose build gives the appearance of strength and quickness in turning, rather than the long, slim build required for fast running over distance.

sow – an adult female pig.

stallion – a male horse of breeding age.

suppuration – the discharge from an infected wound.

swain – a lover or country or country lad.

temerity – rash and bold.

truculent – brutal, hostile or belligerent.

upwind – anything in front of you when you face into the wind.

virgin timber – any mature stand of timber not previously harvested or used.

viscera – intestines or bodily organs.

vixen – a female fox.

vulva – female genitalia.

wheat straw – wheat stalks left after grain harvesting and used for animal bedding.

whelp – to give birth or the babies of dogs, wolves, foxes, coyotes or other animals.

wraith – ghostlike or visible spirit.

Wyandot – a member of the Huron tribe of the Iroquois Nation, including the Mohawks, Oneidas, Onondagas, Cayugas, Senecas, and the Tuscaroras.